Old-school, Nog thought. *... ... ...t.*

The Robert Hooke's operations center had obviously been designed using the tried-and-true circular design aesthetic of most Federation command centers. Judging by the way the walls curved upward into an arch and the pair of auxiliary stairways to his left and right, Nog decided there was one more deck above them.

From where he stood on the transporter pad, Nog could see that the workstations all appeared utilitarian, and moderately well maintained by civilian standards. Lights blinked; sensors pinged; indicators pulsed in predictable patterns; and the fabric covers for the furniture, while worn thin, were not rubbed raw or sprouting foam. Everything about the setting made Nog feel at home.

The only problem, he decided, was the people. To be more precise: the lack thereof. As he and the chief stepped off the pad in unison, each of them looked to his left and right, both searching for a sign of life. They found none. The ops center purred and ticked around them, but was otherwise indifferent to their presence.

"This can't be good," O'Brien murmured.

"That's supposed to be my line," Nog said. "This is why I never want to go anywhere with you."

STAR TREK
DEEP SPACE NINE®

FORCE AND MOTION

JEFFREY LANG

Based upon *Star Trek*® and
Star Trek: The Next Generation®
created by Gene Roddenberry
and
Star Trek: Deep Space Nine
created by Rick Berman & Michael Piller

POCKET BOOKS
New York   London   Toronto   Sydney   New Delhi

Pocket Books
An Imprint of Simon & Schuster, Inc.
1230 Avenue of the Americas
New York, NY 10020

This book is a work of fiction. Any references to historical events, real people, or real places are used fictitiously. Other names, characters, places, and events are products of the author's imagination, and any resemblance to actual events or places or persons, living or dead, is entirely coincidental.

First Pocket Books paperback edition June 2016

POCKET and colophon are registered trademarks of Simon & Schuster, Inc.

For information about special discounts for bulk purchases, please contact Simon & Schuster Special Sales at 1-866-506-1949 or business@simonandschuster.com.

The Simon & Schuster Speakers Bureau can bring authors to your live event. For more information or to book an event, contact the Simon & Schuster Speakers Bureau at 1-866-248-3049 or visit our website at www.simonspeakers.com.

Manufactured in the United States of America

10 9 8 7 6 5 4 3 2 1

ISBN 978-1-5011-1073-3
ISBN 978-1-5011-1078-8 (ebook)

This one is for Tristan.
Thanks for all the walks and talks.

Historian's Note

The main events in this story take place in early January 2386, just after the discovery of the falsework on the Bajoran moon of Endalla (*Star Trek: Deep Space Nine— Ascendance*).

Prologue

Ben Maxwell sat on the low stone wall that marked the border between the campus and the not-campus. He stared into the west, out into Half Moon Bay, and watched the sun settle into the sea, painting both the water and the sky crimson and gold. He was too far up the hill to hear the surf, but, from where he sat, the bay looked as smooth as the ice on a skating rink. Maxwell imagined what it might be like to step off the sand and onto the ocean's surface, push off with his left foot, and slide on west until he hit Auckland. In his prime, he knew he could have covered the twenty-five or thirty kilometers in a few hours. *If I get tired*, he thought, *I'll stop at Motutapu Island and take a breather. Have a beer.*

Maxwell tipped his head back and stared up into the darkening sky. He rubbed his chin and felt the bristles of his day-old beard. It was a cloudless night, like most were during the roiling days of late summer. *Well*, Maxwell thought. *I guess that's a good thing: with a sky like this, we'll see them coming from a long way off.* He paused to consider: *Do Borg cubes have running lights? Are they visible from a distance?* He had read the reports about the Borg back in the day—any good ship's captain would have—but never had the opportunity to see a cube up close, having missed out on the imbroglio at Wolf 359 back in '67. The *Phoenix* had been on patrol on the other side of the quadrant that dark day, and some Starfleet analyst had decided his ship was too far away to arrive in time to make a difference.

I'm probably still alive today because of that analyst, Maxwell decided. *I should track him down and beat him with his abacus.* He chuckled, knowing he would have to mention the image—abacus beads exploding upward as the wooden frame connected with someone's temple—in tomorrow's therapy session (assuming there was a tomorrow). No doubt, Doctor Beeman would ask, "Why an abacus?"

"Wow," Maxwell muttered, "therapy must finally be taking hold." He heard something skitter away. Speaking aloud must have startled some small creature that had been enjoying the heat of the baked rock. He stood up and lightly brushed the backs and palms of his hands on his trouser legs, a move designed to dislodge small things without coming into contact with them. Maxwell had spent enough time in New Zealand to know to be cautious of its creeping, crawling denizens.

A speck of light blinked into existence on the horizon and crossed swiftly from south to north, then disappeared in a wink of blue-shift. *Interesting,* Maxwell thought. Someone must have gone into impulse much too close to the atmosphere. *How could that happen?* The airspace around Earth was usually so tightly monitored no one would think to do such a thing. Whoever it was at the ship's controls must have been woefully ignorant of both common sense and procedure. "Or maybe just very, very desperate," he added aloud.

"Who?"

Maxwell looked back over his shoulder and was surprised to find a figure standing no more than a few meters away, just on the edge of the gravel path that led from the main administrative building down toward the beach. It was Doctor Clark, one of the younger staff members. Like most of the therapists, Clark's taste in garments ran to the simple, even utilitarian, likely because of some colony edict that the staff not be too distracting, as not to agitate the inmates. Occasionally, Maxwell had noted, Clark would wear large, handmade belt buckles inscribed with peculiar logos or symbols that clearly had meaning to him and some sub-sub-subgroup of fellow travelers, but were meant to be mysteries to all others. Maxwell liked him for that.

Shall I answer truthfully or make something up? It probably didn't matter, he decided, so he went with the truth. "Someone did something they're not supposed to do. Went to impulse." He pointed toward the now-dark horizon. "The streak of light. Unless EarthNav has completely thrown up their hands in despair, which I suppose is possible." He couldn't tell if Clark was following him, so he added, "Because of the Borg?"

Clark jerked backward suddenly. He flicked on the torch he was carrying and pointed the beam up into the sky. "Have they arrived?"

Maxwell was confused. He peered at Clark and said, "You would probably know better than me. I'm just an inmate." By the light of the torch, Maxwell could see the deep lines of stress etched into Clark's face. He wasn't being obtuse; he was simply exhausted. And probably terrified. They were, after all, residents of a planet that was the target of the pointy end of a Borg armada. Likely, neither of them would live to see another day.

The doctor's therapeutic training kicked into place. He assumed the soft, compassionate voice. "You're a patient, Ben, not an inmate."

Maxwell knew he shouldn't go down any bumpy rhetorical roads since Clark was new to the staff and, as near as he could tell, a fundamentally decent person. But then the truth shone forth: *Oh, hell. The world is coming to an end. What have I got to lose?* "Oh, great. Then I'd like to check out. I'm cured."

"You know you can't," Clark said, shaking his head.

"Because?"

The doctor paused and Maxwell guessed that the therapist was weighing the same kind of internal math that he had a moment before and, laudably, came to the same conclusion. "Because you're not a patient, you're an inmate."

Spreading his arms wide in welcome, he asked, "Was that so hard?"

"No, Ben," Clark replied, smiling. "It wasn't. Thanks for taking it easy on me."

"But I'm afraid that's all the time we have for today . . ."

Clark waved off the sarcasm. "No more fencing, please. Doctor Gunther sent me to look for you."

Maxwell's spine stiffened. A moment before he had been sitting with his hands on his knees, his shoulders rounded down and forward, comfortable with the way gravity was pulling at him. And then, suddenly, he was standing at attention, pushing against the ground with the balls of his feet, toes biting into the surface. His shoulders were back and his knees were locked. Swallowing once loudly, jaw clenched, he asked, "What did he say?"

Apparently startled, Clark took a half step away. "What I just said," he replied, trying not to sound rattled. "He asked me to find you. You know, Ben, you're supposed to carry your communicator at all times."

But Maxwell wasn't listening anymore. He was running. The flimsy shoes had no support, and the soles of his feet crunched painfully into the gravel, but he didn't slow. He pointed toward the administration building as he ran. Calling back over his shoulder, he shouted, "There? In his office?"

"Yes," Clark called. "But don't run! The sentries will think you're trying to escape!"

Maxwell ran faster, arms pumping, knees high. When was the last time he ran like this—not a jog, but a sprint? He couldn't recall. He thought back to his cadet days, running wind sprints, but then battle scenes flashed through his memory. *I ran then*, he thought, *but not a sprint. Mad dashes. Scrambling. Running for my life.* The brightly illuminated portico of the main administrative building swam into view, blurry through his tearing eyes. *I'm not trying to escape,* he thought. *I'm not. The sentries will be able to tell the difference.* His breath came in sharp gasps. *They'll know I'm not escaping. They'll know I'm going home.*

Abram Gunther's office was on the second floor of the main administrative building and was reached by one of two wide, sweeping marble staircases that framed the building's lobby. Usually the lobby was a busy place, a natural spot for counselors and inmates to meet and converse, but it was late in the evening now, well past the end of even the latest therapy session. Also, Maxwell reminded himself, there was the whole "Borg coming to eliminate us and our way of life" thing. That was the sort of event that motivated even the most devoted doctor to consider heading home for a little family time or to the nearest pub, depending on their predilection. The inmates, the ones who couldn't arrange some form of evacuation, were hunkered down in their quarters sitting in pairs and trios, talking in low tones or trying to contact their families and friends, if they had any left.

Gunther, to his credit, hadn't left his office, despite having a family in Auckland, a husband and two children. A part of Maxwell felt bad about the fact that the head of the colony was still in his office at this late hour, but not so bad that he wished that Gunther had left.

This is it, Maxwell thought as he skidded to a stop in front of the director's formidable desk. As ever, the desktop was a model of tidy organization: a pair of padds lying side by side, a neat pile of isolinear chips aligned nearby. A pair of tasteful holograms floated serenely on each of the corners nearest the two visitor chairs—one an image of what Maxwell had recognized as an antique music player called a Victrola and the other a portrait of the doctor and his family. In the image, the children appeared to be eight and ten years old, though Maxwell knew they were much older.

Maxwell started to speak, but had to lay a hand on

the desktop while he caught his breath. Gunther rose and waved Maxwell toward a chair. He continued, "Take a moment, Ben. Take two. You'll need them."

Unlike most of the doctors and counselors who worked with the inmates at the colony, Abram Gunther had served in Starfleet, a line officer for twenty years. Though he had never commanded a ship of his own, he understood the demands of the service. He had never mentioned Maxwell's former rank—such references were taboo—but Gunther always treated the former captain with the respect of a fellow officer. Part of that respect, Maxwell realized, came in the form of the courtesy to not sugarcoat or prevaricate. He was about to receive bad news.

Maxwell did as he was told and sat down, though he leaned forward, all his weight on the balls of his feet, hands clenching the chair's arms. He managed to ask, "What did they say?"

"What do you think, Ben?" Gunther said, sitting down in his own chair, though he pushed his back into the cushioned fabric. He sighed and rubbed the stubble on his jawline. "They said no."

"*Dammit!*" Maxwell groaned. "I could help!"

"Of course you could," Gunther said, but had the courtesy not to say more. Instead, he leaned across the desk and handed Maxwell a padd.

Dear Abe,
I only have a moment to respond to your request regarding Benjamin Maxwell. I can only imagine how strongly you feel about this situation, given the other challenges you must be facing at this time.

While I understand he has been an inmate of good standing at your facility for the past several years and acquitted himself well in the time since his court-martial, we cannot accept his offer to serve even given the current crisis.

Please extend my thanks to Mister Maxwell and tell him that this is not my decision. I am not making excuses, but merely explaining as best I can in consideration of our history. Tell him I remember our days in the service together fondly. He was one of the finest officers I ever had the privilege to know, despite any actions he may have taken.

Unfortunately, this is not his day. Forgiveness is hard won. Given our current situation, Ben Maxwell may have to face the possibility it may never come at all, at least not in this lifetime.

My best to you and your family, Abe. I understand Mark is in the vanguard, serving on the Constitution. *I have no doubt he will make you proud.*

In haste,
Jason Mark Stratham, Adm.
Highest possible priority via subspace channel

Maxwell's fingers grew numb, and he almost let the padd drop to the floor. Then he remembered that the message had not been addressed to him. It belonged to Gunther, and losing his grip on the padd would be disrespectful in the extreme. He handed it back to the director.

"I'm genuinely sorry, Ben. I thought they'd let you, considering what we face."

"I only want to serve," Maxwell said. "Why not let me?"

"I don't know," Gunther said. "But I can guess." He retrieved a tiny control from a drawer and pointed it at the wall to his right. Panels parted and a large viewscreen appeared. Images flickered as Gunther worked the control. Finally, he stopped on a grainy image: several bright blobs of light in a dark field. In the lower right-hand corner of the screen was the gentle curve of a mass that Maxwell immediately recognized as a planet. He was looking at a long-range sensor image.

Gunther rose wearily and approached the screen. "There are some advantages to having friends in the service," he said. "I have some codes. I found out where the fleet was massing. You probably recognize the planet just from this blurry image, don't you?"

"Yes," Maxwell said. "Of course I do."

"And you see that white blob up there in the left corner?"

"Yes. Deneva."

"And that," Gunther said, circling a blob with red light. "That's the *Constitution*. My son Mark serves on her. First lieutenant. His first rotation on a starship. Weapons officer. From what he's said in his messages, it's not his favorite job ever."

"I'm sure he'll do it well."

Gunther pointed at the blobs nearer the lower edge of the screen. "And you see this one, this one, this one . . . well, most of them?"

"Yes."

"Any ideas what they are?"

"Cardassian. *Galor*-class? They still use those?"

Gunther squinted at the blob and shook his head in mild disbelief. "They're using everything. Everything Cardassia has, they're throwing at the Borg. And do you know why?"

"No," Maxwell said. "I don't. Why?"

"Because we asked them. Despite everything, despite the Dominion War, despite the disasters that have been visited on them, the Cardassians are coming to our aid. Of course, they probably know the Borg would come for them too, but probably not right away. They could be using those ships, even the *Galor*-class, to get their people out, off, away. But they're not. They're helping us."

Maxwell inhaled and sighed deeply. "Makes you wonder."

"What does?"

"Why I hated them so much."

Gunther smiled. He almost laughed. "Ben, I think we both know you had a very good reason to hate them. And, by the way, they hate you too. Your name has *not* been forgotten. Which is, I suspect, why your offer was rejected. If the Cardassians ever found out you were on a starship . . ." He shrugged and flicked a switch. The display darkened.

"So," Maxwell said, collecting himself, "I guess I get to stay here and see what happens."

"Just like the rest of us."

Maxwell rose, his legs still a little shaky. He laid the tips of his fingers on the top of Gunther's immaculate desk and looked at the holo of the family. "Which one is Mark?" he asked.

"The older one." He smiled. "His brother, Arin, isn't

interested in Starfleet. He's studying at the University of Sydney. He's coming home tonight. In fact, I have to go meet him at the station."

"Of course," Maxwell said. "Thank you, Doctor Gunther, for your help and consideration. I guess I knew it was a long shot."

"I thought they'd take you, Ben," Gunther said. "'Every hand to the lines when the storm is breaking.'"

"Is that a line from a poem?"

"No," Gunther said. "Just something my dad used to say."

Maxwell smiled, but only for a second. No sooner did the smile fade than the weariness descended. He turned his back on the director's desk and shuffled through the door, down the steps and outside.

Behind him, the lights of the administration building dimmed.

Above him, clouds began to roll in, obscuring the stars.

Maxwell slept like the dead and rose with the sun the next morning to learn that the Earth, miraculously, had survived and would continue to spin for one more day.

The Borg destroyed the fleet sent to defend Deneva, including the *Constitution* and her Cardassian allies.

All hands were lost.

Chapter 1

January 9, 2386
Runabout *Amazon*

"**A**nd then I found some leather straps out in the barn—
I think they had been traces for a carriage harness
my da made for one of his historical reenactments—and
threaded them through the eyebolts I'd screwed into the
head jamb—"

Lieutenant Commander Nog rolled his eyes and
sighed deeply. "Wait," he said, "Chief—stop. Please. You
know what that sounds like to me, don't you? 'I went to
the *blah-blah* and found some *blahs* and tied them to the
blah in the *blah*.'"

"What do you mean?" Miles O'Brien said, crossing
his legs, folding his arms, and pushing his back deeper
into the copilot seat. "What part didn't you understand?"

"Let's start with traces."

"Traces—leather straps. Long leather straps. You use
them to control the horse or bullock or whatever you have
drawing your cart or carriage." He held his hands out in
front of him at chest level and grasped something imaginary that Nog assumed he was now supposed to be able to
visualize. O'Brien jerked his hands back and smiled, as if
this was supposed to make everything clear.

"Bullock?"

"It's a large terrestrial mammal," O'Brien said mechanically, his smile slipping. "Domesticated. People used them on farms. For labor and transport."

"You made animals work for you?" Nog asked. "Isn't that considered abuse?"

"*No*. And I didn't say *we* used bullocks. But the traces were in the barn."

"A storage building used on farms."

"Right."

"All right, and I know what an eyebolt is."

"Good thing, too, or I'd have to kick you off the station."

"And I guessed what a head jamb is from the context, but I've never heard the word before. It sounds . . ." The Ferengi thought about it for a moment while checking their course. "It sounds like something you would rub on your lobes. Or have someone else rub on for you.

O'Brien winced. "I don't want to hear about your personal life, Nog."

"Medicinally."

"Sure," the chief agreed neutrally. "Can I continue with my story?"

"Of course, Chief. Please." Nog wanted to add, "I'm riveted," but O'Brien would know he was lying.

His fellow engineer continued his tale of a boyhood prank. Nog tuned out just a bit, just enough to recheck the course. The *Amazon* was not the first *Yellowstone*-class runabout Nog had flown, and he was well acquainted with their fussy navigational systems. As one of his shipmates aboard the *Challenger* had once commented, "East is east and west is west . . . unless you're flying a *Yellowstone*."

"So I rigged the cantilever so that when Cully—my older brother, remember—yanked open the door to the upstairs in that way he always did that rattled the whole house, he activated the audio playback and sent the dummy we'd dressed up in Grandma's ratty old dress down the guide wires." O'Brien began to guffaw at the memory. Nog had a sense he was supposed to join in, but wasn't certain, so he held back. It didn't help that he wasn't sure what was supposed to be funny.

Nog asked, "And then what happened?"

"Well, *then*," O'Brien continued, "after he finished thrashing around and gettin' himself untangled, Cully started screamin' like a banshee himself, which only seemed appropriate considering all the stories Bill had been feedin' him for the past week . . ."

Nog knew that O'Brien was coming to the conclusion of the tale. The chief tended to lose the *g* at the end of his gerunds when he became excited. "Bill is your other brother . . ." Nog added.

O'Brien's laughter stalled. "Well, yeah. O' course. Who usually tormented me, but he was just as sick of Cully . . ." His face went slack and he dropped his hands. "Have you been listening?"

"Of course," Nog said, very professionally staring at the sensor readouts. "This is the story of how you and one of your siblings made an alliance to chastise your other sibling because you both felt he was inconsiderably monopolizing resources . . ."

"Taking too much time in the bathroom, yeah."

"Exactly. Monopolizing resources."

"Cully was fourteen. We were ten and eleven and

didn't know . . ." O'Brien sighed in resignation. "Never mind. Forget it. I'm sorry I brought it up."

"Don't be sorry, Chief. I enjoy hearing stories of other people's childhoods."

"Other people's childhoods?" O'Brien repeated. "That sounds ominous. Like you didn't have one of your own. I seem to recall you and Jake running around the station like a couple of puppies back in the day."

"I was already sixteen when Jake came to Deep Space 9," Nog explained. "Hardly a puppy."

The chief narrowed his eyes. "I guess that's true. It's just that you were so . . . you know." He held his hand up so it was parallel to the deck and moved it up and down.

"Short?"

"Well, yes. Especially compared to Jake."

"For a Ferengi, I'm above average."

O'Brien appeared to consult a mental ledger—probably of every Ferengi he had ever met—and then nodded in agreement. "I guess you're right." He shrugged. "No offense meant."

"None taken."

"No brothers?"

"None that I know of," Nog said, trying to sound jaunty. "Just my sister."

"How old is Bena?"

"Five," Nog replied. "Or, wait . . . maybe six?" It worried him that he couldn't remember. Nog had always prided himself on his memory, but small details like remembering names and dates were beginning to elude him. He wasn't *that* old yet. "Time flies," O'Brien said absently, folding his arms over his chest, sliding down, and laying his head back against the chair. "Molly is eighteen. *Eighteen*! She's going to head off for university soon."

"Not the Academy?"

"Not unless there's a need for painters aboard starships that I'm not aware of," O'Brien said, his tone edged with mild annoyance.

"Painters? You mean, like bulkheads? We have 'bots that can—"

"No, not bulkheads. Canvases. Specifically, very large canvases. Very, *very* large canvases. Molly has decided she wants to be an artist." He added, "This week."

"Uh, um." Nog fumbled for the correct words. "Okay." *Or possibly not . . . ?*

"I don't know. It might be. I haven't decided. Neither has she. That's the point: this is something new, the big canvas thing, and it's just come up this month and now it's the *most important thing in her life*." He shook his head dismissively. "And I don't even understand what she's painting. It's all very . . ."

"Abstract?" Nog knew enough about hew-mon art to know it came in a variety of styles, some representational and some decidedly not.

Wincing, O'Brien shook his head. "No, abstract would be fine. Just swell, in fact. If anything, it's all a bit too graphic for my tastes. Lots of *flowers*." He huffed. "*Blooming* flowers."

Nog decided he didn't want to know any more. "What does Keiko think?" he asked.

O'Brien slid his eyes to the side and looked back at Nog out of the corners. "You and Rom got along well," he said, a statement with the overtone of a question.

"I guess so," Nog said. "Sure. We had to get along. It was always the two of us against Uncle Quark."

"So you don't know how teenage girls get along with their mothers, do you?"

"No," Nog admitted, feeling a bit foolish. He thought of his father's *moogie*, Ishka, and what she might do. "Do they form alliances?"

O'Brien snorted derisively. "No," he said. "Or, wait . . . yes, briefly. Usually after some amount of crying. And then the alliance falls apart, and the yelling and throwing of breakable items starts up again."

"That does not sound like something Keiko would do."

"Until she had a teenage daughter."

"You and Yoshi should form a counteralliance."

O'Brien rolled his eyes. "Unlikely. Yoshi is not in the frame of mind to form an alliance, counter or otherwise, with his father these days. He still hasn't decided whether he's ready to forgive me for moving back to the station. Or, as he would put it, 'Uprooted his life and forced him to live in an aluminum can on the edge of a forsaken void.'"

Nog puzzled over the statement and then asked, "I can understand forsaken, but how does a void have an edge?"

"I asked about that too," O'Brien replied. "My son has not yet deigned to explain." He turned to stare out at the streaking stars. "Kids!"

Nog jiggled his head in a manner that would make it appear that he neither completely agreed nor disagreed with the chief's exclamation. He had lived among hewmons long enough to have a general sense of the boundaries of their familial relationships, but no intimate knowledge. He understood that the circumstances under which Jake Sisko—his closest friend—had lived had hardly been typical (even for a Starfleet brat), but no more or less than his. In brief, Nog had no frame of reference, a circumstance that provoked very familiar (if uncomfortable) sensations.

"I miss Julian," O'Brien murmured.

The transition to the new topic was abrupt, but Nog did his best to follow along. "Have you talked to Doctor Bashir recently?"

"No. Not directly. He must be busy, what with the adoration and reverence." O'Brien grinned, but the smile had very little wattage. "He must be hating that."

"*Hating* it?" Nog asked. "I would think Doctor Bashir would be enjoying the adulation. Forgive me, but my impression of the doctor is—"

"Oh, he probably liked it for a bit. Don't get me wrong: Julian has an ego as big as . . . well . . ." The chief raised one of his arms and swept it past the forward port. ". . . the forsaken void." He gritted his teeth.

Grimace? Pained mirth? Something in between the two? Nog couldn't be sure.

"But then, around day two, it would begin to rankle him. A burr under his skin. He'd be asking himself, 'Do I really deserve this?'"

"Doesn't he?"

"Of course he does," O'Brien said, rallying to his friend's defense. "He just wouldn't believe it deep down."

"Why not?" The helm signaled that they would reach their coordinates soon. The *Amazon*'s autopilot dropped them down to warp one.

O'Brien shrugged. "Who knows? Maybe he thinks that everything comes too easy, so he hasn't earned it."

Nog thought about the doctor's now well-known augmentations. *If I could be genetically modified, what would I want? Greater intelligence? Bigger lobes? Sharper teeth?* He dismissed the ideas as both petty and unnecessary. Nog was content with his physical and mental attributes. So, what did he really want? The thought came unbidden and all too easily: *To not feel so alone.* The idea surprised him. It was silly, wasn't it? Nog knew he wasn't alone. He had his crewmates and his colleagues. He had his work . . .

"Anyway," O'Brien continued, "if Julian were here, this would be just about the time we'd log some holosuite time."

"Alamo?"

"No, Siege of Bastogne, I think."

"I don't think I know that one," Nog confessed. He knew about the Alamo, but only because he had installed the holoprogram in his uncle's bar on the first Deep Space 9.

"Oh, it's glorious," O'Brien said, sitting up straighter in his seat. " 'Nuts!' "

"What?"

"I said, 'Nuts.' It's a famous quote from the siege."

Nog looked at O'Brien from the corners of his eyes, uncertain if he was being mocked. "If you say so."

O'Brien settled back down into his chair. "Julian would get it."

"Approaching destination coordinates," the computer announced. *"Scanning. No anomalies detected. Exit warp?"*

Nog took the helm back from the computer and, with practiced ease, disengaged the warp engines and slipped into impulse, the stars shifting from streaks of light to bright pinpricks. He checked the scanner readout. "Nothing," he said. "Except what you told me to expect."

O'Brien rose and leaned forward to get a closer look at the only noteworthy object in nearby space as it rolled slowly beneath the runabout's bow. "Not much to look at, is it?"

Nog hadn't wanted to say, especially as their outing had not been his idea. "But this is where you wanted to be, isn't it?"

O'Brien nodded.

"*Why*?" The Ferengi tried to put as much emphasis into the word as he could without sounding insulting.

"We needed to get away," O'Brien offered.

"*We* did?"

"Well, *I* did. And Captain Ro thought you did too, so she asked me to bring you along."

"Captain Ro thought I needed to get away?" Nog asked, his voice going an octave higher at the end of the question.

"She said you've had a rough few weeks," O'Brien offered. "I had to allow as that might be true, so . . ." He lifted his hand and waved it generally in the direction of their destination. ". . . change of scenery. If only barely."

The station—a *Helios*-class hub—rolled into view. Compared to the glory that was the new Deep Space 9 or, frankly, even the former Terok Nor, this waypost in space looked like an indifferent first-year engineering student had designed it on the morning the assignment was due.

"Looks like a mushroom," O'Brien said, which is exactly what Nog had been thinking.

"I didn't know that Starfleet used these anymore," Nog said.

Seventy or eighty years ago, just as it was beginning its second great age of exploration, the Federation had constructed scores of *Helios* stations and dropped them off as pickets where the newly commissioned fleet could stop and refuel and resupply. The upper decks, or the mushroom's cap, housed the bridge and officer quarters, while the thick stalk was comprised of anywhere from four to ten decks of quarters, labs, work space, and stowage. A bulb at the base of the stalk contained the station's reactor and, just below, the hangar deck. As one of Nog's professors at the Academy had explained, "Every expense was spared." And then she had added mysteriously, "Spam in a can." Nog had always remembered that comment.

"They don't," O'Brien said. "This is privately run."

"By whom?"

The *Amazon*'s comm chirped. The station was hailing them. "This is the Federation runabout *Amazon*. I'm Lieutenant Commander Nog. Please identify."

"No," a male voice replied. *"Or, wait, yes. This is the Robert Hooke. Who are you again? No, wait. Don't answer. We don't care. Just go away. We're busy. We don't want any. That's all you need to know. Go."*

Nog muted the feed. "Friendly," he said. "Do you want to reply? Or just turn around and go home?"

O'Brien made a sour face. "Not exactly what I was expecting." He tapped the companel. "This is Chief Miles O'Brien of Deep Space 9. I filed a flight plan for these coordinates earlier today. Is there a problem?"

Whoever was manning the comm board either didn't

know or didn't care to use the mute button. *"They say they're from Deep Space 9. What should I say?"*

A second voice, deeper, but muffled, answered, *"Ask them why they're here. Politely."*

"All right," the male sighed, and then cursed, perhaps realizing he hadn't muted his pickup. *"No problem, Amazon. We're just not used to visitors. Sorry, but I don't know anything about a flight plan. Is there something I can help you with? You understand this is a private station, right?"*

"I'm aware of that," O'Brien replied. "This isn't Starfleet business. I'm just, that is, *we're* just here to visit a friend."

"We are?" Nog asked *sotto voce.*

"We are," the chief replied.

"A friend?" Hooke asked. *"Who?"*

"Yeah," Nog asked softly. "Who?"

"Benjamin Maxwell," O'Brien said. "I believe he's employed here."

"Benjamin Maxwell?" Clearly, he no longer cared that he didn't know how to use a mute button. *"Who's that?"*

The second, deeper voice said, *"Ben. He means Ben."*

Realization took its sweet time. *"The janitor? Ben the janitor?"*

"Yes," the second voice drawled. *"Ben the janitor."*

Chapter 2

The giant strode across the island. With every step, its wide feet compressed the topmost branches of the olive trees, which sprung back again as the giant marched on.

Doctor Clark cupped his hands around the top half of his face to protect his eyes from the bright midmorning sun and laughed appreciatively as the behemoth strolled down the shoreline. Above the waist, the giant was nothing more than a bare armature, a sketch of a torso: just enough structure to hold the sensor array and the tiny antigrav engines. The legs were the magic, each one over forty meters high, and, though massive in appearance, constructed of superlight materials that didn't have more than a couple hundred kilos of mass.

At the last minute, just before unleashing it, Maxwell had thought to clothe his creation in loose trousers, which flapped merrily in the steady breeze off the water. *Next time*, he thought, *I'll use colored cloth. Something really bright. Rainbow patterned.* But, for the apparatus's first real run, white cloth seemed appropriate.

Clark asked, "How do you keep it from crushing anything?"

Maxwell winced, unsure whether the doctor was merely woefully ignorant of any principles of modern engineering or was simply being a good therapist and giving his patient plenty of room to reply. In either case, he decided, the reply would be the same. "It's pretty simple," Maxwell said. "Microsensors are slaved to the antigravs, and the main processor makes sure the structure maintains enough buoyancy to not come down too hard."

"The feet actually do make contact?"

"Yes," Maxwell explained. "So, the treetops bow a little. There are footprints in the sand. Otherwise, it would look odd. You might not be able to spot exactly why, but some part of your brain would tell you it was all a trick. This way—"

"It looks like a giant pair of legs walking around the island."

"*Strolling* around the island. I worked hard to make sure the gait was correct." He shaded his own eyes with his hand. Stupid to have forgotten his sunglasses. "He's taking it easy. Not in any hurry. He's just . . . taking it all in."

"And isn't that a lesson for us all?"

Down on the beach road, Maxwell watched pedestrians and cyclists stop short as the legs came into view. The rolling landscape, even down by the muddy shoreline, meant it was difficult to spot the giant legs coming from more than a couple hundred meters away. He couldn't see the people's expressions (he should have sent out some probes), but their posture signaled their reactions: awe, confusion, wonder, amusement. No one appeared to be frightened, which was good. It meant Maxwell had correctly calibrated the timing of the legs' pace: no one was alarmed because who could be alarmed about a man out for a stroll?

Colony staff and inmates (*No,* Maxwell corrected himself, *not inmates, patients*) were coming out of the administration buildings and dormitories. Maxwell had timed the event well: just after breakfast, but before the first round of group therapy sessions. People were asking, "What is it?" and "What does it mean?" No one sounded alarmed; most were delighted or, at worst, confused. He flicked his gaze over to Doctor Clark, who was studying him as best he could under the glare of midmorning.

"Well, Ben," Clark asked, smiling slyly, "what *does* it mean?"

"It means I have a degree in engineering with a specialty in repulsor field dynamics," Maxwell replied, watching as the legs briefly paused to avoid a foolhardy pedestrian who wandered too close to its foot pad.

"That's all?" Clark asked, crossing the lawn to stand closer. "Nothing else? No other message?" The wide lawn rolled down before them. Beside Maxwell, a small silver and ivory box chirped and ticked in time with the giant's steps.

"I'm not sure what you're trying to say, Doc," Maxwell said with all the sincerity he could muster. In the months since Gunther had left the colony and Clark had become Maxwell's primary counselor and (he had to admit it) confidant, they had developed a friendly, if contentious, give and take. Maxwell pretended to be ignorant of the doctor's therapeutic ripostes, and Clark pretended not to be annoyed.

"I think you're trying to tell us something," Clark said. "Or maybe only yourself." Maxwell remained silent. Clark sighed. "You're usually not this obtuse, Ben."

"I usually haven't released a pair of giant legs into the wild. I might be distracted."

"And you might be ready to leave, Ben," Clark said, laying a hand on his shoulder. He tightened his grip for a moment and then released it. "It might be time to go for a walk."

"A stroll," Maxwell corrected. "I keep telling you: a stroll."

"Then go for a stroll. I think it's time."

Maxwell stood a bit straighter, crossed his arms, and tilted his head to the left as he regarded his creation. The giant's legs had briefly come to a halt just at the edge of the mucky shoreline. Its posture suggested contemplation and rest. Its white pants fluttered like banners. A tern swerved around the left leg, banked, and landed atop the hip armature, happy for the vantage point, a new place to study the water for his midday meal. Maxwell said, "Maybe you're right. Not much left to do here, is there?"

"That's what I've been telling you."

"It's a penal colony, though. I might need some more penalization."

"It's a therapy center," Clark said. "And we're long past the point where there's any more therapy we can offer." He laughed. "Hell, most of the other patients think you're on the staff."

"I do have an air of command," Maxwell noted. "I keep trying to get rid of it, but can't seem to shake it."

"Stop trying," Clark said. "It's baked in."

The giant legs marched south and west, along the shoreline, and disappeared behind a low hill covered in grape vines. "So, time to go?" Maxwell asked as the spectators at the bottom of the hill returned to their chores and errands.

"Yes," his therapist said. "Time to go."

"Just one question."

"Only one?"

"Only one important one: Where?"

January 9, 2386
Ops Center
Robert Hooke

Finch leaned forward, briefly entering Sabih's personal space, and tapped a control stud on the comm panel. Being in Finch's orbit always meant coming into a complex mélange of aromas: sandalwood, green tea, and something metallic. It was pleasant, but unexpected.

"This is the mute button," Finch rumbled. "Pray learn to use it." He sat back in his padded chair with a huff. "What are you planning to say to our Starfleet friends?" Anatoly Finch was a large man. His generous frame was hard on furniture, especially furniture as old as some of the pieces in the Hooke common areas. "Quickly now, lad," he prodded. "They'll be getting suspicious right around now."

"Go away?" Sabih suggested, fidgeting with the closer on his jacket. He had only worked for Finch for a few months and didn't always know what his employer wanted when he posed questions of the sort he was flinging at him. Life would be ever so much simpler if Finch just *told* Sabih what he wanted to happen.

Finch shook his head and rubbed the neatly trimmed whiskers on his chin with the ball of his thumb. "While they have no formal jurisdiction here, our Starfleet friends will no doubt find some pretense for boarding. Try again."

"Tell them Ben isn't here?" Sabih asked, wishing there was someone—*anyone*—else in the ops center who might offer an opinion. But it was late in the station's workday, and the communications center typically wasn't manned in the "evening" hours.

"Unrealistic," Finch sighed. "Especially since they could contact him directly. I suspect that may occur at any moment. Their contacting him through us may be only a courtesy."

Sabih's mind raced. His palms were sweating. Getting rid of the 'Fleeters didn't seem to be an option, so the other logical option was . . . "Invite them aboard?"

Finch smiled and raised his hands in mock salute. "Well done, lad."

"And hope they don't see anything they shouldn't see?"

To Sabih's utter dismay, Finch grinned so broadly his molars showed. His eyes narrowed mischievously. "Oh, no," he said, his deep baritone voice reverberating off the ops center's dingy walls. "Show them *everything* and ask them what they think. But, before we do, let's find out more about our Lieutenant Commander Nog and Chief Miles O'Brien."

Runabout *Amazon*

"What is this place?" Nog asked, though he had already submitted a search to the computer. "And who is Robert Hooke?"

"You've never heard of Robert Hooke?" the chief asked.

"No. Should I?"

"Have you heard of Isaac Newton?"

"Of course," Nog replied. "He was a physicist." His mind raced. *Or a baker?*

"Well, you wouldn't have heard of Isaac Newton if not for Robert Hooke," O'Brien replied. "Hooke figured out most of the rules for the motion of planets, work that Newton later completed."

"*Most* of the rules? Why not all? That seems like something you'd want to finish."

O'Brien shrugged like he was making excuses for a friend. "Hooke was easily distracted. He had lots of other interests: microscopy, experimental physics, surveying. You know the type."

"I know the type," Nog said. "So he asked his friend Newton to take over?"

"They hated each other. I don't think Hooke wanted Newton to finish his work. He just did. Newton was like that."

"How do you know all of this?" Nog asked, impressed despite himself.

"Ah, well. No trick to it. I looked it up when Captain Maxwell told me he was stationed . . . well, *working* here."

"*Captain* Maxwell?"

"I should be more careful," O'Brien admitted. "He hates it when I call him that."

Captain Benjamin Maxwell. The name rang a bell. *And not a good bell,* Nog thought.

"Look it up, Nog," the chief said. "It's quicker than me telling you."

The computer had already retrieved the search about the Robert Hooke, but Nog nudged the results to the side and opened another search pane. Official Starfleet reports were the first results, including an image of Benjamin Maxwell, a middle-aged hew-mon, slight of build, gray-haired, with pleasant features and warm blue eyes. He was smiling slightly in the image—unusual for official Starfleet portraits—and there were crinkly lines around Maxwell's eyes that made Nog want to smile back.

"The image is old," O'Brien said. "Almost twenty years."

"Captain of the *Phoenix,*" Nog said, quickly scanning the article.

"And the *Rutledge* before that," the chief added. "He was my commanding officer."

Nog scrolled through the high points. Most were very impressive. The last one was not. Nog didn't need to read the details; he remembered hearing the story in the Academy, a cautionary tale of a captain who lost his way and decided he knew better than the admirals and analysts. "You were on the *Enterprise* then."

"Just a couple years before I went to the station," O'Brien added.

He skimmed through the text and stopped to read the brief of the court-martial in more detail. "Maxwell claimed the Cardassians were rearming for another push into Federation space. The science station was a supply depot?"

"Probably," O'Brien said. "It was never proved definitively, but Captain Picard said the evidence strongly suggested that Captain Maxwell . . . that Mister Maxwell . . . that he was probably right."

"Captain Picard even offered to testify on his behalf at the court-martial."

"I would have spoken too," O'Brien said. "But they never called me. He'd already confessed to everything. There was no need, but I would have. He didn't have anyone left."

Thirty-eight Years Earlier
Puerto Vallarta, Mexico, Earth

There hadn't been much left to bury, not that Maria would have wanted to be buried on Setlik III. "This isn't home," she had said on more than one occasion and never in earshot of the kids. They'd only lived at the colony for two years, but it was the longest either Carlo or Sofia had stayed in one place—the itinerate life of a Starfleet brat—so they considered it home, but not Maria. Earth was home, or, more accurately, Mexico, and his wife had every intention of settling there someday. The operative word was *someday*, as she was happy to say given any opportunity.

Maxwell looked at the tiny container that held his wife's remains: mostly just ash and a few bone fragments. Cardassian torpedoes were legendarily brutal, designed to instill maximum terror and damage. "If it helps," the recovery specialist had told Maxwell, "if it means anything at all, they never knew what hit them. These things burn so hot . . ."

He knew the specialist had been lying. They were trained to lie, trained to conceal and comfort and help the bereaved find some modicum of peace. Maxwell knew this because, being a captain, you just know these things. It was the curse of being a captain—knowing things, even the worst things. You had to know because you had to make sure you could be prepared, prepare your crew, prepare the people who depended on you.

"Thank you," Maxwell had said. "That . . . helps." For good measure, he added, "And at least they were all together in the end."

He looked at the two other tiny containers, both burnished to a gleam, even in the low light of the ship's tiny makeshift chapel. All three containers would remain there until the *Rutledge* reached Earth and Maxwell could bring Maria home. He would bury the containers on the hillside near Maria's parents' home. Her brothers would help him. Marco and Miguel would cry all afternoon as they carved out the graves and squared them off. They would cry through the funeral—quiet, manly tears—and cry afterward when they filled in the graves and replaced the sod they had carefully removed. They would cry some more at the dinner and all the time they were getting gently yet deeply inebriated on the tequila they distilled in the garage behind Marco's house.

They would give Maxwell a shot of the tequila and tell him to drink, which he would. They would tell him, in low tones, that it was all right to weep, to release his grief, to wail and curse God. Maxwell would smile and thank them. He would, too. He would when the time was right. "I'll cry," he promised, "when the tears come."

But he knew that he never would. Tears had to come from someplace inside you, but there was nothing left inside Benjamin Maxwell except perhaps ashes. He felt them there, inside him.

He studied the small silver containers in his ship's chapel, but he didn't dare touch any of them. His hands were too heavy, too clumsy. He knew he would break the containers open if he tried to handle them, and the ashes, the ashes, they would fill the room and be sucked away by the air scrubbers until they were shot out into space. His wife and children shot out into space, disbursed, and never to be recovered.

January 9, 2386
Ben Maxwell's Quarters
Robert Hooke

Maxwell opened his eyes and silently counted backward from ten. He tried to remain still, not wanting his cabin's motion sensor to detect him and turn on the light. He wanted the dark to remain dark.

. . . Seven, six, five . . .

Years of therapy kept him in the moment, experiencing the feelings, letting them wash over him.

. . . Four, three, two . . .

He heard the voices of his counselors in the back of his mind, all of them speaking in low tones, offering encouragement: *Stay with it. Feel it. Don't deny the emotions.*

Maxwell thought about the ocean, thought about surfing. Despite living in New Zealand for years, he had only tried surfing a couple times, and only in curated areas. Having spent most of his childhood living near or on the water, knowing what dwelled beneath the waves, he had too much respect for those creatures to play on the roof of their home. He had told Doctor Gunther, "There are great whites down there." Gunther had been one of the best surfers at the hospital, he and his sons. "You know what one of them can do, don't you?" Maxwell had asked. Gunther had only laughed. Of course he knew. He'd lived his whole life on the waves. He knew everything about the water, everything above and below. He respected the hunters, but never worried.

. . . One, zero . . .

The dream was locked down. He had it, the gist of it, in any case. Not so much a dream, Maxwell knew, as a distillation of memory. He reflected on his feelings, about those days: discovering the bodies, bringing them home, and laying them to rest. His wife. His children. Maxwell remembered how he had felt, or, in truth, hadn't felt anything at all.

Counselors had asked, back when he woke up every night, chest heaving, sheets soaked with sweat. *Only in the hospital or at the colony, though.* Never when he was on his ships, not the *Rutledge* or the *Phoenix.*

"How did you sleep back in those early days?" every counselor had asked.

"Like a rock," Maxwell had said.

He almost laughed now to think about it.

He hadn't had that dream in years. He thought about that day. His wife and children, dead now for so many years, were never far from him. But did he dream? No. Not so much.

"So why today?" Maxwell said aloud. The cabin sensors heard, naturally, and the tiny light in the corner near the hatch flickered on just in case he needed to go to the head. He rolled over onto his back and put his hands behind his head, considering the bulkheads. *Oh,* he thought. *Of course.*

And, naturally, just at that moment, the intercom chimed. Anatoly Finch intoned, as if from the heavens (which was, in a sense, true), *"Ben? Are you awake?"*

Maxwell replied, as one does to a minor deity, with respect and good grammar. "I am," he replied. "What can I do for you?"

"You have some visitors, Ben. Starfleet. They're asking about you. Do you want to see them?"

Them? Maxwell wondered. *Who did Miles bring with him?* He shrugged. It didn't matter. He sat up and massaged some of the kinks out of his neck and shoulders. The Hooke beds were too soft. "Of course," he said. "Where would you like me to meet them?"

"The hangar bay, I suppose," Finch replied.

"Can't right now. Both bays are being used." Finch never paid any attention to log entries that didn't involve the labs.

"Ah," Finch said. *"Of course they are. I suppose we'll have to receive them up here then, shan't we? Ops, in five minutes?"*

"Make it ten, please." Maxwell said. "I need to tidy up."

"Very well," Finch drawled. *"And Ben?"*

"Sir?"

"We will be having a discussion about your having guests show up unannounced, won't we?"

"Check the logs, Mister Finch," Maxwell said, repressing his irritation. "It's all there."

Finch paused, but did not sign off. Clearly, he was checking his log. *"Of course it is, Ben. But still . . ."*

"If you say we're going to have a discussion, Mister Finch," Maxwell conceded, "we'll have a discussion. It's your station, after all. I just work here."

"Indeed," Finch intoned. *"Indeed."*

Chapter 3

"Thank you both for agreeing to meet me here," Nog said.

"Hey," Danny said. "Glad to help." He tugged on the knot of his necktie, loosening it just enough that he could slip a finger down his collar and scratch his neck. Then Danny tilted his head to one side, moved his mouth in a way that might have been interpreted as a smile, and said, "Sorry I couldn't find Vic for you. He's . . . ah . . . busy?"

"That's okay, Danny," Nog said. "It's always good to see you. How's business been?"

Danny squinted and looked down at the inside of his wrist like he was reading something very tiny someone had written there. "Business has been okay. We've been knocking around a couple possibilities. Rusty has an idea."

"Rusty?" Nog asked.

Danny shrugged wearily, like he didn't have the strength to comment, and sat back in his club chair. The hologram flickered once and then again.

"My brother's still having problems with his holosuites?" Rom asked from where he sat. Nog's father fidgeted, first rubbing the arms of the chair, then touching the lobes of his ears, and finally tugging on the cuffs of his expensively

tailored shirt. Despite having been the grand nagus for more than a decade, Rom still did not present any evidence of being comfortable with the higher-quality fabrics his wife, Leeta, rightly insisted he wear while serving in his official capacity.

"What kind of suites?" Danny asked.

Rom, seated in front of his personal holographic array in his office on Ferenginar, grinned, remembering that *this* hologram was not self-aware like Vic Fontaine. *"Danny, you look good."*

"You too, Rom," Danny replied. "How're the wife and the kid?"

Rom smiled hugely, showing his back teeth. *"The treasures of my life."*

Danny dipped his head and turned away as if he was embarrassed by the display of unbridled happiness. "How is it," he asked wryly, "that a guy like you is in charge?"

Rom's grin faded. *"I think,"* he said uncertainly, *"because the economic indicators are up one point six percent over projections for the quarter, largely on the basis of the depreciated tariffs we've introduced for both Federation and Cardassian goods. In the past three quarters, we've seen slightly smaller increases, though we've managed to leverage the improved reputation of Ferengi mining so that—"*

"Father?" Nog asked.

"Yes?"

"Please don't get started on economic reforms. Beaming in your hologram from home is very . . . costly."

"I can afford it," Rom said brightly.

"I mean, Uncle Quark is bound to notice sooner or later and wonder what we're doing."

"*Oh,*" Rom said, shrinking slightly, which seemed so ridiculous to Nog. His father had infinitely more wealth and prestige than his uncle, and yet Rom still acted like he was afraid Quark was going to walk in at any moment and tell him to clear a dirty table. "*All right, then, what are we doing?*"

"Yeah," Danny said. "What's the deal?"

"I need some advice," Nog began.

"*Oh,*" Rom said, and sat up straighter. "*Of course, son. What can I help you with? I mean, what kind of advice do you need? Financial information? Questions about career options? Uh, decorating suggestions? You do have new quarters, don't you?*"

"This isn't about women, is it?" Danny asked. "If it is, I can go get Rusty."

"No. No," Nog said. "No, and definitely *no,*" he said. "It's just that . . ." He searched for the right words despite the fact that he'd been rehearsing the conversation for the past couple days. Crossing his arms over his chest, he lowered his head and said, with as much meaning as he could muster, "Life has been very *odd* lately." He looked up from under his brow to see what kind of response his statement had generated. His father was now leaning forward in his chair, palms of his hands resting on his knees. Now that Rom had something to do, a task to engage in, he had ceased fidgeting. Danny maintained a demeanor of polite, modulated concern. Interestingly, a small table had materialized beside his chair and Danny was sipping from a tumbler of brown liquor.

No one said a word for several seconds.

His father looked back and forth between Nog and

Danny. *"So?"* Rom asked, apparently mystified. *"You're on Deep Space 9. Life is* always *odd there."*

Danny pointed toward Rom without taking his eyes off Nog. "I concur."

"It's been *extra* odd," Nog amended. "As in 'more so than usual.' I . . . I'm afraid I can't tell you about all of it." He shook his head, an indication of his frustration. "Orders." Rom frowned at him as if to say, *So?* Nog added, "From the top. The *very* top."

"But you're okay?" Danny asked.

"Nothing physical," Nog explained. "Nothing permanent, anyway." He rubbed his forehead and stood up straight. Besides the two chairs and the table, the room was starkly simple, with paneled walls and a lush wall-to-wall carpet based on the kinds in gentlemen's clubs a person like Danny might have frequented back in the twentieth century, though purely for business reasons, naturally. Nog enjoyed walking around on the carpet. He felt like the soles of his feet were being massaged by tiny, furry springs.

"Then what?" Rom asked.

"Yeah, kid. What he said. *Then what?"* Danny asked. "Afraid you're being a bit too cryptic."

"There's no one to talk to!" Nog said, surprised by his own words. He had been thinking about this conversation for some time, but now that he had arrived at the crux of the matter, he was surprised—and not a little bit embarrassed—to hear the words come out of his mouth. This was the source of his spiritual malaise? That he didn't have anyone who would listen to him complain?

Danny and his father looked at each other. Two overlapping but competing thoughts blipped through Nog's mind:

These two glancing askew at each other is costing an astonishing amount of latinum.

The holograms look great.

"Well . . . ," Rom began.

"You could . . . ," Danny hemmed. "Ah . . ."

Both fell silent and became very intensely interested in their manicures, waiting for the other to continue.

"You could call me anytime," Rom said, rising and spreading his hands.

"All you have to do is drop in," Danny added, uncrossing and recrossing his legs.

Nog waved them both away. "This isn't about making you feel guilty. Or worrying about me. I know how I sound. I know this is kind of . . . " He searched his feelings for the correct word. " . . . pathetic."

"Not at all," Danny said. "It's important. And something you need to get all the kinks out of because if you don't, it can turn nasty."

"He's right, son," Rom said. *"It is important. Everyone needs someone to talk to about this sort of thing. If I didn't have Leeta, I don't know what I'd do. Thoughts whizzing away at warp speed, one way or another. A million things to ponder every day. It's enough to make a man's lobes throb."*

"What did you do before you met Leeta?" Nog asked.

Rom sat down again and slumped into his chair. Nog was touched by the momentary expression of wistful sadness on his father's face. *"Well,"* he said, *"I had you."* He furrowed his brow. *"And Quark, who can be a surprisingly good listener when you pay him enough.*" He frowned, but then brightened. *"And Morn!"*

"Morn?" Danny asked.

"I miss him," Rom said, momentarily lost in the mists of nostalgia.

"Sure," Danny said, playing along.

His father remained quiet for a count of four and then asked, *"What about Jake?"*

Well, Nog thought. *Here we are.* He kept his answer brief. "Married. Baby."

Both men shrugged and looked at opposite corners of their virtual room.

"No counterproposal for that," Rom said.

"It happens," Danny added.

"Yeah," Nog sighed. "And I'm happy for him."

"Of course you are," Rom said. *"But I understand what you're saying,"* his father added. *"What it means. But it's one of those things that happen to everyone. People change. They grow up. And sometimes . . ."*

"People get left behind," Danny concluded.

No one spoke. They all stared for what seemed a very long time, but was probably only ten strips of latinum.

Finally, Nog asked, "So, what do you do?"

Rom looked at Danny, who looked back. They shrugged as one.

"Move on," Danny offered.

"Make new friends."

"Or see a shrink," Danny added.

Nog shook his head at the last suggestion. "No. This isn't that sort of thing. I'm not looking for therapy. Just someone who wants to . . . I don't know. There's a word . . ."

"Hang out," Danny offered.

"That's two words," Rom corrected.

Nog rolled his eyes.

"What about the chief?" Rom asked.

January 9, 2386
Ops Center
Robert Hooke

"What about this Chief O'Brien?" Finch asked.

"What *is* a chief?" Sabih asked, scrolling through large chunks of data at rapid speeds. One of his skills—his *only* skill, he would admit when he was being honest with himself—was his ability to quickly and efficiently search for and retrieve data from a variety of nonintegrated databases. Starfleet, he knew, was all about cohesive, curated databases, but not everyone else in the Federation (and definitely not outside it) was fortunate enough to possess its refined resources. Sabih also knew he could look up the answer to his own question before Finch could reply, but he wanted to buy himself some time. Also, sometimes he enjoyed listening to his employer pontificate.

"A *chief*," Finch began, leaning back with fingers steepled, "is a noncommissioned officer, which means he or she has been promoted up through the ranks of enlisted personnel and did not receive a commission. There are many types of noncommissioned officers—or noncoms, as they are sometimes called—but most of them share the distinction of being particularly talented in some complex, specialized skill, such as piloting a particularly nasty form of craft or mastering a weapons system. Chiefs frequently know more about the actual subject than the lieutenants and captains to whom they report."

Finch exhaled, as he often did when completing one of his complex and perfectly phrased sentences. Inhaling, he began anew. "Now, our *Chief* O'Brien is likely some sort of engineering specialist—the most common use of the term in Starfleet—and holds sway over some section of specialists . . ."

"Actually," Sabih said, having located O'Brien's public records, "he's the chief engineer of Deep Space 9. In fact, he's one of the primary designers and architects."

". . . Or, as I was about to say," Finch continued without missing a beat, "sometimes the title is retained by individuals who, in fact, have a much wider swath of responsibility and authority. Obviously, such is the case with our erstwhile visitor. And his associate?"

"Nog? Hang on, let me check." As Sabih had immediately recognized the name as Ferengi, he needed little time to find a Starfleet lieutenant commander from that world. There was, in fact, only one, named Nog or otherwise. "Lots of impressive information here, assuming I'm reading this correctly. But one fact stands out: Lieutenant Commander Nog is the son of the current grand nagus, Rom."

Finch was not often rendered speechless. Sabih observed the spectacle from the corners of his eyes, not daring to stare directly at a minor miracle. Finch's gaze, meanwhile, appeared to be flickering from one imagined vista to the next. He lifted his chin and rubbed the underside with the tip of his thumb. "*Really?*" he breathed. "How very *interesting.*"

"It is, isn't it?" Sabih commented. "Why would the son of the grand nagus waste his time working for Starfleet? He must be worth more latinum than, well, the space station he works on."

"The newly built space station," Finch said. "And our nearest neighbor of any note if you don't count Bajor."

"Don't you count Bajor?"

"No," Finch said. "Bajor is too concerned with *Bajor* to have much interest in our activities. But a Starfleet station . . . I've been meaning to focus some thought on them, but, you know . . ." He gestured significantly in an "up-there-thataway" fashion. "Busy, busy."

"But now they've come to us," Sabih added, and then corrected, "To *you*. They've come to you."

"They *have*," Finch growled. "But *why?*" He suddenly remembered. "Ah, yes—Ben. Ben the janitor."

"You know, he's not really exactly a *janitor,*" Sabih said, wishing to present a fair and balanced perspective.

"He is if I say he is," Finch replied, pulling his cuffs through the sleeves of his jacket. "But clearly there's more to our Mr. Maxwell than was unearthed by his background check. How does he command the attention of two such eminences?"

"I'm not sure," Sabih said, scrolling as fast as he could. "I'm not finding anything actionable. It's not exactly the easiest name in the word to disambiguate. *Benjamin No-Middle-Initial Maxwell.* He could be anyone."

"Check for a Starfleet connection."

"I thought of that," Sabih said, mildly insulted. "I found a stub of a record about an officer named Benjamin Maxwell."

"A stub?"

"Something left after something has been edited. Or purged."

"Purged. An interesting term, my lad. Why *purged*?"

"It doesn't say. That's more or less the point of a purge. So no one knows. Again, I note that Benjamin Maxwell is a common name." He knew he would pay for these last comments—Finch did not appreciate being the target of sarcasm—but Sabih was tired and hungry and had been working for more than sixteen hours with neither rest nor consuming anything he considered real food. This internship was not working out the way he had hoped. If only he had worked a little harder at university, maybe he wouldn't be in this ridiculous situation, forced to kow-tow to every whim of this strange, strange man.

"Hmph," Finch grunted. "Yes."

Oh, yes, Sabih thought. *I'm definitely going to pay for that last comment. Unless I can distract him?* "They're waiting for a reply."

"Of course they are," Finch said, standing up straight and tugging his jacket down over his barrel chest. "Where are our manners? Lower the ramparts and invite the venerated inside. And, as soon as they're comfortable, we'll take them up to meet *her.*"

Runabout *Amazon*

"And who is this fellow Finch when he's not at home?" O'Brien asked.

"Well," Nog said, "to start, he *is* at home. The Hooke is his home, his only home. Or at least it's his only known address."

"He owns it?"

"He's the landlord. An Orion bank owns it. He didn't have much of a down payment. The loan terms are not optimal. Interest rates are . . . well, my uncle would need to have a lie-down with a damp cloth on his forehead if he ever had to pay these rates."

O'Brien glanced at the column of numbers Nog indicated. "Or have a little private party if he was the lender," the chief observed.

Nog grinned. "He might invite a close friend or two with these kinds of rates."

"So he's a landlord. What else?"

"A scientist," Nog recited. "A researcher—genetics and biotechnology. An entrepreneur."

"Not a term you hear much these days," O'Brien said.

"But not a very good one," Nog said. "Finch has had his successes." He pulled up a long list of filed patents. "And some failures." He pulled up an even longer list of lawsuits.

"Aren't lawsuits one of the operational hazards of aggressive capitalism?"

"Not if you're doing it right."

"Hmmm," O'Brien said, realizing that while Nog was the least Ferengi-like Ferengi he had ever met, he was still steeped in the arcane workings of finance. "So, Finch managed to purchase—well, *mortgage*—this station out here in the middle of nowhere and lured some other researchers to come along. Why? How?"

"Because they couldn't find anyone else who would let them do their work?" Nog theorized.

"Possibly," O'Brien said. "Do we have any data about Finch's tenants?"

"No," Nog said, having obviously attempted several searches. "Not public information."

"So they could be crackpots."

"Crackpots?"

"Fringe scientists."

"Ah," Nog said. "High-risk researchers. Understood. Then, if I may ask, do you have any idea why Captain . . . I mean . . . *Mister* Maxwell . . . is out here with them?"

O'Brien was reassured by the fact that he wasn't the only one tripping over what to call Ben Maxwell. "I think," he said, "because he believed he didn't have anywhere else to go."

The comm cheeped. *"Gentlemen,"* boomed the deeper male voice, presumably Finch's. *"My sincere apologies for keeping you waiting. We've contacted Ben—Mister Maxwell—and asked him to meet you here in our operational center. The transporter platform has been cleared. Please be aware that we use a slightly older integrator, so set your pattern buffer to—"*

"Got it," O'Brien said, checking the schema on the transporter panel and finding it mildly alarming. *Maybe I should offer to do an upgrade while I'm here,* he thought. "Thanks for the warning. We'll use your coordinates but *our* transporter"

"I apologize for not being able to let you use our docking facility," Finch continued. *"But both of our transports are in for minor repairs."*

"No worries," O'Brien said. "Give us a minute to secure our ship and we'll be over. *Amazon* out."

O'Brien pointed at the transporter schema and Nog winced. He stood, brushed off the front of his uniform tunic, and then sighed deeply. "I hope you won't mind, but I have to ask you this, Chief."

"Go ahead."

"Why am I here?"

O'Brien answered, "Like I said, you've had a rough couple months and Captain Ro thought you looked like you needed to take a little trip."

"Remember where we went the last time we 'took a little trip' together?"

"No," O'Brien said uncertainly.

"Empok Nor."

"Oh," O'Brien recalled. "Right. That could have gone better."

Nog walked to the transporter pad. O'Brien joined him. Neither of them commented further.

O'Brien opened his mouth to issue the order, but then snapped it shut as he remembered that Nog was, officially speaking, the senior officer and entitled to give the command.

"Computer," Nog said, "beam us to the *Hooke.*"

The transporter replied, *"Energizing,"* and the interior of the *Amazon* dissolved.

Chapter 4

Miles O'Brien rolled over onto his stomach and searched the deck for his bedside chrono. Naomi Chao cursed when his movement yanked the sheet off her chest. "Why do you keep this cabin so cold?" she griped.

"It's not cold," O'Brien replied, patting the deck. "You just need to eat something besides broccoli and soy paste."

"I *like* broccoli and soy paste," Chao muttered, and half-heartedly socked O'Brien in the back.

"I'm going to make you some mutton stew," O'Brien said. "And you won't be cold anymore. My mother loves mutton stew, and she's never cold." This, strictly speaking, was not true. O'Brien suspected that his mother, like most women he had encountered so far in his life, was *always* cold, but like any good Irish countrywoman, she knew the virtue of thick wool socks.

"What is mutton?" Chao asked. "It's sheep, isn't it? Or baby cows. Which? Never mind. They're both disgusting and I won't eat it."

"Then you'll always be cold."

"Not if you would turn up the heat!"

O'Brien chuckled, pleased with the reaction. Though they'd only been lovers for a few weeks, he enjoyed knowing he could get under Chao's skin when needed. He found his chrono and held it up so she could see it. "Oh-two-thirty," he said.

Chao groaned. "I can't believe you did this to me *again*. I have to get up in four hours."

"So do I," O'Brien protested.

"Right," Chao said, dragging the sheet back to cover her chest and legs. "You sit at tactical and pretend you're looking at sensor readouts for a few hours. I actually have to *work*."

"Staring at sensor screens is work," O'Brien said, mentally adding, *Especially if you're waiting for a Cardassian ship to pop out of warp and run the blockade.*

"Not compared to ops," Chao said. O'Brien had to admit this was probably true, especially when Captain Maxwell was on the bridge. The captain was, as everyone who served on his ship agreed, a genial and gracious commander, but he did not tolerate shoddiness or incompetence. Chao leaned over and began to search the deck for her discarded uniform.

"You don't have to go if you don't want," O'Brien said. "Marcus is on leave, so I have the cabin to myself."

"That's not the problem," Chao said, standing and pulling on her undergarments. "It's one thing to be seen leaving your cabin in the middle of the night and something entirely different stepping out into a busy corridor just as alpha shift is beginning. Especially if my uniform looks like it probably does." She sighed and said, "Lights. One-quarter." The lights came up, though only barely. She was holding up her uniform blouse, inspecting the creases. "I *hate* this fabric."

"I hear they may be changing them again," O'Brien said off-handedly. "One-piece."

Chao slipped on the uniform blouse. "I *heard*," she moaned. "What genius do you suppose came up with that idea? It wasn't a woman, I can tell you that much. I mean, how are we supposed to go to the bathroom without completely disrobing?"

O'Brien considered possible solutions. "Snaps?" he offered.

Chao pulled on her jacket and tugged the flaps snugly over her breasts. "Hey, mister," she warned. "Don't get snappy with me. Not if you ever want to see any of this again *without* a uniform." She waved her hand in an all-inclusive motion. O'Brien didn't tug on the dangling thread of her metaphor. He most definitely *did* want to see Chao without her uniform again. While he was reasonably sure she enjoyed some warm feelings about him, he also sensed that the balance of power in their still-new relationship was decidedly in her favor. O'Brien knew she could live without ever seeing him again.

He watched silently, arms crossed over his chest, as Chao gathered together and donned the last straying bits of uniform. She worked quietly and efficiently, the same manner in which she approached most tasks.

After she had shaken out her second sock and was slipping it over her foot, O'Brien asked quietly, "You want to have dinner tonight?"

Chao slowed her movements as if suddenly worried she might be making too much commotion or noise. Without looking at O'Brien, she said, "I don't know, Miles. This seemed to work when we were just . . . when it was just a casual." She paused to consider her words. "When we weren't breaking any major rules . . . any of the captain's major rules. You know what I mean. He gets it—that people need to blow off steam."

"And eat dinner," O'Brien reminded her.

"Yes, but . . . if you eat dinner together every night and then slip away to someone's cabin every night, people begin to notice."

"They've already noticed, Naomi."

"*I know they've already noticed*," Chao said through clenched teeth. She inhaled once deeply and then released the breath slowly. "That's my point."

O'Brien was surprised by how much effort it required to continue breathing at a regular rate. After three exhalations, he said, "I'm sorry you feel that way."

Chao sighed, finished tugging on her second boot, and stood. She looked at the mirror, attempted to rake her hair into some presentable shape with her fingers, but then seemed to surrender. "I'm not sure how I feel, Miles. I know that I like you. I know that I have fun with you." She paused, clearly searching for a third item to complete the set. "And I know that I'm never going to try mutton. Do you think you can accept that for now?"

Understanding that he had just been given parameters gift wrapped in a reprieve, O'Brien smiled and nodded. "I think I can do that."

"Good." She came back to the bed, leaned down, and kissed O'Brien on the cheek. "I appreciate it. Maybe when things settle down here we can figure this out."

"Settle down?" O'Brien asked skeptically. "You think the Cardassians are going to just give up and go back home? Do you think *we're* going to pack up and leave, especially after what they've done?"

Chao sat on the corner of the bed and laid her hand on O'Brien's chest, not with any sensual intent, but simply, he thought, to comfort or, perhaps, to take measure, or to see whether she could read his thoughts through his skin. "No," she said finally. "I suppose not. When you put it like that." To O'Brien's great surprise, Chao folded backward so that her head landed on his shoulder, then pulled his arm up around her like she was tugging on a blanket. They lay there together for a good few minutes, neither one of them speaking. Then, so softly that O'Brien could barely hear her, Chao asked, "How do you think he does it?"

O'Brien was fairly certain he knew what Chao meant, but he was sure this was one of those times when he should have his pronouns sorted out. "How," he asked, "does who do what?"

"The captain," she said. "Keep it together. How does Captain Maxwell keep it together—keep all of *us* together—so well after what he's been through? After what those . . . *Cardies* . . . did to his family."

And everyone else on Setlik, O'Brien added silently, but decided that this was not Chao's point.

"I don't know," O'Brien replied gently. "But I also don't know anyone else who possibly *could*."

"Me either," Chao said. Suddenly, O'Brien understood that there might be another reason why she had some second thoughts about spending her meals and nights with him (regulations notwithstanding). To his great surprise, O'Brien found that he did not feel particularly slighted by the realization. She squeezed his hand, the one she had pulled around her shoulder. "You come pretty close," she said with something like her familiar bravado. Kissing him again on the cheek, this time with a little more commitment, Chao sat up and rolled off the bed. "See you on the bridge."

"And later?" he asked. O'Brien couldn't help himself.

"Later's later," Chao said as the door to the main corridor snapped open and she stepped through. "Let's worry about it when it gets here."

January 9, 2386
Engineering Deck
Robert Hooke

Not enough sleep, not enough sleep, not enough sleep, Maxwell thought, jogging up the stairs that lined the inner wall of the Hooke central module. *I'm getting too old to just shake it off like I once did.* He moved easily enough despite his eighty-plus years, lifting each foot just enough to clear the top of the riser, not scraping the bottom of his thin shoes or putting any more stress on his knees and ankles than absolutely necessary. *The muscle and bone parts still seem to be doing okay,* he decided, though he was a little concerned about the twinge in his lower back. *The mushy stuff in my skull—there's the area of greatest risk.*

Maxwell didn't have to climb the stairs. He could have taken the turbolift just like everyone else. The turbolifts worked—more or less—primarily because Maxwell made sure the turbolifts worked. Essentially, everything on the Hooke that wasn't controlled or managed or owned by the individual researchers continued to function because of Maxwell's cajoling, insults, and—when required—willingness to make shameless promises that he had no intention of keeping. Thus, the life-support system continued to support life, and the toilets emptied when the levers were pulled.

As he puffed up the stairs, Maxwell listened to the Hooke expand and contract around him just the way he had once listened to the surge of his ship's warp engines. It pleased him to note that nothing sounded like it was going to break down anytime soon. It was, Maxwell had to admit, the most fulfilling relationship he had managed to maintain for several years.

And now Miles has come by to say hello. Maxwell groaned involuntarily and almost stumbled on a step.

During his years of incarceration and treatment following his crime, many of Maxwell's former colleagues and crew—everyone from mission specialists to admirals—had come forward to offer assistance and support. Most of them had been genuinely concerned and not merely morbidly curious to observe a precipitous fall from up close. As weeks became months, which in turn became years, Maxwell's story mutated from a news story to a teaching moment or cautionary tale, depending on who was telling the tale.

Over time, most of the observers had fallen away, not the least because Maxwell had encouraged them to do so. Did he not want their support or had he simply grown weary? Or, as Doctor Clark had suggested, "Have you simply changed into another person?" Maxwell wasn't sure, but there was one fact about which he was certain: Miles O'Brien had been a constant, gracious presence. The chief never intruded, but Maxwell always knew he could count on his old tactical officer for a moderately raucous note and a bottle of real Bushmills on his birthday.

O'Brien's constancy was an inspiration. Maxwell knew he should be grateful. He knew this in his heart of hearts, but, for reasons he couldn't satisfactorily articulate, the idea of O'Brien coming for a visit felt like an intrusion. "You're a terrible man, Ben Maxwell," he mumbled as he reached the landing. "A terrible, terrible man."

Far below, in the depths of the core, the Hooke's overburdened atmosphere reclaimers chugged, scrubbing out the carbon dioxide and spewing forth breathable air. One deck below the scrubbers, and the station's primary reactor, was the hangar bay where the *Wren* and the *Aubrey* awaited last touches of paint before Maxwell considered their refits completed. He had come to love both spacecraft: rugged workhorses with the same basic engineering of the Federation's *Erewon*-class transports, but smaller and more manageable. Keeping the craft healthy was one of Maxwell's principal joys. If one of the ships was outside the bay, as was usually the case, O'Brien might have brought his runabout in and given them a chance to chat briefly before encountering Finch. Perhaps that would have been the kind thing to do. *Finch Without Warning* felt like it could be the title of a moderately disturbing children's book.

Maxwell pressed his thumb against the electronic lock, but suddenly froze. He looked out of the corners of his eyes, right and left, without moving his head.

He was, he knew, being watched.

She's here, Maxwell thought. *Great.*

He felt her eyes on him. If he moved his head and looked around, then there was a chance she might drop down on him. Sometimes, though, when these spells of watchfulness were on her, if Maxwell didn't challenge her by locking gazes, she would simply let him pass. *It was a game to her*, Maxwell thought, though there was more to it than simply that. She considered the central core to be *hers* and mildly resented Maxwell for using the stairways. He mentally conceded the point: the core *was* hers or, at least, she had been made for such spaces. *Well,* Maxwell thought, mentally shrugging, *her and her sister. But I never see her down here.*

He sighed and tilted his head back to look up at the underside of the stairway slanting off over his head. Eight jewel-like beads, two much larger than the other six, glittered back at him. "Hello, Ginger," Maxwell said. A pair of delicate chelicerae parted and clicked back together, a motion that Maxwell had learned to interpret as a kind of nod, a greeting. She dropped out from under the staircase on a slender, deceptively fragile-looking thread and allowed the air current in the core to spin her slowly in a clockwise direction. The grayish-green marking on her exoskeleton made it very difficult to see Ginger in low light, but now that she had slipped into the relatively modest illumination provided by the staircase lamps, she was easy enough to spot.

She dropped lower, and then lower, until she hung less than a meter above Maxwell. He had to tilt his head so that his neck was completely exposed, the muscles tight, so that he could look up into the arachnoform's complex eyes. If she, for any reason, decided to release her hold on her thread, she would undoubtedly land so hard on Maxwell that he would be sent tumbling back down the stairway or, conceivably, over the rail to the bottom of the core. But she wouldn't do that, Maxwell knew. Ginger loved him.

Well, Ginger loved Maxwell as much as a giant spider weighing roughly thirty kilos could love a man. He suspected this was a lot.

"Where's your sister?" he asked. Ginger and her sister, Honey, were near-constant companions, the one exception being Ginger's periodic forays into the core of the Hooke in search of Maxwell. It wasn't that Honey disliked Maxwell (or so he hoped). They had a cool, professional relationship. They knew—and were respected by—a lot of the same people. In brief, Maxwell believed that Honey considered them to be *colleagues*, which seemed a desirable state of affairs. The exceptions, naturally, involved the moments when Maxwell worried whether Honey might feel some *personal* animosity, which their creator, Nita Bharad, claimed was impossible.

Whenever he had voiced his concern, Nita had simply stated, "I like you, so they like you. That's the way it is."

"But, Nita," Maxwell frequently replied. "One of them likes me a lot more than the other. What about that?"

"Sometimes I like you more than at other times," Nita explained. "It's complicated. Emotions are complicated. They're complicated for us with all this squishy gray stuff up here . . ." At this juncture, Nita would usually point to her skull with two fingers (which Maxwell always found curiously endearing). "Imagine how it is for them!"

"Because they're spiders?"

"They're arachnoforms," Nita said matter-of-factly. "Not spiders. And, no, imagine what it's like for them being so smart."

"Smarter than we are?" Maxwell always asked, at which point Nita would always shrug and finish her drink.

"They won't tell me," she would say. "I keep asking, but they're being coy."

"Do you need something, Ginger?" Maxwell asked, tapping his thumb against the electronic lock. She swayed in the breeze. She chittered, a mild gurgling kind of sound that, fortunately, never produced moisture. Streams of drool would be more than Maxwell could handle, though he believed Ginger too polite to drool.

She continued to spin above his head. Usually, if Ginger spent this much time near him, it meant one of two things: she was worried about him *or* she thought Bharad needed something. Maxwell asked, "Does Nita need help with something?"

Chelicerae clicked.

"Ah," Maxwell said. "Well, I have to go meet some people in ops. Can I go see Nita after I take care of the visitors?"

Ginger exhaled sharply. *Annoyance.* The tips of her long hind legs touched the thread from which she dangled and contracted three times in rapid succession, pulling her back up into the shadows under the stairway. There was a vent cover there, Maxwell knew, that Ginger must have pried away and stuck to the wall with her silk. The sounds of the core covered most of her movement, but Maxwell was able to just barely detect the clink and clatter of the arachnoform squeezing into the vent and replacing the cover. He briefly considered turning around, going back down the stairs, and returning to the storeroom/bolt-hole he had set up as his private lair. It was secure against every manner of intrusion—Ginger, O'Brien, Finch, everyone. He looked back down the stairs and considered his options. *Why not?*

His wrist communicator chirped and Maxwell tapped it. "Go ahead," he said.

"Hey, Ben. This is Uchiha on deck four. You know, toward the back?"

"Sure," Maxwell said. Uchiha worked with complex decahydric polymers—something to do with either construction material or long-term food storage. "Hi, Ken." Maxwell always tried to address everyone by his or her first name. "What's up?"

"Uh, something with the toilet." Uchiha sounded embarrassed. *"I think someone tried to flush something down it that maybe they shouldn't have. Could you come take a look? When you have a second?"*

"Of course," Maxwell said, tapping his thumb to the lock. "I'll be right there." The door to the corridor swooshed open, and he stepped through. "Duty calls."

Ops Center
Robert Hooke

Old-school, Nog thought. *I like it.* The Robert Hooke's operations center had obviously been designed using the tried-and-true circular design aesthetic of most

Federation command centers. Judging by the way the walls curved upward into an arch and the pair of auxiliary stairways to his left and right, Nog decided there was one more deck above them.

From where he stood on the transporter pad, Nog could see that the workstations all appeared utilitarian and moderately well-maintained by civilian standards. Lights blinked; sensors pinged; indicators pulsed in predictable patterns; and the fabric covers for the furniture, while worn thin, were not rubbed raw or sprouting foam. Everything about the setting made Nog feel at home.

The only problem, he decided, was the people. To be more precise: the lack thereof. As he and the chief stepped off the pad in unison, each of them looked to his left and right, both searching for a sign of life. They found none. The ops center purred and ticked around them, but was otherwise indifferent to their presence.

"This can't be good," O'Brien murmured.

"That's supposed to be my line," Nog said. "This is why I never want to go anywhere with you."

The doors to the turbolift snapped open, nearly causing Nog to jump. A tall, thin man stepped out carrying a tray laden with several beverage containers. The thin man nearly tripped as he stepped out of the lift, moving as if propelled from behind; the beverage containers swayed precariously. Both O'Brien and Nog bounded toward him to see if they could steady the load, but were forced back when the thin man did not check his pace. A deep voice boomed out from behind the thin man, "Forward, my lad. Forward, forward, ever forward. Now step to the side. And halt. Good."

A large man stepped out of the lift pushing a trolley before him. One of the trolley's wheels wobbled and squeaked as it rolled. Several plates, each protected by a domed cover, rattled as the trolley rolled to the only open space large enough to accommodate both it and its driver. "Gentlemen," the man intoned. "Please excuse our tardiness. Just as we broke off communications, it occurred to me that you might require some form of repast. Not knowing what time of day it is for you, we—my associate and I—decided we should try to assemble several different options." He pointed at the thin man. "Sabih, please set the tray down over there." He indicated the console to the thin man's right. At a glance, Nog decided the thin man was setting down a tray of drinks on the atmospheric control console, which worried him.

The large man—Finch, Nog assumed—lifted lids off plates, describing the contents of each in brisk tones. "A bit of smoked *krelt,* which, if you've never had, it's a bit like haddock with a troubled past. Please try the Stilton, though let it warm up to room temperature." He retrieved a cheese knife from the platter and carved off a chunk, which he popped into his mouth and chewed thoughtfully. "Definitely a few minutes. I just took it out of the preserver. As I said, we weren't aware you were coming." He lifted another lid. "And these are . . ." He studied the morsels carefully.

Nog inhaled. "*Yak-ja?*"

"Ah, yes." Finch poked at it. "It rather catches the light nicely, doesn't it?"

"When it's properly writhing," Nog said, "yes."

"Ah, a connoisseur! Excellent! Sabih, offer them beverages!"

Sabih asked, "Can I get you a beverage?"

Chief O'Brien, who Nog could see was casting a skeptical eye at the proceedings, said, "I appreciate the consideration, gentlemen, but I've really come to see Ben Maxwell. If you could page him, we'll clear out of here and . . . is that Guinness?"

"It is a dry stout, sir," Finch said, tugging a stopper from the mouth of a large brown bottle. "Made in my own lab. One of the advantages of knowing a great deal about microbiology is you can always find the means to get the little buggers to dance when you call the tune. Can't claim it came all the way from Dublin, but it's a fair approximation of the venerable beverage. Would you care for a half-pint? It should pair nicely with the duck."

"Well," the chief hemmed, "to be polite. Seeing as you've gone to the trouble." He watched the large man carefully pour the beverage into a glass. "No, that's too much. No, wait. Very nice pour, yes." O'Brien accepted the proffered glass and sipped appreciatively. "That's lovely, thanks. But, about Ben Maxwell . . ."

"He's on his way, Chief O'Brien. He'll be with us as soon as possible. He might even want to join us, though I believe it's rather early in his day for him to want to enjoy a libation." He slurped the foamy head off his own glass and smacked his lips. "But perhaps not. I'm afraid I don't know as much as I might about Ben's proclivities."

Nog looked down and was mildly surprised to see he was now holding a mug of something deep red and slightly foaming. He took a sip and found the flavor pleasant, though this might have been partly because his upper palate had gone immediately numb. "What do you think of that, Commander Nog? It's a wine made from unga-berries. I've never developed a taste myself, but some of my Ferengi investors swear by the vintner."

"Ith verra nith," Nog said, but then stopped speaking to concentrate on sucking on his tongue so he could get some feeling back into it. "Thank kew," he continued. "Ith . . . *it's* very nice of you to greet us in this fashion, but I'm afraid you have us at a disadvantage. You know who we are, but . . ."

"Of course!" Finch bellowed. "Of course, of course! How ridiculous of me! Introductions! Just because your fame has preceded you doesn't mean we should make any such presumptions. Well, in my case, anyway. I can't think of a reason in the world why you should know Sabih." He presented his associate. "Sabih Ali, my director of communications and marketing. Recently of . . . where are you from, Sabih?"

"New Samarkand," Sabih offered.

"Nice town," Finch added. "Good restaurants."

"Yes," Sabih agreed flatly. "And universities, hospitals, shipyards, *my home* . . ."

"Yes, yes," Finch said, waving his hand dismissively, already moving on. Sabih frowned and narrowed his eyes. "And I, of course, am Anatoly Finch, the director and owner of this temple of inquiry." He bowed at the waist with his arms extended out to each side like a pair of wings. Finch was surprisingly flexible for such a large man, the crown of his head dipping down as low as his knee.

"Owner," Nog said.

"Yes," Finch replied, a small smile—practically a smirk, Nog thought—playing around his lips.

"It's always strange to hear a . . . well, a hew-mon use that word," the Ferengi said. "At least, with any depth of conviction."

"Is it?" O'Brien asked, lowering his glass from his mouth. He had a small foamy mustache on his upper lip.

"It is," Finch said. "I know *precisely* what you mean, Commander Nog. *Precisely.* Sometimes, I feel I have to apologize when I use the word in the presence of humans. Well, Terrans." He nodded toward Sabih. "And Alpha Centaurians. It feels practically *salacious* somehow. Perhaps a Ferengi soul became lost and found its way into this somewhat ample frame after its last incarnation."

"The majority of Ferengi don't believe in reincarnation," Sabih began. "Inasmuch as there can be said to be a major religion, it's basically an extension of their nearly religious belief that the value of a life is measured in material gain. In fact—"

"Stop," Finch said, snapping his fingers together like he was pinching Sabih's lips together. Sabih ceased speaking. Finch never stopped staring at Nog. "One of the virtues of a liberal arts education," he said, "is that one can drone on endlessly about so many topics. Wouldn't you agree, Commander Nog?"

"You don't have to call me Commander Nog," Nog said, embarrassed. "Just Nog is fine. Or Commander."

"You honor me, sir," Finch said, sitting upright, his back straight. The front of his jacket pouched out a bit, bumped from the inside by his belly. "And, please, call me Anatoly."

"This is lovely," Chief O'Brien said, wiping away his foam mustache. The pint glass was one-quarter empty. "And you made it here?"

"Indeed yes, Chief," Finch said. "Only one of our wonders. A minor miracle. Would you care to hear about some of the major ones?"

Nog looked down at his beverage, which was still foaming, though in a much more desultory fashion than a couple minutes earlier. He set it down on the tray and wiped his hands together, checking to see if he had splashed any liquid on himself. "Sure," he said. "Why not? It's not like we're doing anything else right this moment."

Chapter 5

"**M**ost of my tenants are what I like to call *free-thinkers*," Finch said, running through his recitation more or less on autopilot. The holodisplay unit at the center of the main comm unit lit up on cue and images began to flicker into focus: first, the thoughtful faces of individuals clearly engaged in rigorous intellectual exercises. "Beings who discovered they didn't fit neatly into the scientific or academic institutions of their homeworlds. Or, sadly, discovered that their talents, or their work, wasn't valued." A new set of images followed, these more abstract: complex data displays, mathematical and chemical formulas, engineering schematics. "Lab time is always an issue, even on worlds where they claim resources do not come between a researcher and his work. We understand each other here, do we not, Nog?" The Ferengi, who had been watching the display, turned slightly to meet Finch's gaze. He nodded in a polite, but neutral, manner.

Finch resumed his spiel. "Amongst my cohort are a Tellarite cyberneticist who is developing a means for telepathic communication with autonomous robots. Do not chuckle, Chief O'Brien. Consider the applications in deep-space engineering." A brief video of a Tellarite, wearing an elaborate telepresence rig on his head and focusing his gaze meaningfully, twinkled past.

"One of our great successes—Doctor Nita Bharad of Earth—can be seen here with her greatest achievements." The image of a small, dark-skinned woman with a round, cheerful face and bright eyes, materialized. Finch winced inwardly. Bharad was, by any objective measure, a successful and appealing researcher, with scores of highly cited papers to her credit, but she insisted that any promotion that included her also prominently feature Ginger and Honey. O'Brien and Nog reflexively smiled back at Bharad's image when she appeared and then recoiled as the surreal visages of her "pets" dropped into the frame, multiple eyes glimmering, mandibles flexing.

"What the *hell?*" O'Brien exclaimed.

"Wait," Nog cried. "What? The spiders—"

"Arachnoforms," Finch corrected.

"—they're what?"

Sabih paused the presentation, but did not—could not—roll it back to show Bharad and her creations. Finch explained, "They're artificial life-forms. Arachnoforms. They're really quite . . . unique?" He was momentarily at a loss for words. "Really remarkable. Highly intelligent. Mildly telepathic or empathic, the doctor can't decide which it is. She believes they'd be very useful for assisting disabled individuals or working in low-gravity environments. Actually, the applications are endless if you can get past the fact that . . . well . . . . Really, only some people have problems with the fact that they're . . ."

"They're remarkable," Nog said. "I'd have to get a better look at them. Can we meet them?" The engineer looked back and forth between Finch and O'Brien, eyes bright.

"Really?" Finch asked.

"Yeah, *really*?" O'Brien whispered. "I mean, Nog, come on. They're giant *spiders*, for mercy's sake. I mean . . ." He shuddered.

"They remind me of a *dhara* I had when I was a boy, back before we came to the station." The Ferengi held his hands up, wrists together, so that his fingers dangled to each side. He wiggled them. "You know . . . a *dhara?* No?" All of the humans, Sabih included, shook their heads in the negative. "Well, they're adorable. And so affectionate. Their suckers can . . ." Nog intuited he wasn't going to receive the reaction he expected. "Never mind."

"I'm sure Doctor Bharad would be happy to have you meet her creations," Finch said. "Thank you, Nog, for your enthusiasm. Your response has confirmed a belief I've had since we met—you truly are able to appreciate what we're attempting to accomplish here on the Hooke."

O'Brien cleared his throat while putting down his pint. "Oh," he said. "Sorry. Never mind. Carry on."

"Yes," Finch said. "I will." He stood, attempting to convey his excitement. Sabih cleared the holodisplay, but now Finch was lit dramatically from below. "I think, Nog, that you would take a keen, *keen* interest in my work: a project that has consumed me for the better part of the past five years. Allow me to demonstrate. Sabih, show us Deneva. First, as it was."

Light from the holodisplay dimmed, then flared. An image coalesced: a blue and green world as seen from high orbit, its northern pole crowned with an iridescent icecap. Bands of cirrus clouds streamed over the verdant continents. The lights of mighty cities twinkled far below. "Home to five billion souls. Long considered the most gracious, the most cultivated, the kindest world in the Federation. Deneva was a jewel, a beacon of civilization and civility, an abode of balance, humor, and grace." Finch paused meaningfully.

The edges of the blue and green world blurred and faded into a soft gray. When the image sharpened again, all color had disappeared. Deneva was now nothing more than a chunk of charcoal, all but indistinguishable from the sea of black in which it floated.

"And then the Borg," Finch intoned. He watched as expressions hardened and lines appeared around the Starfleeters' mouths and eyes. *Not desk jockeys. They were, if not warriors, soldiers.* "Now Deneva is nothing but a memory," he continued. "As are many other worlds." The cinder that was Deneva disappeared and was quickly replaced by fleeting glimpses of a half-dozen other planets, some completely stripped of life, others only partially ravaged.

"Despite the best efforts of the Federation and her allies, Barolia, Acamar, Ramatis, Korvat, and Deneva were ravaged. The Borg weapons not only crushed and burned, but also left behind a putrefying malaise. They became diseased sepulchers where nothing would ever live again." The view dove down into the atmosphere of one of the planets and showed what appeared to have been a continental shoreline, but the land was no more than an ember and the ocean only a sickening phosphorescent sludge. Finch had searched long and hard to find this particular landscape. *It tells our story,* he had said to Sabih, who had wordlessly agreed.

"Chief O'Brien was on the *Enterprise*," Nog murmured, his voice almost too low to be heard. "The first time they encountered the Borg. He—"

"We know all of this," O'Brien snapped. "Everyone knows this. The Borg didn't want to assimilate us—they wanted to *annihilate* us. And they might have . . ." Stopping himself, the chief studied Finch, wondering if he was playing them.

"They might have," Finch agreed. "But they didn't, thanks to brave people such as yourselves. I thank you." He bowed stiffly. "But the Borg have taken their toll. Worlds lie burning, their citizens not even given the grace and dignity of a peaceful resting place, their lands toxic, their atmosphere defiled, their oceans venomous. And, these worlds can never be healed . . ."

The image of the wasted shoreline faded into an ashy gray and then went blank.

Finch waited, counted down in his head, *Three, two, one . . .* The display blinked back on. Finch thought, *Let there be light,* as he always did at this point in the presentation, and said, "Or can they?"

Deck Four
Robert Hooke

"Well, here's your problem," Maxwell said, extracting the bolus of congealed resin from the mouth of the drainpipe with ceramic tongs. He let the fist-sized glob touch the mat he had laid on the deck and watched to see if there was a reaction, chemical or otherwise. One of the first things he had learned during his tenure on the Hooke was to never assume substances yanked out of toilets, drains, or ventilator shafts were inert. Back in his first month, a blob—not unlike the one he had just extricated—had burst into flame when exposed to light. Maxwell knew he should routinely scan everything with his tricorder, but he wasn't patient enough or, frankly, worried enough to make the effort.

"I didn't do that," Uchiha said.

"Didn't say you did," Maxwell replied, carefully rising to a standing position. "Something like this had to accrete over a long time. Enough of the right things have to get disposed or, you know, flushed."

"You think it's organic?" Uchiha eyed the bolus carefully.

"Well, partly, sure. The question is how much?"

"Do you mind if I take it?"

Maxwell suppressed a shudder. He replied, "As long as you promise to dispose of it properly when you're finished doing . . . whatever."

Uchiha fished a pair of heavy gloves out of his lab coat pocket and picked up the sticky, irregularly shaped object. "Of course," he said, carrying the bolus in one hand, rubbing his chin with the other, and not watching where he was walking. "Thanks, Ben."

"No problem." Maxwell wiped down the tongs with a dry cloth and replaced them in his tool chest. Resetting and resealing the head would be the work of only a few minutes. Once again, Maxwell found himself admiring the designers of the *Helios*-class stations. Nothing on the station was fussy or overcomplicated, and most of the problems he encountered in his daily routine could be fixed with a hammer, a sonic driver, and a couple of self-sealing stem bolts. *Was the same true for a starship?* he wondered. *Hard to recall for sure since mostly I just pointed at things.* He chuckled at the mental picture. *I must have done something else. I'll have to ask Miles . . .*

He winced. *Miles.* He was up in ops with Finch. *How long since they had called?* Maxwell checked the time. *Crap.* He sighed and shoved the toilet back into place. *You're a terrible man, Ben Maxwell.* He tapped his wrist communicator and asked for ops, but received no reply. *This is bad.* It meant Finch had set the privacy seals, which meant he was making a pitch. Which meant that he might be talking about her. Which meant that she might be invited out to meet someone. But who? Miles O'Brien? Maxwell shook his head and reset the toilet's seals. *I have to see this,* he thought, and tossed the remaining tools into his kit, not taking as much care as he usually did. *A terrible, terrible man.*

Ops Center
Robert Hooke

"I have some little friends," Finch said. The holo displayed the image of the burned-out shoreline, still alight with the phosphorescent glow. But now, instead of fading into gray, the image brightened as the sky over the scene lightened, and the sickening radiance dimmed. "They don't care for the Borg or their works. Indeed, they defy them. They *consume* them." The phosphorescence disappeared as the line of the horizon glowed. In time-lapse splendor, the arc of the sun rose above the distant peaks and painted the sky a rosy pink, which quickly deepened into healthy and hearty blue. The line of shadows that defined the memory of a shoreline softened. Clouds gathered overhead, but, strangely, their shape and shade did not betoken despair, but a sense of hope and rebirth. The sensors cut to a close-up of a patch of pallid, ashy soil and lingered expectantly. Finch pitched his voice low and said, "And they make something new."

A drop of rain exploded into the center of the frame and excavated a tiny crater. More drops; more craters. The soil grew soft and malleable. The edges of the individual grains became indistinct as the sensors zoomed in farther and the resolution shifted to the microscopic, augmented with animation. Tiny beasts roamed across the field of the mote of earth and absorbed the sickly green blobs. The animators intentionally left the details vague, but the tenor of their movement seemed very deliberate.

"They're eating the Borg poison," Nog said, as if on cue.

Couldn't ask for a better audience, Finch thought.

"How is that possible?" O'Brien asked. "Federation scientists have tried every kind of bioremediation in existence, but the Borg toxins have been intractable."

"They can't resist this," Finch said, quite pleased to have the opening. "We've made something much smarter, much more fierce, than anything the Borg could ever create."

The young engineer grinned wildly. "This is incredible," he said. "If it's true, you've got to bring this to the Federation Science Council. They'll go . . . they won't know how . . ." He looked up at the station owner, the light from the display flashing on his gleaming teeth. "You're going to be rich!"

"Perhaps," Finch said, rubbing his chin with his thumb. "That would be lovely. I can't deny it. It's not my primary goal, but, certainly, financial remuneration would be an acceptable outcome. But this isn't even the primary project," he continued. "These organisms are merely an offshoot of my research, an opportunity I saw to bring my creation to the attention of a larger audience."

Sabih shut off the holo and brought the main lights back up.

"I'm confused," O'Brien said, shaking his head. "What's your primary project if not this? And, why are you showing this to *us*?"

"I have to ask the same question," Sabih said. The boy seemed annoyed, a mood Finch had never seen him display. "Aren't you worried who they might tell? I thought we wanted to keep this all a secret until you've heard from some of your potential customers."

"Don't worry, Sabih," Finch said. "These gentlemen are men of honor. They won't reveal what they've seen."

"Customers?" Nog asked. "So, you're in discussions?"

"With several interested parties, including the Federation. Though I fear all my labors may come to naught, and worlds will continue to lay in ruins."

"Why?" Nog asked. "What's wrong?"

"I can guess," O'Brien said. "The genetic code."

Finch tipped an imaginary cap toward the chief as he wandered back to the trolley to see if any of the Stilton remained. Presentations always gave him an appetite. "They all want to know how the bread is baked. I say to them, 'You all know what's in bread. You don't need to know the exact recipe.'"

"What are you afraid of?" O'Brien asked. "The Federation has laws to protect intellectual property."

"The Federation," Finch said, plucking a piece of cheese from the tray, "is in the business of governing, and any government is only one crisis away from either anarchy or totalitarianism." He popped the morsel into his mouth and let it melt on his tongue. "Or haven't you heard about the tenure of President Baras?" The Starfleeters exchanged anxious glances. Finch sensed he had scored a hit. Bacco had been assassinated on Deep Space 9. For all he knew, one of these men might have been nearby when she was felled.

"This is all very interesting," said Nog, withdrawing from his enthusiastic position in regard to Finch's future earnings. "But I don't see how anyone would be willing to let you use your organisms without knowing more about them."

"Perhaps if you vouched for me," Finch said, his tone dry.

"Excuse me?"

"You heard me. Perhaps if *you* vouched for me. You are Nog, son of Rom, the current grand nagus, aren't you?"

"Yes," Nog admitted. "I don't see what that has to do with anything."

"Really? Hmph. And I'm usually such a good judge of character. I thought you wouldn't have to be dragged all the way into the river before you realized you were dying of thirst."

"What?" Nog demanded.

"Or perhaps I should quote the Ninth Rule of Acquisition."

" 'Opportunity plus instinct equals profit,' " Nog said. "So?"

"Wouldn't your father look upon your visit as an opportunity? What are your instincts telling you?"

"My instincts," Nog replied, "tell me that you don't know anything about my father."

"And mine," Finch replied, "are telling me it might be time for you to meet the Mother."

"What?" Nog asked.

"Who?" O'Brien asked.

"No!" Sabih shouted, rising from where he sat. "No! That is a *terrible* idea! You can't just . . ." He dug his fingers into his curly hair as if he was planning to tug out fistfuls. "I don't understand you!" he continued, his tone nearing hysteria. "You can't resist, can you? *Every* time!" Sabih threw his arms up into the air and shrieked. "That's *it!* I'm *through!* I really wanted to be a part of this, Mister Finch, but I can't stand this anymore. I'm going *home!* You can keep the damned credit!" He stalked to the turbolift, which, embarrassingly for Sabih, took several seconds to arrive, during which all he could do was fume.

Finally, the lift arrived, the doors parted, and Sabih stormed off.

No one spoke for several seconds until Finch said, "Apologies, gentlemen. I've had concerns about that one. He's young, excitable . . ."

"Where's Ben Maxwell?" O'Brien asked. "I think I've had—"

Ignoring his comrade, Nog asked, "Who or what is the Mother?"

"The first question," Finch replied, "I could answer if you'd like, with the touch of a button. The second question, if you really want to know, I can answer too, but you'll have to come with me." He pointed at one of the pair of stairways that led up to the topmost deck—his private lair. "Be prepared to have your life changed."

Chapter 6

"That's all that's left?" Maxwell asked.

"That's it," Brody said.

"Damn."

"Yeah," Brody said, drawing out the word in a typical island fashion. He poked the toothpick he always seemed to have in the corner of his mouth into whatever crevice he was working at the moment. "Damn." This last word he said like there was iron at its core, as if he possessed the power to really, truly *damn* something. He jammed both hands into his jacket pockets, burrowing for warmth. He hadn't bothered to find gloves before escorting Maxwell over to the cottage. "Still," he mused, "could be worse."

Maxwell stared at the remains of his mother's house. He could barely see the outline of the foundation, but only a charred, blackened concrete slab. Any wood or plaster that had been part of the structure was gone, reduced to ash and blown out to sea. "How could this be any worse?"

"She coulda died of old age," Brody said. "Your mum, she wouldn't have liked that. Struck by lightning, though. It suited her."

Maxwell carefully played back Brody's words for any

sign of sarcasm or insincerity or even just plain cruelty, but no . . . he couldn't find any. Maxwell had known— or known of—Cyrus Brody, his mother's best friend (and companion—he couldn't ignore the possibility) for well over twenty-five years and was reasonably certain the man could not express an insincere sentiment. It wasn't in his nature.

"Your mother was probably content about being vaporized in a freak lightning strike on the day before her hundred twenty-eighth birthday."

Maxwell reflected, *It would have been nice to hear something like regret.*

"She was a fine woman," Brody continued. "Your ma was . . ." He exhaled, vapor puffing from his mouth and nostrils. He turned his head away and rubbed his cheeks with his surprisingly long fingers. Maxwell knew that in addition to being one of the best fishing guides on the island, Brody was also a fine pianist. He remembered a family get-together, almost fifteen years ago—one of the handful of times he had brought Maria to see his mother—when Brody had spent the evening sitting at the old upright in the parlor cycling through a program of Brahms, drinking songs, and Elton John, utterly charming Maxwell's wife. Turning back into the wind, Brody rubbed the corners of his eyes with the tips of his index finger. "We miss her," he said. "Everyone misses her."

Maxwell wanted to say—he truly, deeply, and sincerely wanted to say—"I miss her too," but all he could manage was, "Thanks." He knew that he loved his mother, always had, but he couldn't honestly say that he had thought about her very often over the past thirty years except on the occasions when he needed to announce significant passages: when he had married, when the children had been born, when they died, when he was sent to prison. *What a strange litany,* Maxwell thought, absently counting the events by touching the tips of his fingers to his palm.

When he was released from the penal colony, Maxwell had been forced to consider, *Where do I want to go?* Somehow, Nantucket had seemed like the best idea. There were two things he could count on there: the sound of the ocean and his mother's comfortable silence. Never much of a talker, Maxwell knew he would have been able to sit on the porch or in the kitchen and just stare out at the water for as long as he liked without her asking him what he planned to do next. Mom had been good that way: she didn't ask many questions because she didn't care about the answers.

He hadn't been surprised when she didn't respond. She rarely replied to any kind of communication unless she had something very specific to convey. Brody had been the one to meet him at the dock, which had initially pleased him, and then alarmed him, and then simply confused him when the old man began, "There was a storm last week." A storm? Of course there was a storm: it was Nantucket. A freakish lightning storm in mid-winter? Unusual, but not unknown. Lightning striking a house? Also unusual, but not out of the question . . .

All Maxwell could do was shake his head and say, "Was there anything left? In the house, I mean."

"Just bits and bobs," Brody said. "What the fire didn't take, the wind and the rain did. It was over a day before anyone even noticed what had happened, her living out here on her own." His mother had lived on a lonely spur, a spot that Maxwell imagined as the closest she could come to being on the bridge of her tug as a land-bound structure could be. Brody pulled a small parcel from his pocket. "I saved this—pretty much the only thing I thought anyone might want." He handed the package to Maxwell, who, feeling the rectangular shape and the four corners, guessed what the object might be, in general terms if not specifically. Brody didn't say another word, but only stared at Maxwell as if waiting. Though he didn't really want to do it, Maxwell felt like he was expected to open the package at that moment, so he carefully tore the paper away from one corner.

It was a photograph, as Maxwell had suspected, a flat, two-dimensional image, the kind his mother had always preferred. She felt holograms were too fussy to take on an oceangoing vessel, so she never had much patience for them. He tore away another corner of paper, and a sudden gust of wind ripped it out of his hand so the scrap went skittering down the beach and out into the breakers. Maxwell stared at the half-revealed photo. He remembered the moment it captured, but couldn't remember sending it to his mother, which meant Maria must have done it. He was kneeling on the ground, smiling up at the camera, his son and daughter both standing beside him. Carlo had that bad haircut he got when he was four, so Sofia must have been three. They were both pointing at the fourth pip on his collar, both of them grinning proudly, like they understood what it meant. Maria must have been the photographer.

"This is from the day I was promoted to captain," Maxwell said flatly. "The day I got the *Rutledge*."

"I know," Brody said. "She had it on the mantel. Made sure anyone who came into the house saw it."

"Really?"

"Sure."

"I don't remember ever seeing it."

Brody shrugged. "It was always there, long as I can remember."

Drops of rain wet the glass protecting the photo. Maxwell slipped the parcel into the big side pocket of his coat. "Thanks for saving it, Brody."

"No worries. Figured it belonged to you. Found a couple other things that I kept for myself—nothing that would mean anything to anyone else."

"Okay. Good." He didn't know what else to say and so, as his mother would have, Maxwell said nothing at all.

Without another word, the two men turned away from the burned-out building and trudged back up the beach to where Brody's small vehicle waited. Maxwell was thinking about jamming his feet up against the heater. After living in New Zealand for so many years, he had completely lost the ability to cope with the kind of cold weather you got on Nantucket.

"So," Brody asked, clearly having waited as long as he could to do so, "what're you going to do now?"

Maxwell chuckled, though the sound was probably

lost in the wind. He rubbed his chin and felt the stubble. "I really have no idea," he admitted. "Kind of thought I was going to stay here for a while, but, well . . . not much chance of that now, is there?"

"No," Brody allowed. "Guess not. Got any friends you can stay with?"

In his head, Maxwell answered, *Friends? You mean, like former shipmates? Colleagues? Men and women who I served with, commanded for twenty-five years? People who don't think I betrayed their trust and nearly started a war? The friends I haven't heard from or tried to contact for the past ten years? You mean those friends?* To Brody, he said, "Yeah, *probably*. I'll have to make a couple calls, but I can think of a couple."

"Because if you need someplace to stay, I have a room you're welcome to use. Not much. Just a bed and a dresser and a chair, but it'd be nice to have some company." He looked back at the spot on the beach where the cottage once stood. The island, Maxwell realized, was already taking back the spot. Except for the charred ribs of the cottage and the outline of the slab, it was difficult to see where his mother's home once had stood.

"To be honest, Brody," Maxwell said, reaching for the handle to the passenger side door, "I don't think I could stand winter here anymore. My blood's thinned out. I need to go someplace warmer."

Brody nodded and pulled open his door. When they were both in the vehicle, he pushed the heater up to maximum, much to Maxwell's relief. Brody said, "Or you could go back into space, I guess."

"Space?" Maxwell asked.

"Well, that was your job, wasn't it? What you trained to do."

"Sure, but . . ." He let the words trail off, waiting for Brody to catch up to the obvious point.

"You don't have to be the *captain,* you know," Brody said. "Ship only has one of those, but there are lots of other jobs. Captain wasn't the only one you ever had. Just the last one."

Maxwell rubbed his hands together to try to get some circulation back into his fingers. He looked out at the surf as Brody revved the accelerator and the vehicle began the slow slog up the potholed road. He lifted his eyebrows and cocked his head to one side, letting the idea sink in. "I guess that's true," he allowed.

"Somebody somewhere needs something that you know how to do."

"Thanks, Brody."

Brody nodded his head and clamped both hands on the manual controls. The guidance system on a vehicle as old as his probably needed some help anyway. "And, just so you know, most people around here think you got kind of a raw deal."

"Thanks, Brody."

"Your mom, too," he added.

"Thanks, Brody." Maxwell felt foolish repeating himself, but couldn't think of anything else to say. Also, he was fairly certain that Brody was lying. It was nice of him to lie, though, and there was no reason, Maxwell decided, to abuse the courtesy. He also decided there was no good reason to point out how cold a person could get in space if one wasn't careful.

January 9, 2386
Finch's Lab
Robert Hooke

"What the hell is that?" the chief asked.

"That—*she*—is the Mother," Finch declared in what Nog considered to be a defensive tone. He let it pass. One should be defensive about a Mother, any Mother.

"It's . . . it's," O'Brien said in a tone that mingled disgust and awe.

"*Sir*," Finch said, drawing himself up as tall as he could and standing on his dignity (which appeared to be quite profound), "choose your words more carefully."

The chief shot his fellow engineer a sidelong glance, the kind that Nog knew meant "Get *this* guy." Nog cocked his head at a neutral angle, neither agreeing nor disagreeing. He was trying to be politic. He studied the Mother and found her, on the whole, to be quite beautiful.

The tank was ten meters long and wide and perhaps half that high, meaning it was (he did the math in his head) five thousand liters. The liquid—presumably some kind of nutrient solution—was completely clear and the sides of the tank were utterly and completely unstained, which meant Finch took very good care of the Mother's enclosure and Nog's view of her was unobstructed. She floated tranquilly in the exact center of the tank, approximately half its length and breadth and height, a rosy red tinged with lilac highlights. In simple terms, she was a blob. Shapeless, she undulated, a study in soft curves. Eddies in the tank—probably from some sort of exchanger—made her ripple and shimmy, but whenever a tendril or globule moved too near the tank's inner surface, an invisible agent gently pushed her away. *Some kind of force field,* Nog thought. *Or maybe just an antigravs supporting the mass.*

"What is it?" O'Brien asked.

"And why do you call it Mother?" Nog added, though, in the safety of his own head, he wondered what other name she could be called.

"I am in the business of creating designer microbes," Finch began, caught in the grip of a sales pitch. "Not a new concept by any stretch of the imagination, but still an expensive and laborious one. And, in the Federation especially, there are certain—how shall I say it?—prejudices against genetic enhancement." Nog sneaked a glance at O'Brien to see how Finch's comment landed, given the chief's friendship with Doctor Bashir, one of the few genetically enhanced humans either of them knew. But the chief appeared to be unmoved, except for a raised eyebrow, a sign for Finch to continue. "The microbes I demonstrated earlier—the Borg-waste consumers—normally would have required years of development and an intensive breeding program to ensure stability and longevity, but, using my new process, I've shortened that time frame considerably, all thanks to the Mother."

O'Brien shook his head. "I'm still not following you."

"Or why you call it Mother," Nog added.

"It's my little joke," Finch said, smiling and smoothing the front of his jacket over his considerable midriff. "Are either of you gentlemen familiar with how vinegar is made?"

"Vinegar?" Nog asked, who knew of the substance from his years of working in his uncle's bar.

"In theory," O'Brien replied. "Wine gone bad?"

"More or less," Finch said. "A fermenting liquid will produce a substance composed of cellulose and acetic acid bacteria. It's a gel-like substance that can be added to wine or cider, which will in turn transform it into more vinegar. These acetobacters, propagated and maintained over many generations, are called mothers because of their boundless fecundity and giving nature."

"I'll never look at fish and chips the same way," O'Brien said.

"Nor should you," Finch replied, unfazed by the chief's tone. "My grandfather made vinegar. Perhaps that was the beginning of my fascination with microbiology. I remember his mother, a grand creation of unfathomable depth and maturity. When I completed my work and gazed upon my creation hovering elegantly in her watery abode, I was struck by how much this Mother reminds me of my grandfather's. And so she was named."

"But I still don't understand what it . . . she . . . is," Nog admitted.

"She is a ready template," Finch said. "A source of life, but herself alive."

"Less poetically, it's a baseline that he can program similar to how a replicator rearranges matter," O'Brien said.

"Nothing so ignoble," Finch said, "though correct in concept. The Mother is the basis for all the programmable cells I create. She is modular, undifferentiated, but it takes only a few adjustments to create viable descendants."

Understanding finally dawned for Nog. "You've already solved ninety percent of the problems in nurturing a new life-form."

"Correct," Finch said, grinning.

"And you just have to make sure you don't harm anything when you create the specialization."

"You have grasped the fundamental concept correctly."

"That's wonderful," Nog said, genuinely impressed.

Finch bowed.

"I'm not a biologist," Nog said, "but it's obvious when you think about it, so . . ."

"Why hasn't it been done before?" Finch completed the question. "It has been tried. Endlessly, in fact. Maintaining a stable yet open genetic code is a complex business. The organism is extremely susceptible to free radicals and environmental degradation. And the inclination of cell lines is to differentiate and specialize. Suspending that propensity, yet keeping the organism viable, is difficult."

"But you figured it out," O'Brien said.

"Indeed I have," Finch said, preening.

"But you won't explain to anyone how you've done it."

"Not unless they pay my price."

"That's not science," O'Brien stated, crossing his arms over his chest.

"Perhaps not," Finch said, "but it *is* good business. I can demonstrate the efficacy of my tailored organisms if given the chance. I would even be willing to donate my services if that led to an agreement. But I will not open my notes to the scrutiny of bureaucrats and functionaries."

"That is an old business model," O'Brien said, his anger evident. "One I've heard plenty of times: 'First taste is free.'"

"Chief," Nog said, surprised by the tone of his voice, "we're guests."

"I know. But I didn't come here to see *this.*" O'Brien nodded toward the tank and the oily blob floating in its center. "I came to see my—"

"And he's here," said a voice from the stairwell. "Sorry I'm late. Had to tend to a small problem. Well, not that small. Just big enough to clog the waste extraction system."

A man stepped out of the shadows and strode forward, hand extended. "Hello, Miles. How are you? It's good of you to come all this way." Maxwell was smaller in stature than Nog had expected, accustomed as he was to craning his neck back to look most hew-mons in the face. He was fit, compact, and stood with his shoulders back and chin up in the manner of most career Starfleet officers. He glanced at Nog as he crossed the room, grinned, and nodded, and the engineer felt as if he had actually been *seen* and not merely viewed. For just a second, Nog imagined what this man must have looked like standing on the bridge of a starship and thought, *I would follow him.* All this, despite Maxwell's stained shirt, wet boots, and the lingering smell of a potent disinfectant.

Maxwell and O'Brien shook hands enthusiastically. The chief grinned and looked for a moment like he might try to embrace his former captain, but Maxwell took half a step back, then turned to Nog. He nodded again and said simply, "How do you do, Commander? I'm Benjamin Maxwell. I've heard a bit about you. It's a pleasure to finally meet you."

Nog was startled, but pleased. He reached out and took Maxwell's hand. "Heard about me? From whom?" Maxwell glanced meaningfully at the chief and then shrugged as if to say *Who else?* Nog laughed, confused but delighted.

"Well, I have to talk about *something* when I write," O'Brien said.

"I take it Doctor Finch has been keeping you entertained while you waited?"

"I guess that's a word for it," the chief said. "Good beer, anyway."

"No room for another one?" Maxwell asked.

"I didn't say that."

"Then come with me. I know someplace we can go and get caught up. Unless you had something else you needed me to do, Doctor Finch?"

Finch waved him off. "As we both know, Ben, you know more about what needs to be done around here than I. If you're going to take Chief O'Brien with you, perhaps you'd like to chat a bit more, Commander Nog?"

"Oh," Nog said. "Uh, sure. I guess." He had thought he was going to accompany O'Brien and Maxwell, but suddenly he became aware that he might not be welcome at just that moment. It made him wonder again, *Why am I here?*

"I'll come find you, Commander," the chief said. "Just a bit of a chin wag first. Talking about people you don't know and wouldn't care about."

"Sure," Nog said, as graciously as he knew how. "Not a problem. Have a good time."

O'Brien and Maxwell departed immediately in a cloud of *bonhomie* and chatter. Two old friends, reunited, they spoke in their mutual language. Nog felt deflated and a little trapped, like he was a small child who had just been dropped off at a dreaded relative's house for an unknown length of time.

"Perhaps," Finch said, drawing nearer, his face wreathed in purple light reflected from the liquid in the tank, "you'd like to hear more about the Mother?"

"Sure. That would be . . . great." Nog's mind raced, but he didn't feel as if any gears were catching. An image of friendly faceted eyes popped into his head. "Or maybe we can go see the giant spiders?"

Chapter 7

"What's the worst day you ever had?" Jake asked.

"What?" Nog said, surprised by the question. The two of them had been lounging in Jake's living room, Nog in the big easy chair and Jake sprawled on the couch, each of them with their padd propped up on their knees, neither of them talking or really paying attention to the other.

"I said, 'What's the worst day you ever had?'" Jake repeated.

Nog turned to look over at Jake, just to be sure he was asking a serious question. Hew-mons, he knew, had a tendency to harass each other, sometimes out of boredom, as a sort of test that Nog didn't really understand, but nothing about Jake's expression or demeanor indicated he was teasing. "I don't know," Nog replied. "I'd have to think about that. Why do you ask?"

"It came up in school today. Mrs. O'Brien told us a story about when she was a girl, when her family went to a park on a picnic."

"Where?"

"Where what?" Jake asked, confused.

"Where was the park?" Nog replied. "If you're going to tell a story, set the scene."

"Oh. Sorry. In Japan, I guess. She grew up in Japan. Do you know—"

"I know where Japan is," Nog said. "Okay, Mrs. O'Brien was telling you all . . ."

"Not all of us," Jake said. "Just the older kids. She breaks us up into groups sometimes, by age. And we'd been reading this short story called 'A Perfect Day for Bananafish.' Have you ever heard of it?"

"No."

"Well, it's old. Like, from the twentieth century. It's about this guy who was in a war, he comes back, gets married, and goes to a resort with his wife. And then—I'm not too sure about this part—he has a conversation with this little girl on the beach about bananafish."

"What are bananafish?"

"I don't know. I think he made them up. Or they're extinct. One or the other. Anyway, then he goes back to his hotel room, where his wife is taking a nap . . ."

"Yeah?" Nog was suddenly more interested. Were the man and his wife going to have sex?

"And then he takes out a gun and shoots himself in the head."

"Oh," Nog said, startled. "I didn't see that coming."

"No. Me either. I think that's the point."

"What happens then?"

"Nothing. That's the end."

"Really?"

"Really. But that's not what I was going to tell you. Mrs. O'Brien was talking to us about this story—the historical background and the critical reaction and why it's important, you know—the kinds of things teachers tell you."

"No, I really don't," Nog said, "as you already know."

"Right, right, sorry." The situation with regard to Nog and not attending school was already a sore topic. "But then she suddenly stops and tells us how when she was a little girl, she went with her family on this picnic and wandered off into the woods and found this man hanging from a tree limb."

"Hanging? Like, what? Holding on to a branch?"

"No. Not *hanging*, like grasping, but *hanged*. With a rope around his neck. Just dangling there a few feet off the ground. She said there was a little stool nearby on the ground. Kicked over. Mrs. O'Brien said she always remembers that detail because she saw the stool *first*, before she saw the man, and wondered, *Why is there a stool on the ground out here in the forest?* And then when she saw the man, she said she wasn't scared—I think she was like five or six years old—but confused. She thought it was part of a show or a play and that she had accidentally wandered onto a stage."

"What did she do?"

"She ran back to find her parents and told them what she found. Her father went to see, and when he came back his face was wet, like he had been crying, but she didn't understand why. Mrs. O'Brien said she kept asking him why he was so sad, but he wouldn't tell her, even after the police came."

"Was she scared?"

"No," Jake said, leaning back into the couch. He had been leaning forward, the telling of the tale lifting him up out of his seat. "She said that mostly she was just mad because they didn't get to have their picnic, and when they finally got home—there were lots of people talking, she said, some of them asking her questions—the little tea cakes they'd gotten for the day had gotten all runny from the heat. The icing dripped off, I guess, and she had really been looking forward to having hers."

"Oh," Nog said, unsure what the appropriate response was. "Did she ever find out what happened?"

"I asked her that too. She said her parents told her that the man had been very sad and had died. For a while after, she had thought they meant you could die from being sad. Which is true, if you think about it . . ."

"Sure. I guess."

"But, then, when she was older, she finally figured out she could look up the police records on the database and find out who he was. The man had had a family, two kids and a wife. They died in an accident. 'A toxic event,' whatever that means. Two years before."

"Two years. Huh. That's a long time."

"Mrs. O'Brien said she figured he gave it some time, to see if he would get over it. Probably what the counselors and his friends would have said. But he couldn't get over it, so he killed himself."

"That's really sad," Nog said, surprised at how the tale was affecting him. Working in a bar, he had overheard people from many worlds tell every manner of miserable story imaginable, but their sorrow had bounced off him. Nog had just assumed it was part of being a Ferengi and a businessman. People were despondent. His role was to profit from it.

"It is," Jake agreed. "But the worst part was knowing

he had probably tried to get over it, tried to feel better, and he just couldn't."

"I'm surprised the counselors couldn't help him."

"Counselors can only help you if you let them," Jake said. "You have to be willing. I . . . I know something about that." He looked down at his padd, scrolling through the menus like he was looking for something important. "After my mom died, I remember my dad, he spent a long time—a *long* time—hurting and he didn't want to do anything about it."

"What do you mean?"

"I'm not sure I understand it myself," Jake said. "It was like he was there, but he wasn't really. He was somewhere else, some*time* else. I remember thinking he was going to drift away someday, like a balloon when the string breaks."

"Huh," Nog said, picturing the moment. "What happened? He's not like that."

"No, not now. The *opposite*, if you know what I mean." He laughed. "I don't know exactly. We came *here*. He had his encounter with the Prophets, and when he returned, well, he was back again. Back in the *now*. He tried to explain it to me once, what they said to him, but, honestly, I'm not sure I understand it yet. Not sure if I ever will."

"So was that *your* worst day?" Nog asked. "When your mom died?"

Jake jerked his head back. He looked at Nog like he wasn't sure how to reply, but, after a pause, said, "Yeah, was it yours?"

Nog shrugged. "I don't know. I mean, I barely knew my mother. Even if my father had stayed married to her, I probably *still* wouldn't know her. That's how things are."

"Oh," Jake said. "I didn't know that." He frowned. "Now that I think about it, I've never seen a female Ferengi."

"And you probably never will," Nog said.

"Why?"

Nog threw his hands up. He knew that this was a concept most hew-mons had trouble grasping. "Because you won't," he said. "They rarely leave Ferenginar. It's *cultural.*" He had learned that this word carried a lot of weight with hew-mons, some kind of pass. Not much got past *cultural* if you didn't want to let it.

"Oh," Jake said, predictably. "Okay." He settled back onto the couch. "So was that *your* worst day? When your mom and dad broke up?"

"No," Nog said. "I barely remember it. I just remember coming here, to the station. I remember my dad was kind of sad or mad or something, but he was trying to put a good face on it. I was relieved to be getting away from my grandfather. Have I told you about him?"

"No," Jake said. "What was he like?"

"He was . . ." Nog stumbled. He didn't have a very clear idea how to describe his feelings about Dav. "I don't know. Scary. Loud." He shrugged. "A terrible businessman." He couldn't think of anything else to say, though he knew the truth of it was that his grandfather had been a very *good* businessman. His father, on the other hand, was not.

"So what was your worst day?"

Nog shook his head. "I don't know. I'll have to think

about it." He looked down at his padd. He had been scouring the station's auction sites for new listings of erotic figures to add to his collection, but found he was no longer interested in finding any. He flicked off the padd and found himself looking at a photo of himself and Jake on the upper level looking down at the Promenade. Jadzia had taken it a few weeks ago and sent it to the two of them with the note, "Boys will be boys." Nog still didn't know exactly what she meant by the sentiment, though he hoped it was some kind of flirtation (though he doubted it). He brightened. "But I do remember my *best* day."

Jake was intrigued. "Really? When?"

Nog pointed at his friend. "When you and your dad came to live here."

Jake rolled his eyes.

"No, really. It's been *way* more interesting since you two came here. Not that I didn't have some fun before, but, you know."

"Yeah," Jake said. "I know. Our lives *are* chock-full of interesting." And then he threw a pillow at Nog's head.

Nog responded in kind, and the fight continued until Commander Sisko came home and made them stop and clean up the wrecked living room.

But, afterward, on his way back to Quark's for his evening shift, Nog passed by the turbolift where he had first seen Jake and his father, the pair of them stepping out and looking around at the Promenade, both of them appearing a bit lost and forlorn. He remembered looking at Commander Sisko's stance, his straight back and outthrust chin. He even remembered how the pips on the commander's collar had gleamed in the low light of the artificial evening. He remembered Jake too, standing there, eyes narrowed, curious, but cautious.

But, mostly, for some reason, the detail Nog remembered most clearly was the pips and thinking, *Those look good. How do you get them?*

January 9, 2386
Ops Center
Robert Hooke

"Don't let Finch get to you, Miles," Maxwell said, guiding the chief to the main bank of turbolifts. "He comes off as a bit self-aggrandizing, but he's actually pretty clever. I take it you met the Mother?"

"I did," O'Brien said, radiating mingled revulsion and concern. "And I have to wonder if it's safe, that thing just hovering there in a tank. What happens if something . . . I don't know . . . cracked the side of it?" He gestured for Maxwell to precede him onto the lift. *Still deferring to the captain,* Maxwell thought.

"It can't crack," Maxwell explained. "Or, I should say, it *could*. Anything can crack, after all. I mean, there are actually some pretty sophisticated safeguards in place. Finch wouldn't have talked about those. Not interesting enough. No show in it."

"Sophisticated? How sophisticated? Like what? And where are we going?"

Maxwell pushed the button for deck six. "There's only one place to get a beer here. Not as good as the stuff Finch makes, but not bad."

"Yeah, and what about that? Brewing beer and splicing genetic material in the same lab. That can't be right."

Maxwell chuckled. "He's colorful. I'll give you that."

"I didn't say that," O'Brien protested.

"But you were thinking it."

"No," O'Brien said. He crossed his arms over his chest and watched the numbers over the door change as the car descended. "I wasn't."

"I don't think he really does that. It's just an image Finch likes to project."

"Really?" O'Brien huffed.

"I don't suppose it will come as a surprise to hear that some of the scientists on the Hooke are into some unconventional areas of research."

"I heard about the spiders," O'Brien replied flatly.

"Ginger and Honey. Right. You'll meet them soon enough. Hardly the strangest thing you'll find here if you start poking into the corners. There's an Aldebaran on deck four who's working on a shrink ray."

"A shrink ray?"

"Yes, for shrinking."

"Well, sure," O'Brien said. "What else would it be for? But you were saying about safeguards?"

"Oh, right." The car coasted to a halt and the doors parted. "The usual sort of thing in most of the labs: disinfectant sprayers, quarantine doors. Some labs can be vented directly into space. The station is programmed to transport all personnel to a sterile zone if something nasty escapes containment. And, in a few of the labs, including Finch's, we have a directed radiation pulse that would kill anything inside the burst radius."

"Ouch," O'Brien said. "Nasty."

"Yeah, it is. But it shows Finch is not as cavalier as he might like to appear."

"But why seem cavalier at all?"

Maxwell shrugged, directing O'Brien to turn left. "I've given up trying to figure out why most people do most anything. It satisfies a need, Miles. Finch needs to believe he's someone or something in particular. Neither you nor I can see what that is or why, but that doesn't really matter, does it?" Maxwell pointed at a door. "Here we go: the Public House."

O'Brien turned into a room as the doors parted, hesitant at first, but then clearly pleased by what he saw: a dimly lit space with a handful of small tables and unmatched chairs scattered around them. The walls were decorated with cheap posters of entertainers or sports stars from a half-dozen worlds. There was a four-meter-long bar with a small sink and a rack of various glasses and mugs arrayed behind it, and rickety stools arrayed in front.

Faces turned to check out the newcomers when they entered, but then everyone saw Maxwell and returned to their conversations. The lone figure behind the bar, a small, dark Terran woman, called out, "Hey, Ben. Get your butt over here and take a look at the tap. I think it's busted again."

"I keep telling you, Nita," Maxwell said, "that you can't *yank* on it. You just *pull*. Gently. You have to baby it, or the keg will fill with carbon dioxide."

"That's what I said: it's busted."

"Calm down, Nita," Maxwell said, sliding around behind the bar and pointing Miles to an empty stool.

"Say hello to my friend Miles O'Brien. Miles, Doctor Nita Bharad."

Bharad slipped past Maxwell in the narrow space, not taking care to avoid contact. "Hi, Miles," she said. "So, it really is true that Ben used to be in Starfleet?"

"Um, well," Miles said, quickly glancing at Maxwell for confirmation that he could speak of such matters. Maxwell shrugged. "Yes. A long time ago. We were shipmates."

"He's being circumspect, Nita," Maxwell said, checking the hoses on the tap. The rig was handmade out of odds and ends that Maxwell had found around the station, so it was fussy. Carefully unscrewing one of the connectors, he felt a hiss of compressed gas on the palm of his hand. "It was much worse than that: I was his captain."

Bharad guffawed and slapped the top of the makeshift bar. "Captain of *what*? Do they have ships that just clean up the mess after the big ships are finished doing whatever they need to do?" A couple of the people at the tables chuckled.

"Something like that," Maxwell agreed, screwing the connector in place. "It wasn't very prestigious, was it, Miles?"

"No," O'Brien agreed.

"Napoleon said an army marches on its stomach," Maxwell said, finding a clean pint glass. "But you need latrines too."

"Well, he was too refined," O'Brien added.

"The French," Maxwell explained. "They're a refined people. Here, Miles. Try this." He handed over the pint.

"He was Corsican." O'Brien accepted his glass gratefully, careful not to disturb the masterful head.

"They're refined too," Maxwell said, half filling another clean glass. Holding it aloft, he said, "To refinement."

"Refinement," O'Brien repeated, and touched his glass to Maxwell's.

Bharad watched the two men like she was observing a tennis match, head bobbing back and forth in time. "Clearly, you two had plenty of time to work on your routine."

"Yes."

"Yes."

"Keep working on it," she said, hopping up onto the stool beside O'Brien's. "And get me another beer."

Whoever this man is, Miles O'Brien thought, *I'm not sure he is Benjamin Maxwell.* He watched as his former captain plucked another pint glass out of a rack of (hopefully) clean dishware, lifted it to the tap, pulled the lever, and patiently watched the amber liquid flow. Smiling, Maxwell half listened while Nita Bharad rambled about the latest round of havoc her "babies" (presumably the giant spiders) committed around the station, and her staunch defense thereof. *Mischief* was Bharad's word. O'Brien suspected *mayhem* might be a better fit. Remembering that he had spent too many years drinking synthehol beer, he thought, *Pace yourself, Miles.* He took a small sip from the pint. Rolling the stout around in his mouth, he smiled.

"Not bad, right?" Maxwell said. "Microbiologists make the best beer."

"Obviously," O'Brien said.

"Though botanists are valuable too," Bharad inserted.

"Couldn't agree more," O'Brien said, smiling and leaning back. "Married to one."

"Well, then you know."

"How is Keiko?" Maxwell asked. "And the kids? Let me think—Molly should be eighteen and Yoshi is . . . twelve?"

"Thirteen."

"Wow. Huh." He shook his head. "Amazing. Time flies."

"It does," O'Brien replied. "Faster than I can stand sometimes. They're all fine. Or, well enough. Molly is driving Keiko mad and Yoshi . . ." He shrugged. "Honestly, I don't know what to tell you about him. A bit of a mystery, that one. I don't think either of them knows exactly what they want or where they want to be."

"Did you at that age?"

"At eighteen?" The chief snorted and puffed out his chest. "I wanted to be on a starship and I wanted . . . well, I wanted to do something worthwhile." He let his shoulders sag. "But at thirteen? I think I wanted to ride bulls in the rodeo."

"And look where you are." Maxwell lifted his half-pint in a toast, though he didn't drink from it.

"I suppose," O'Brien said. "Though there are days on the station that feel a lot like bull-riding."

"I wanted to study spiders," Bharad said. "At thirteen and eighteen. And eight, now that I think of it. And thirty-eight." She tossed off the rest of her pint and turned to O'Brien. "Have you heard about my babies?" she asked, her words a bit blurry from beer.

"Yes."

"Would you like to meet them?"

"Well, I might not have time. We're only supposed to be here for a few hours, Doctor Bharad."

"Call me Nita," Bharad said. The rapidity of her speech appeared to ratchet up as her alcohol intake increased. "And there's plenty of time. Or hasn't Ben told you that wherever he goes, Ginger is never too far behind?" She directed her gaze above O'Brien's head and smiled brightly. "Oh, here she is now."

The chief glanced over at Maxwell, who was grinning maniacally. He groaned inwardly, unwilling to offend the geneticist. O'Brien tilted his head back and looked up.

There was Ginger (presumably) dangling from the ceiling, spinning slowly on a silken thread. Right over the bar. Centimeters above his head.

O'Brien felt a shudder rise up; suppressing it, he slipped off his stool so he could observe the creature from a discreet distance. Ginger checked her spin by touching one of her hind legs to the wall. Her mouth bits moved in a manner that O'Brien felt could only be described as "thoughtful."

"Say *Hello*, Miles," Maxwell said.

"Ahhhh . . ." O'Brien began. "Hel—" Alarm bells were going off. Something was wrong. Something was terribly, terribly wrong. He dared to take his eyes off Ginger and glanced at Bharad, and then Maxwell. They were looking up at the ceiling, eyes twitching back and forth. Bharad was frightened, Maxwell was alert, amusement evaporated. "Wait," O'Brien yelled so as to be heard over the din. "What is that?"

"It's a contamination alert!" Maxwell shouted back. Everyone in the bar froze for a half second, all except for Bharad, who reached up and pulled Ginger to her chest.

"What's happening?" O'Brien tried to set his pint

back on the bar, but he stumbled on the stool and the glass tipped over, his stout spilling across the bar top.

Bharad's eyes were wide with trepidation, but she was quiet. Ginger had folded her legs around the geneticist's torso, either protectively, or possibly seeking protection. "Ben," Bharad said, "get to the shuttle! We need you! You can't fix this by yourself—" But before she could finish her statement, the transporter beam had immobilized her. A moment later, she disappeared.

All the other barflies had been whisked away, too.

O'Brien and Maxwell were alone in the Public House.

Maxwell pulled a small device from a pocket and pointed it at the ceiling. The alarm faded away. He pocketed the device. "Come on, Miles," he said, dodging around the bar and racing for the door.

"What's happened?" O'Brien cried at his former commander's back.

"Don't know," Maxwell shouted back. "Not exactly. Some disaster or another." The doors parted and Maxwell ran out. O'Brien followed, adrenaline pumping, his ears still ringing from the klaxon, though calm had descended. He'd been in too many situations like this to be rattled for more than a moment. Just one thing really bothered him and that was just how *delighted* Ben Maxwell had sounded when he shouted the word *disaster*.

Chapter 8

Lieutenant Commander Travis Higgins rapped a knuckle on the top of the low wall that separated his desk from his office mate's. "Hey, Javi." Travis's friend and colleague Javier Rodriquez was also a lieutenant commander and an incident report investigator. As usual, Rodriquez had his personal transceivers jammed into both his ears, eyes scrunched tightly shut, and was likely listening to the cockpit chatter of the transport whose crew's luck ran out and they corkscrewed into an asteroid. It was, as Rodriquez had commented on more than one occasion, not a pleasant duty, but someone had to do it.

Higgins rapped harder. "Javi!" he said, raising his voice. No response. Rodriquez was mouthing the words he was hearing through his headphones, trying to make sense of the murmured jargon and personal asides bandied back and forth between the bored helmsman and exhausted navigator.

Higgins tossed a stylus at Rodriquez's head. Rodriquez caught it midflight, held it lightly in his hand, and raised a middle finger. Then, slowly, he lowered it. He then lifted his index finger, requesting a moment of patience. Higgins held his peace until Rodriquez finished whatever he was doing and tugged the transceivers from his ears. "Yes, Mister Patience?"

"Come take a look at this."

"At what?"

"A recording of a deposition."

Rodriquez tilted his head to one side and squinted at Higgins. "Because I've never seen a deposition before? I mean, you *do* know what we do here, don't you?" He indicated the rows of desks to his left and right, ahead and behind. "All of us? And, if not, what have *you* been doing the past couple years?"

Higgins made a *very-funny-ha-ha-ha-hilarious* face. "No, really. Come here and check this out."

"Why?"

"If I tell you that, there's not much point in you seeing the recording."

Rodriquez slumped down in his chair, which silently reconfigured itself to give him maximum back and hip support. "You know, I have my own work to do. I can't just drop everything . . ."

"I don't need you to do my work. This is . . ." He lowered his voice. "I want to make sure I'm not missing something really important here. Can you just stop being such a . . . so *you*."

Rodriquez rubbed his face, stood up, and straightened his tunic. Protocol was that to visit another officer's work area you put on your jacket, but Rodriquez decided to flout convention. He walked around the front of their desks and plopped down into Higgins's guest chair. "Show me," he said, leaning forward. His large, brown eyes were bloodshot. *Probably staying out too late with the new girlfriend*, Higgins decided.

"This is from the *Darius* hearings. I told you about this the other day at lunch."

"The freighter," Rodriquez recalled. "Snared by pirates. What were they? Cardassians?"

"No, Cardassian ship, but probably an Orion crew. They bought up a lot of old Cardassian ships after the war ended, especially the *Hideki*-class."

"I get the same briefings you do, Trav."

"Yes, but do I assume you *read* them? No, I do not."

Rodriquez pursed his lips and made a sour face. "Continue, please."

Higgins complied. "So, these poor bastards were attacked just outside the Regulus system, out in that big, empty space that borders the Neutral Zone, you know what I mean?"

"Yeah. Lot of activity there recently."

"Right, well, no one mentioned it to the captain of the *Darius* apparently. Or he was just rolling the dice."

"What kind of ship is the *Darius*?"

"Good question. *Xepolite* built. I can't pronounce the class name. *H'rut?* Something like that with a glottal in the middle. You know, the kind with the dense hulls?"

"Particle scattering, yeah."

"Right." Higgins leaned back into his chair, settling into his story. "So, the *Darius*'s captain decides to make a run for it."

"Brave. Not that they had much choice."

"No argument. No way is a *Xepolite*-class outrunning a *Hideki*." He bounced forward, the chair back following, contouring to his spine. "Except they *do.* Because they have this helmsman who apparently knows everything there is to know about wringing every joule of energy out of a warp core."

"Really?" Rodriquez was interested now. Higgins felt vindicated. "What happened?"

"The *Darius* managed to stay ahead of the pirates, avoided their tractor beam, and was heading like a bat out of hell for Starbase 46."

Rodriquez squinted, drawing a star chart in his head. "Okay," he said. "Yeah, that makes sense. If they could hail the starbase, they could get help."

"That's what the second-in-command said was the plan."

"Second? What happened to the captain?"

Higgins frowned. "This would be the point where the pirates opened fire."

"Really? Surprising. That's not the usual *modus.*"

"No, it's not. That's why this is so interesting. The Orions, or whoever they were, must have been aggravated enough by the *Darius*'s moves that they stopped worrying about catching her intact and just decided, 'What the hell.' And they start peppering her with disruptor fire, not full power at first, judging by the sensor readings, but enough to shake her up pretty bad."

"And the captain died."

"Yeah, she was under a major power coupling when it came loose."

Rodriquez made a sympathetic face. "That's rough. Any other casualties?"

"No. But I saw the interviews with the second, and he

didn't look to me to be the sort to stay calm under fire. I figure the helmsman was calling the shots. I mean, he had the crew's lives in his hands at this point."

"But they're taking fire."

"Their aft shields collapse. And I expect the Orions—or whoever—were about to take out the engines when the helmsman decides that this would be a good time to drop out of warp . . ."

Rodriquez tipped his head to one side. "Okay."

"And let the pirates get in front of him . . ."

"That would happen, at least until they dropped . . ."

"Then as soon as they flew past, he went back into warp."

"Now that's just crazy."

"Wait, it gets better. He goes *right* for them. Warp six. And he's firing his phasers, these tiny, little units that can't do any more than melt debris when you're in orbit."

"No way that's going to have any effect on a *Hideki*."

"Not supposed to. Camouflage for the real attack."

"Which is?"

"He'd had the cargo master tractor out some of the shipping containers they were carrying. Guess what's in them?"

"On a Xepolite ship?" Rodriquez shrugged. "Something borderline illegal, I expect."

Higgins jabbed a finger at his friend. "And we have a winner. Depleted uranium. To be used for who-knows-what? Best not to ask, perhaps. Very dense, though. And if you split open the cargo container just a few hundred meters away from the pirates and let the uranium pellets spread out in a fusillade . . ."

Rodriquez winced. "Ow."

"Ow is right. The only thing left of the *Hideki* was a smear in space."

"A highly radioactive smear in space."

"Which is why there was an official hearing. If it had just been a pirate hit-and-miss"—Higgins shrugged—"I doubt we'd even have heard about it. We had to send out a couple SCE ships to clean up the mess. No one was happy, believe me."

"I would imagine not," Rodriquez conceded. He raised his hands in a gesture halfway between surrender and a shrug. "But is this such a big deal? I assume it has something to do with the helmsman."

"Of course." Higgins smiled in a manner that he hoped could be described as sardonic. "Check this out." He touched a control, and the small viewscreen on his desk came to life. They were now looking at the image of a human male, late middle aged, sitting behind an anonymous table in an anonymous chair. Higgins thought the interviewee looked as if he was expending a tremendous amount of effort to keep his posture relaxed and casual.

"Where did you get the idea to use part of your cargo as a shrapnel grenade?" asked an off-image interviewer.

The man shrugged. *"Something I read once. There was a time, we're talking a couple hundred years ago, when starships used to fight that way, before phasers and disruptors. You had to just throw things at each other and then run away as fast as you could."*

"But now ships have shields. The pirates had shields. You knew that."

"Sure," the interviewee said. *"But* Hideki-*class ships*

have a flaw: their shield generators. They're great with energy weapons, but they can't distribute kinetic energy. The Cardassians would never bring them into battle situations for that reason—too much debris. They would always position them at the edge of the field of battle and pick off stragglers from afar."

Higgins heard the interviewer snort, impressed despite himself. *"And you know this how?"*

The man smiled self-deprecatingly. *"I like military history."*

"You like military history."

"Yes."

"And you can make a freighter move like an attack vehicle."

"I don't know about that. *The Darius is a good ship— tough. And, past a certain point, any kind of space battle is just luck. We were lucky. I was lucky."*

"Lucky?"

"You keep repeating what I say without asking any questions."

"Apologies, sir. Just collecting my thoughts."

"I understand." The interviewee crossed his legs and sat back in the chair. He never took his eyes off the interviewer.

The interviewer was quiet for a few seconds, but then continued—rather lamely, Higgins thought—*"Do you have anything else you wanted to add to your testimony?"*

"No. Other than I'm sorry about the mess. Please extend my apologies to the SCE. Those poor bastards always have to deal with this sort of thing when everyone else just runs on to the next . . . well, you know."

"Sure."

"If you have the opportunity, please extend my condolences to Captain Selim's family."

"Couldn't you do it yourself?"

The interviewee shook his head. *"No, I'm leaving right after we're finished here. That's okay, isn't it?"*

"I think we have everything we need. Leave your contact information in case there's any follow-up, but . . ." The interviewer paused. His tone of voice shifted, going from the professional to the purely personal. *"Why are you leaving? You just saved these people, the entire crew. They owe you their lives."*

The man shrugged and, finally, looked away from the interviewer. His head dropped so that the bright, overhead lights cast long shadows down his face. He murmured a reply, but even the room's sensitive pickups couldn't make out his words.

"Pardon?" the interviewer asked.

"I said, 'Not all of them,'" the man responded.

"You mean, not the captain?"

The interviewee shook his head and seemed genuinely puzzled. *"No,"* he said. *"I meant, not the pirates."*

"You think there was a way that you could have gotten away without killing the pirates?"

"Yes. Of course. There's always a way."

"Well, Mister Maxwell, I've investigated a number of incidents and, frankly, I usually don't have the luxury of speaking to survivors, let alone an entire ship full of them. Most of the time, I just listen to the captain's logs and look at the scans. It's not usually this . . . well . . . this happy an outcome. You should cut yourself some slack."

The man—Maxwell—nodded his head and seemed

to smile, but the smile didn't reach his eyes. *"Are we done here?"*

"We're done," the interviewer said. The commander froze the image.

Higgins asked, "Do you know who that was?"

Rodriquez glanced over at Higgins, a squiggle of a question mark in his brow. "Someone named Maxwell? Should I know who that is?"

Higgins sighed extravagantly. "Did you ever study?"

"Me?" he asked. "I seem to remember being twentieth in our class and you were like, what, two hundred fifteenth?"

"Two twelve, but that's not the point. Benjamin Maxwell. Doesn't that name mean anything to you?"

Rodriquez shook his head slowly. "Should it?"

"The *Phoenix*? Killed a bunch of Cardassians back before the war with the Dominion? Years before anyone had any idea what they were up to?"

"I have a vague recollection," Rodriquez said. Higgins was sure he was lying. "And I also recall it wasn't as simple as that. You're making it sound like Maxwell was prescient or something, but the way I remember it, he was just . . . angry. Or traumatized. Something like that. And the only reason you recognized him is because you've always collected these kinds of stories."

"What kind of stories?"

"Sob stories."

Higgins waved away Rodriquez's ambivalence. "The point is that that's him." He pointed at the holo. "Jockeying some freighter, except he's not anymore, because he saved a bunch of people doing a crazy stunt that not one helmsman out of a thousand could pull off, but he feels bad about it. Don't you think that's the sort of thing I should maybe report up the line?"

"Why?"

"Because he disappeared. I checked. The contact information he left was totally bogus. And here's another thing: if you look up his record, a lot of it is redacted. Someone's covering up for him."

Rodriquez rose from his chair. "You're crazy. No, worse—you're bored and making up things. Stop it or you're going to get in trouble."

"I'm not going to get in trouble! There's something hinky here. Maxwell has completely disappeared."

"People are entitled to be anonymous," Rodriquez said, leaving Higgins's cubicle. "I think we actually fought a war about that once."

"No, we didn't."

"I think we did. Look it up. Apparently you don't have a problem wasting time not doing your job for other reasons."

"C'mon, Javi. This might be important!"

"Believe me: it isn't."

Higgins stood up so he could see over the low wall between his desk and his friend's. He felt like there was still something to say on this topic, but wasn't sure what, so he settled for, "You want to get dinner tonight? Maybe go to the club?"

"Sure," Rodriquez said without looking at Higgins. "As long as you promise not to talk about this all night."

Higgins weighed his options. Decided. He filed his completed report, closing the case. "Sure," he said. "Whatever you say."

January 9, 2386
Ops Center
Robert Hooke

"What's he doing?" Nog asked, pointing at the sub-optimal image on the display. Finch ran his hands over the controls for what he grandiosely called "the security console," but the resolution became neither better nor worse.

The klaxon was still blaring, though Finch had found the volume control and managed to crank it down from mind-numbingly loud to simply annoying. Nog's sensitive inner ear canals throbbed in time with the alarm. He had been so close too, so very near the exit door, or, at least, the lift door. The pitch had been deafening. Finch was turning it down.

Then the alarms started ringing.

And the calls started coming in.

Training and instinct had kicked in. Nog sat down at the communications console and began to field questions from distraught scientists, all of whom had the same basic questions: What the hell is going on? Why was I transported to the hangar? And, *really*, what the hell is going on?

Nog replied, "I don't know, but keep calm. I don't know, but keep calm. I *really* don't know, but *keep calm*." Sometimes he followed up with, "We'll get back to you as soon as we know anything."

And now, like any good officer, Nog attempted to collect intelligence.

About a non-Starfleet research station that he was *visiting* for a couple of hours.

With Chief O'Brien, whose idea it had been to come here.

Who had left him forty-five minutes ago.

Why do these things always happen to me? Nog wondered. *It's not that I don't want to have an interesting life. I just don't want it to be* so interesting.

"I don't know what he's doing," Finch said. "Which is to say, I don't know what he's already done. This is a playback, we must speak in the past tense."

The images flickered and scritched, footage from a low-resolution sensor. Sabih Ali had entered Finch's lab sometime in the past ten or fifteen minutes and was carrying a hand tool of some sort in one hand and a canister or sample collection device in the other.

The Mother swam contentedly in its tank, unaware of Sabih's proximity. *It's unaware*, Nog thought as he watched, *because it's devoid of intelligence. It's a mass of tissue and nothing more.* And yet, Nog could not rid himself of the impression that there was *something* in the Mother's movements. Expectant, even. She . . . *it* . . . seemed to float closer to Sabih as he approached its tank. He held a tool near the tank's locking mechanism; an aubergine tentacle flicked out and tickled the tank wall.

"Look here," Nog said, pointing at the security system readouts, which was playing back its logs as they watched the vid. "He overrode the locking mechanism. The top of the tank is open."

"I see," Finch said. "But Sabih missed an important . . ."

At the edge of the image's field of view, security doors slid out of the walls and covered the two stairwells. Cracks appeared in the tank walls as the air pressure dropped. Vents opened and the atmosphere was blasted out into space.

Sabih dropped to the deck clutching his head and chest. Nog thought he saw liquid flow from the young man's eyes, nose, and mouth, but then he dropped out of sight behind a console. Mercifully, there was no audio.

In the tank, the Mother's writhing tentacles seemed to freeze in place, but then Nog realized that it wasn't the Mother, but the playback. Exposure to vacuum, bafflingly, had damaged the cameras. The screen went blank.

"What happened?" Nog asked, suddenly finding that the tips of his fingers and the lobes of his ears were numb. Nog had been in battles, seen beings killed more often than he cared to think about, but he had never before witnessed anyone die in such a *senseless* fashion.

"Exactly what was supposed to happen," Finch said blandly, leaning back in his chair.

A chill ran down Nog's spine. He glanced at Finch from the corner of his eye, somehow afraid to look at him directly. "What do you mean?"

"I mean," Finch said, folding his hands over his ample middle, "that the security system responded exactly as intended. Antiseptics were sprayed. Atmosphere vented." He looked down his nose at a readout on the console in front of him. "Hmm. No radiation blast, though. For some reason, it didn't activate."

"So, the Mother might still be . . ."

"Of course not," Finch said. "Don't be ridiculous."

"So what should I tell all these people?" Nog pointed

at the communications console. "And what's happened to all of them? None of them seems to know . . ."

"They're supposed to board the transports," Finch said. "The *Wren* and the *Aubrey*. They were all briefed when they signed on. Or should have been." He waved his hand dismissively, seeming to banish any thought of the researchers. Then he stroked his chin while staring fixedly at the blank screen. Nog was surprised to see that Finch's eyes were shimmering moistly. "They'll be fine there." He pulled on his whiskers and repeated in a hoarse whisper, "They'll be fine."

Nog realized he was fundamentally alone in the room. Finch had gone away. He needed reliable intelligence. He tapped his combadge. "Nog to O'Brien"

"O'Brien here."

Nog suppressed the desire to scream, *Every time! Every damned time! Why does this happen every time I go anywhere with you?* Instead, he said, "I'm in ops. Doctor Finch is . . . preoccupied. Sabih tried to break into the Mother's tank and activated the security measures. He's dead, I think. I'm pretty sure most of the station personnel have been beamed into the hangar bay."

The chief did not reply, but Nog could hear a quick murmured conversation, presumably with Ben Maxwell. O'Brien's next clear statement was, *"We have two options: tell everyone to get off the transports and go back to work, or send them on to DS9. One idea appeal to you more than the other?"*

"DS9," Nog said, thinking about his cabin. "Definitely DS9."

"Agreed," O'Brien said. *"Could you contact the trans-*

ports and send them on their way? We'll meet you up in ops after we make sure the station is cleared out. Then we'll get back to the Amazon *and call it a day."*

Nog turned to look at Finch, who was still staring at the screen and pulling on his beard. Tiny clumps of hair littered the front of his shirt. "Hurry," Nog said.

"We're on our way."

Chapter 9

Nita Bharad thought, *Panic sounds the same in every language.*

She spoke six languages fluently and could muddle through another five or six, enough, at least, to order tea or get directions. Bharad had lived in a dozen cities or towns on ten different worlds and had heard this sound, this cacophony, how many times? Four? Five? It seemed like it should be more, but she couldn't think clearly at the moment.

Instead, she pulled Ginger closer to her chest and felt the arachnoform wrap her limbs tightly around her torso. Neither Ginger nor Honey particularly liked being touched, but they tolerated their creator in the rare moments when she violated their personal space. At least, for now. No telling how they'd behave when they had passed through their adolescence.

The rest of the mob—the yammering, pulsating, querulous mob—pushed and pulled at each other, trying to make room, trying to make sense, trying to talk, either to each other or on their various communication devices. She heard the same words spoken over and over again so that they almost sounded like a chant at a sporting event, "Ops? Finch? Ops? Finch? What's happening? What's happening? *Whatshappening?*" It sounded like a children's song, or a nonsense rhyme, or a riddle.

If anyone came too close to Bharad, they backed away when they saw what she carried. She stroked Ginger's head and worried about Honey, despite the fact that she was much more sensible than her sister. Honey would find her way to safety, one way or another.

Beside her, someone screeched and stumbled, fell to the ground, knocking the legs out from beneath two others. Bharad reached down to help lift up the fallen, a young man whom she didn't recognize, but the youth cowered back, pointing up past her head. Bharad turned and looked up. "Honey!" she called as the arachnoform descended on a slim thread, her chelicerae parting and closing, parting and closing, the thinnest thin stream of mucus dripping down.

Honey stopped a few centimeters above Bharad's head. Her calm demeanor was a sham, Bharad knew, since Honey only ever drooled when she was anxious.

The young man who had fallen scrambled to his feet and pushed his way back into the mob, gibbering incoherently about invaders. The more-seasoned members of the community glanced up at Honey and then turned away, once again intent on their communication devices.

"Hello, sweetheart," Bharad murmured, reaching up to stroke the ridges over the arachnoform's eyes. She didn't have to speak loudly; Ginger and Honey both had excellent hearing. "Thank you for finding us." Her wrist abruptly began to buzz, spooking Honey, who climbed a few centimeters out of reach. She glanced at the name on the display of her wrist comm: *Ben*. She tapped the ball of her thumb with her middle finger, answering the call.

"Are you safe?" Maxwell asked without preamble. He wasn't using visual, only audio, and he sounded like he was exerting himself—running, most likely.

"I think so," Bharad said. "Safe as anyone. Ginger and Honey are with me."

"Good," Maxwell said. *"Someone from ops should be contacting everyone in a minute, explaining what's happening, but I wanted to make sure."* He panted hard, obviously climbing or pushing past something heavy. He didn't continue the thought when he came back. *"We're evacuating the station. Something may have gotten loose."*

"One of Finch's?"

"Of course."

Of course, she thought. No one else on the Hooke was working on anything dangerous enough to merit a complete evacuation. Well, *almost* no one. She worried about some of the things Mireault on deck four had been talking about: alternate dimensions and vibrational frequencies. Poppycock. Pseudoscience. She clutched Ginger closer to her breast. "Are you going to make it down here in time?" she asked.

"Don't worry about me," Maxwell said. *"I get to ride in style with Miles and his friend. They have a runabout parked nearby. We'll probably be to the starbase before you are."*

"Starbase?"

"Deep Space 9," he said.

"Federation," Bharad replied, wincing. "They'll quarantine us. They'll try to take Ginger and Honey."

"Don't worry about that," Maxwell panted. *"We'll*

make sure—" Again, he broke off. This time Bharad heard another voice asking, *"This way?"* and Maxwell replied, *"Yes, yes."* When he came back, he said, *"Sorry. I have to go. Listen, make sure you get on the* Aubrey."

"Faster?"

"Better seats."

Most of the mob had quieted down and were listening to their devices. Bharad looked over their heads and saw the twin hulls of the two transports, side by side in their bays. Hatches were opening on both and lights were coming on inside.

"Which one is the *Aubrey*?" Bharad asked. "Left or right?" But there was no reply. Maxwell had signed off. *Better seats*, she thought. *Like anyone will want to sit!* She looked up at Honey, made sure she had her attention, and then pointed at the right, the farther of the two transports. Most of the mob would pile into the closer.

Honey bobbed on her thread in acknowledgment and began to climb. She would make her way back to the ceiling, cross to the transport, and meet her creator at the hatch. Ginger struggled, asking to be released, but Bharad resisted. Ginger just wasn't as trustworthy. If she were released, she would just go find Ben.

The crowd began to move in a slow, steady fashion toward the transports, no longer a mob. Bharad found herself thinking of New Delhi and the train platform near her apartment where she had lived after university. If her time on the Hooke was over, she thought, maybe she would move back there. Ginger and Honey would like the city.

Maybe Ben would visit them. She was mildly surprised how much the idea pleased her. She hugged Ginger to her breast, which made the arachnoform struggle.

The doctor pushed her way past the clump of humanity that was predictably forming around the nearer transport and slipped into the much less frantic queue that was threading into the hatch of the second. Glancing up, she noted the name painted on the hull: the *Wren. I should call Maxwell and let him know.* But she decided, he was probably busy, and, after all, they'd see one another soon enough.

Ops Center

"What's our status, Nog?" O'Brien asked, stepping through the hatch. O'Brien's calves and thighs ached after climbing six decks' worth of stairs, but pride wouldn't let him reveal his discomfort in front of Maxwell.

His former captain glanced briefly at Finch, but then marched from console to console checking the readings. "Nice job, Commander," he said, nodding to Nog. "You didn't take any time at all to stabilize the reactor. Those gas exchangers are fussy, but you didn't seem to have a problem."

"Not too different from the system we had back on Deep Space 9," Nog said, waving away the compliment. "The old one, not the current one. Actually, I recognize a lot of these sub—"

"Great, great," Maxwell said, walking to a console on the other side of the room. "You do that." Nog fell silent, and his face sagged in disappointment. Maxwell continued: "They've loaded up the shuttles. Engines are primed. Autopilot programmed." He glanced at O'Brien. "You sure this isn't going to be a problem? Two dozen somewhat cracked pots all showing up at the same time?"

"If this is the most interesting thing that happens this week," O'Brien began, but then felt surprisingly awkward about being flippant while Nog looked so downcast. "It won't be," he finished awkwardly. Maxwell wasn't listening in any case.

Tapping a control stud, Maxwell spoke calmly: "Everyone settled in?"

The first transport pilot said, *"Uh, I guess so. Yeah, Wren is ready."*

"Aubrey is ready, too."

"Good. Cycling the atmo. Bay doors should be opening."

"I think . . . yeah, they are. Thanks, Ben."

"No worries. Should have you on your way in—"

Klaxons whooped. Lights on a dozen separate panels flashed. O'Brien lurched toward a console, temporarily hobbled by the unexpected cramps in his legs. "What's happening?" he asked as he collapsed into the nearest chair. Even Finch, who had seemed all but insensate, was leaning forward and checking monitors.

"Hull breach," Nog said. "Deck four. Lost all the atmosphere in a lab . . . I can't read this schematic."

"Six," Maxwell said. "Look for the icon at bottom left."

"Right. Six. Oh, and seven."

"Mother . . ." Maxwell began, but snapped his jaw shut as more and more lights began to blink. *"What* is *happening?"*

"Could it be the sensor grids?" O'Brien asked. "Some kind of flaw in the system giving false readings?"

As if annoyed by his question, the entire station lifted and bucked beneath them.

Nog, who had been leaning too far forward, fell out of his chair and landed face-first on the console. Maxwell tumbled backward and landed hard on his tailbone. Struggling to stand, clutching his lower back and grimacing, he grunted, "Decompression." O'Brien knew he was right. Nog nodded even as he peeled his face off the console, a trail of mustard-brown blood dripping from one nostril. Both of them had felt that unmistakable heave enough times in their careers.

"The breaches," Finch said, speaking in a monotone, "are not coming from inside the station."

"Someone's shooting at us?" O'Brien pulled up the exterior sensors and scanned the space around the station. No sign of a ship, though there were plenty of potential assailants who could have cloaking devices. But, no, there was no trace of any energy weapon. Ballistic projectiles? He scanned for chemical trails, but found none.

"No one is shooting at us," Finch continued. "Those labs—all of them had small reactors. Not terribly well shielded. Didn't need them to be. They weren't dangerous to humans."

"So?" Maxwell asked. "Did they blow?"

"I *said*," Finch hissed, lurching to his feet, "that the breaches are starting *outside*, so, *no*, the reactors did not blow. They were merely . . . appetizing." He giggled as if he had just said something singularly witty.

The overhead lights flickered off and then back on

again. O'Brien heard Nog's breath catch in his throat, or maybe he was simply trying to clear blood out of his sinuses.

"What are you talking about, Finch?" Maxwell snapped, not looking at his employer as he worked the consoles, trying to make sense of the readings.

Finch carefully picked his way over to the tray of left-over food, snagged a morsel of dried-out cheese from the cutting board, and popped it into his mouth. He brushed together the tips of his fingers, removing invisible crumbs. "It's simple," he said. "She's hungry."

"What?" Nog said, pinching the bridge of his nose.

"Not *what*," Finch said, chortling. "But *who*."

"Stop playing games, Finch," Maxwell snarled. "What are you talking about?"

"It's Mother," the scientist said proudly. "She's outside the station, but she wants to come back inside for a snack. She's *hungry*."

Maxwell and Nog both stared at Finch slack jawed.

O'Brien wanted to ask a question, an obvious question like, "What the hell are you talking about?" But some part of his brain, maybe a flywheel, was spinning around and around, not catching.

Maxwell spun and slapped a control on the console he had been using to speak to the transports. "Do *not* launch! *Aubrey! Wren!* This is Maxwell! I repeat: *Do not launch!*"

But it was already too late. O'Brien saw the blip on the sensor readout from the corner of his eye go from green to blue to bright orange and suddenly bloom a bloody red rose. A warp engine had been initialized—a bubble of sculpted space-time elegantly building—and then folded catastrophically in on itself.

One of the transports had been flattened out into a bright trail of radioactive matter smeared across a crumpled tear in space.

"Which one?" Maxwell wanted to say, but he didn't because a part of him knew it was the wrong question. He felt the words in his brain, felt them traveling down his spine and into his gut. *Which one?* Maxwell thought, but, instead, he asked, "Status?"

Nog and O'Brien exchanged a meaningful look. *They've been through this before*, Maxwell thought. *One way or another, they've been through this many, many times.* He remembered the experience from his years on the bridge of a starship, the way a crew coalesces, becomes a shared mind. These men had learned to work a problem together effortlessly, wordlessly. To a civilian, the engineers' brief glance might have looked like hesitation, or even confusion, but an old hand like Maxwell knew differently: they were exchanging ideas.

Both blinked and almost imperceptibly nodded. Nog returned to the sensor console and ran his hands over the controls, collecting and collating data. O'Brien checked the communications console and attempted to raise the remaining transport, but, predictably, no luck. Local space-time had just ruptured. It would take time for the warp and weft of subspace to settle down before any communication was possible.

"One of the transports is still out there," Nog said, frowning at the readouts. "Not moving, but not adrift, either."

"Is it intact?" Maxwell asked.

"Impossible to say with local interference, but I think so."

"Why do you say that?"

The commander shrugged but didn't look at Maxwell. "Not reading any biological matter in space."

Maxwell nodded, grasping Nog's point. If the hull had ruptured, there would be bodies or parts of bodies. "Has it got power?"

"Some," Nog replied, but shook his head as he said it. "But not much. Whoever is flying the transport knew to take the core offline. They're on batteries."

"Which means they've got about two hours of life support, if they split up the personnel fifty-fifty," Maxwell said. "What can we do from here? What are our options?" Somewhere deep inside him, Maxwell knew it wasn't his place to ask these questions—at least not in the tone he was asking them—but he couldn't help himself. And he also couldn't deny that he was experiencing a sensation like walking out of the ocean after an unexpectedly long and difficult swim. He felt leaden, but light, every muscle stretched, but relaxed.

Neither of the Starfleet officers objected. Maxwell wasn't sure whether this pleased or alarmed him.

"Do we have transporters?" Nog asked.

O'Brien had already run a diagnostic. He shook his head. "Whatever's happening, it's already all through the station. Hull integrity is down. Can't really say exactly how much. These stations were built to endure a lot, but they weren't equipped with the kinds of external sensors that you'll find on a Starfleet vessel."

"Or station," Nog added.

"Plus, there are at least three big holes in the outer hull. Probably microfractures all through the structure at this point. Power is down or unreliable. Targeting sensors . . ." O'Brien trailed off, aware that he hadn't answered the question. "Transporters are down."

"What about your runabout?" Maxwell asked. "Can you patch into it and order it to transport over any life signs it can detect?"

"When the interference dies down," O'Brien said. "Which shouldn't be too much longer. Twenty-three minutes by my estimate."

Maxwell wanted to say, *They might not have twenty-three minutes!* But he had known Miles O'Brien long enough to not say anything so stupid out loud. The chief knew exactly how much time they had left.

"And," Commander Nog began, but then stopped to clear his throat. "Maybe," he resumed hesitantly, but then sat up straight and spoke clearly. "No, not *maybe*. We *should* think very carefully about transporting *anything* onto the *Amazon*. Or at least, anything that may be contaminated."

"Do we believe him?" O'Brien asked, pointing at Finch. The station's owner had stopped giggling. The only motion Maxwell detected was a slow rising and falling of his chest. Finch appeared to be asleep.

"Meaning?"

"That his blob . . . Mother . . . is somehow responsible for all of this?"

"Any other theories that fit the facts?"

"I can think of a few," O'Brien replied. "An attack. Finch may have irritated some people at some point in his life. People who may have lost patience with him."

Maxwell pulled a chair in front of the sensor console and began to run scans. "Possibly," he said, urging O'Brien to continue with a small wave of the hand.

"Space debris. An experiment gone wrong. Not *his* experiment, but some kind of explosive. Who knows what else was being done here?"

"Good point," Maxwell said. "I tried to keep track of as much as I could, but someone may have been hiding something dangerous."

"There were giant spiders," O'Brien continued, leaning into his thesis.

"Arachnoforms," Nog corrected.

"Right, arachnoforms," Maxwell agreed. "Spiders could never get that big. No lungs."

"And they shouldn't," O'Brien said. "Who knows what other things that shouldn't have been were happening here?"

Maxwell concluded his scans. "Probably a lot." He pointed at the readout. "But that wasn't the problem. Look." Biochemical data scrawled across each of their stations, all of it notated for the nonbiologists. The engineers tipped their heads down and scanned the text. Nog restarted the feed. Finally convinced, he sat back in his chair.

"Son of a bitch," O'Brien murmured.

"Agreed," Maxwell said. "The sensors' range is limited, thanks to the explosion, but they don't need it." He tapped the monitor. "It's out there. The Mother. In space. On the hull. Probably working its way into the station too. Disparate parts working independently, but all following the same impulse: find energy."

Nog pulled a tricorder off his belt and scanned the room. "But not in here."

"No," Maxwell said, unsurprised. "Ironically. We're clean. Maybe it's scared of this room, given everything that happened close by."

"*Scared*?" O'Brien asked. "You think it has emotions?"

"No. Not really. I don't know what to think. Maybe because the room is filled with antiseptics?"

O'Brien shrugged.

"But we could beam to the *Amazon*," Nog said excitedly. "Once the radiation dies down."

"Maybe," Maxwell replied. "And then what?"

"Contact Deep Space 9," Nog exclaimed. "Explain the situation. Get help."

"It would be too late for the people in the transport."

"We could try beaming them back here," Nog said. "That would give them some time."

"Or we could tow them," Maxwell said. "The *Amazon* has a tractor beam."

"Could the transport endure a tractor?" O'Brien asked.

"No way to know," Maxwell admitted. "But my guess is no."

"The Mother has not gotten to the *Amazon*," Nog added.

"Not yet, anyway. But there's a cloud all around the station expanding outward. It might grow weaker the more tenuous it gets, but as soon as it found the *Amazon*, it would begin chewing through the hull," Maxwell said. "At least, that's the theory I'm working with until something better comes along."

"How could it have mutated so quickly?" Nog asked.

Behind him, Maxwell heard Finch stir. He spun his chair around in time to see the geneticist rise from his chair, arm extended, like a hammy actor chewing on the scenery. "She doesn't mutate," Finch declaimed. "She *adapts*."

"Into an anaerobic creature?" O'Brien asked. "An extremophile that can survive in a vacuum and survive—no, *thrive*—on hard radiation?"

"I'm a *genius*," Finch said, grinning maniacally.

"You're a monster," O'Brien corrected. He rose and, for a moment, looked as if he might rush forward and strike Finch. Maxwell tensed, ready to intervene if necessary, but O'Brien subsided, then finished, "Or a monster maker, at least."

"We need a plan of action, gentlemen," Maxwell said, looking at the Starfleet officers. "First order of business: save the people on the transport, or determine if there's anyone worth saving. Second order of business: find out if anyone saw what happened." He turned to Nog. "Do you think the runabout's sensors could pierce the interference and get a better read on the transport?"

The commander considered. "Probably," he said. "And we might even be able to speak to them. Do you think we should head back to the *Amazon*?"

"I do," Maxwell said. "And do whatever you think is appropriate. Miles, just do me one favor?"

"If I can."

"Let me know if you decide to leave."

Nog interjected, "We're not leaving without you . . ." He almost said, "Captain." Maxwell heard it in his voice.

"All right, then," Maxwell concluded, grabbing Finch by the sleeve of his jacket. "Good luck to all of us. Now, please, move like you have a purpose."

As he was guiding Finch to the deck where they would (hopefully) find a couple of environmental suits, Maxwell heard, just below the low hum of the transporter, O'Brien say, "*That's* what I was talking about. *That's* Captain Maxwell."

Chapter 10

"**W**hat did you do to the captain?" Naomi Chao asked, entering the ready room.

O'Brien hadn't been prepared for the anger in the first officer's tone. He hadn't known she was aboard. When Captain Picard asked O'Brien to stay on board the *Phoenix* and brief the new commander, the chief had no idea that he would be relaying the disturbing news to his former shipmate. "What did *I* do to the captain?" O'Brien asked, retreating half a step and banging the backs of his legs into Captain Maxwell's desk. "I didn't *do* anything," he said, trying to recover his composure.

"He just walked past me on the bridge, calmly announced I was in command, and stepped into the turbolift," Chao snapped. "Five minutes later, the transporter chief called to say the captain has beamed to the *Enterprise*." Chao looked around the room and wondered aloud, "Why does he always keep it so dim in here? Lights up one-third." The room brightened.

O'Brien watched as Chao brought up the captain's log and scanned the latest entries. "Damn," she whispered. "He stepped down. He's in custody." She looked up at O'Brien. A lock of dark hair fell out of her hairclip, and she brushed it away from her face. "Miles," she asked, voice cracking, "what's happening? Why did . . . ?" Chao touched her collar, the tips of her fingers stroking the pips, and then jerked her hand away.

Willing her back straight, Chao took a deep breath. The panic left her eyes and she said, "Chief O'Brien, status report. We were in pursuit of a Cardassian vessel, which we believed was carrying weapons and matériel. The captain ordered us to break off pursuit. The *Enterprise* appears to be preparing to go to warp with Captain Maxwell in her brig and I'm in command. The crew . . . *my* crew . . . is in shock. What can you tell me that will help them?"

O'Brien had not seen Chao for several years, not since a chance encounter and a quick drink on a starbase, how many years ago? Seven? Eight? She appeared largely unchanged from their days on the *Rutledge*. Still round-faced, still trim and athletic, she seemed tougher now, with an edge, though that could be the anger and exhaustion boiling out of her. "Commander," he said, but found it difficult to know where to begin. "Perhaps . . . maybe." O'Brien hesitated, feeling a fool. "It might help if you told me what Captain Maxwell has been telling you for the past few days. About your mission . . ."

"Our mission?" Chao cocked her head to the side. "Our mission is to intercept the Cardassian supply ships and stop them. They're starting another war, Miles. The captain had intel. The brass at Starfleet Command wanted proof. What? What are you doing? Stop that . . ."

O'Brien realized he was shaking his head, unconsciously attempting to stop Chao before she said any more. "No, Commander," he said. "Naomi, listen: that's not what happened."

The lines around Chao's mouth tightened. "What are you saying? We had our orders. He said, 'We have orders.'"

Without thinking, O'Brien stepped around the desk and gripped Chao by the shoulders. It was a terrible breach of protocol—she was the captain of a starship now—but he couldn't think of any other way to break through her denial. "Listen," O'Brien said, and slightly tightened his grip. "There were no orders. I'm sorry, but there weren't. It was all just him."

Chao's eyes widened and her mouth hung open. For the first time, O'Brien could see the lines of exhaustion around her eyes and mouth. The commander flinched and collapsed into the chair—the captain's chair—covering her mouth with one hand and gripping the edge of the desk with the other.

Pushing with her feet, Chao spun the chair away and stared out the port at the *Enterprise*, her hand still over her mouth. The strand of hair had come loose again and swung back and forth as she breathed deeply. Thirty seconds passed. A minute passed. The only sound in the room was Chao's breathing. And then, speaking in very low tones, she said, "Shit, Miles. *Shit.* I knew it . . . I knew it . . . I did. I knew something was wrong, but I didn't . . . I didn't . . . *dammit!*"

O'Brien knew that the ready room's sensors were likely recording everything being said, so he had to think quickly. "You couldn't have known everything," he said, trying to steer Chao away from destroying her career.

"I knew enough," she groaned. "Enough that I was

able to keep the crew placated when they began to come to me with their questions, their suspicions." Chao pinched the bridge of her nose, and O'Brien heard her snuffle back a sob. "Dammit, Miles. I knew . . . enough. Enough to be scared, but I didn't ask him. I didn't demand to see the orders or—"

"That's not your job," O'Brien said.

"No?" she snapped, lifting her head. "Then what *is* my job? I'm the second-in-command. It's not *one* of my jobs, it's the *main* job: you watch the center chair. You ask questions. You keep him honest, to himself if no one else . . ." She gasped and then let the breath out slowly. As the air left her lungs, Chao drew into herself. "Shit," she said again. "Just . . . *shit.*"

O'Brien stepped away, retreated to the other side of the desk, the side where chiefs stood.

By the time he was in his spot, Chao had spun her chair back around and was looking the chief in the eye. "Mister O'Brien," she said, "could you see that any relevant information that may help the crew understand what's happened is transferred to our central database?"

"I'm sure that's already been done," O'Brien replied. "Captain Picard is very conscientious about protocol, but I'll be happy to confirm."

"Thank you." She nodded. "Please ask Captain Picard whether I can speak to Captain Maxwell before we go into warp. I'd like to check if he has any . . . I don't know . . . recommendations? Requests?"

"I'll ask," O'Brien said. "I'm sure there are regulations about this sort of thing, but I'm damned if I know what they are."

"Me too," Chao sighed. "I suppose I'll find out so[...]

"Anything else?" O'Brien asked, but then felt em[...]rassed by his informal attitude. "I mean, excuse me . . ."[...] straightened. "Is there anything else I can do for you, [...]

"No, Chief," Chao said. "Thank you. You're dismiss[...]

"Thank you, Captain," O'Brien said, and turned to l[...]

Before he reached the door, Chao spoke again. "Mi[...] she said, her tone softer, more familiar. "Did I hear [...]rectly that you got married?"

O'Brien turned, surprised, but pleased by the mor[...] of familiarity. "Yes. Just a couple months ago."

"How's married life treating you?"

He laughed. It felt inappropriate, considering the [...]cumstances, but he couldn't help it. When O'Brien re[...]ered, he rubbed the side of his nose with his index fi[...] and said, "Well, so far, so good, I guess."

Chao smiled, which made her look even [...] exhausted, though she seemed genuinely pleased. Fol[...] her hands in her lap, she asked, "Is that a recomme[...]tion?"

The chief thought about the question, inspected [...] booby traps, but found none. "Yes."

Chao nodded and then, almost as an afterthou[...] said, "Dismissed."

The chief headed for the transporter room [...] returned to the *Enterprise*.

O'Brien volunteered to appear on Maxwell's beha[...] the court-martial, as did Chao. Whenever he tried to [...] her and speak with her, Chao seemed to disappear, li[...]

spirit or ghost who could fade into the neutral gray paint of any interior room.

Despite Starfleet Command's request that she remain as captain of the *Phoenix*, Naomi Chao resigned her commission after Benjamin Maxwell was sentenced.

January 9, 2386
Runabout *Amazon*

As soon as the transporter released him, Nog asked, "What do you mean, 'That's Captain Maxwell'?"

"What I mean," O'Brien said, "is at that moment, you were seeing the man I remember from my days on the *Rutledge*."

"Oh," Nog said. "I thought that's what you meant." He cleared his throat, then asked, "Computer, any unusual or unknown microorganisms in the transporter filters?"

"Define unusual,*"* the computer requested.

"Anything . . . dangerous?" Nog added.

"The transporter filters removed four different forms of virus that are considered a nuisance to seven species and fifty-seven known varieties of bacteria or related microorganisms that are considered infectious in two hundred fifteen species. None of these is classified as dangerous *under current Starfleet protocol."* The computer paused, as if gathering its thoughts. Nog cocked an ear. He knew the computer would leave the best for last. *"Also, two uncataloged species of microorganisms were detected and isolated. Genetic scans will be sent to Starfleet Medical, though initial sensor readings indicate they are benign to most known species."*

O'Brien nodded in satisfaction and moved toward the cockpit. Nog, less easily assured, asked, "Nothing dangerous to the runabout?"

The computer paused, possibly because it was having difficulty parsing the question. Finally, it answered, *"Affirmative."*

"Good," Nog said, satisfied. He moved to the cockpit and sat down in the copilot's seat. The primary engines came online as the chief studied whatever data the sensors were able to read about local space. "Anything?" Nog asked.

O'Brien grunted the all-purpose dissatisfied grunt of the seasoned engineer, followed by the similarly all-purpose, "Let me try something." He pushed the pilot's seat back, squatted under the console, and removed an access panel. A couple tweaks of a probe and a yanked isolinear chip later, the chief was pulling up a fuzzy map of local space. A moment's study and he slid the display over to Nog's station. "It isn't pretty," he said.

Nog studied the scan. "No," he agreed. "It's not." The good news—the *only* good news—was that the transport's warp core hadn't cracked until it was a decent distance away. Otherwise, Nog realized, they wouldn't be having their current scintillating conversation.

"As it is," O'Brien continued, "no subspace communications to Deep Space 9 until we're out of this interference. Look at that ripple." He pointed at the crescent-shaped wave of disrupted subspace extending from the explosion's point of origin out toward the edge of the sector.

"Do you think the station's sensors will pick up the explosion?" Nog asked.

"Eventually," O'Brien said, pulling up the communications interface. "They'll send out a probe to investigate. Hopefully, we'll be home before the probe returns to explain what happened." He tapped in the code to unlock the subsystems and swiped past a couple of graphical interfaces until he found the subspace transmitter's guts. After bypassing a couple of safety lockouts, he knit up the system and pointed the runabout's primary comm dish directly at the still-stationary transport.

"How do you think they're doing?" Nog asked nervously.

"Let's find out," O'Brien said, and sent a hail.

Nog wasn't sure what he expected to hear in response to the hail, but he was unprepared for the squelch of white noise followed by the timorous, *"Hello?"*

The chief responded in kind. "Hello?" he said. He cleared his throat and continued in a more decisive tone, "This is Chief Miles O'Brien. Who am I addressing?"

The respondent also cleared her throat and replied, still softly, *"This is Nita, Chief. Nita Bharad. You might remember we had a drink earlier today with Ben."*

"Of course," O'Brien said. "How are you, Nita? What's your status?"

"Our status, Chief," Nita replied breathily, and Nog imagined her looking around at her colleagues, all of whom would have nodded in agreement. *"Yes. We're all really, really scared."*

"I'm only getting audio, Nita. Can you send an image?"

"Oh," Nita said. *"Hold on a moment. How's that?"*

The viewscreen blinked on. Bharad's face filled the

center of the screen. In the fuzzy middle ground, Nog saw what must have been the bodies of a couple of other passengers. The background was a milky white, like the cabin was filled with cotton fibers. There were stress lines around Bharad's mouth and eyes. The doctor looked like she might have been weeping or, perhaps, perspiring heavily. Under the circumstances, either would have been entirely understandable.

"That's fine, Nita. How many people are with you? Are any of you injured?"

"Twelve people," Bharad said, still speaking very softly. *"And Ginger and Honey. They're here with me too. Could you pass that along to Ben when you have a chance? Tell him we boarded the* Wren *and not the* Aubrey, *like he suggested. I'm sure he's right about the chairs on the* Aubrey, *but it looked like so many people were boarding her, and I didn't want to crowd Ginger and Honey. And I figured, how long are we really going—"*

"I'll tell him, Nita. What about injuries?"

"No injuries. We're all fine. For now. We saw what happened. We're not idiots." Her voice went higher, and her words more staccato. *"Until this thing flies apart and we all—"* Bharad bit down on her words and looked away. *"Dammit,"* she said, speaking even more softly. *"I said I wouldn't do that. I said . . ."* She closed her eyes and Nog watched as a single tear trickled down from the inner curve of her eye, following the laugh lines down around her mouth. She did not appear to be the sort of person who cried often. *"What happened to the* Aubrey, *Chief? What's going to happening to us? Don't mince words, please. We're all scientists here. Well, most of us."* Without warning, the

eyes and mandible of one of the giant spiders loomed large in the screen. It must have been down on the deck or on Bharad's lap and suddenly decided it was time to see what was happening, like a dog waking up from a nap while riding on its mistress's lap.

O'Brien strangled back a gasp. The spider ducked back down from view. Nog couldn't repress a delighted "Aww!" O'Brien continued, "We think that Finch's bug, his tailored microorganism, escaped confinement. He thought blowing it out into space would kill it, but it didn't. It adapted to vacuum. It feeds on high-energy particles. At least, that's the theory we're working on."

Fear left Bharad's face. Instead, she appeared to be gripped by what Nog would have described as curiosity bordering on wonder. *"That . . . that's incredible,"* she said, her voice rising above a breathy whisper. *"How do you think . . . ?"*

"I have no idea," O'Brien said. "And Finch appears to have, uh, temporarily vacated the premises."

Bharad cocked her head to the side, momentarily confused, but then straightened and nodded. *"Oh, I see."* She returned to the previous line of questioning. *"But how did the Mother reach the* Aubrey?*"*

"We're not sure, but our best guess is part of the Mother was vented into space when Sabih inadvertently activated Finch's emergency procedures. Contrary to expectations, the Mother survived in the vacuum. The *Aubrey* must have passed through it when they left the hangar and the Mother hitched a ride, then found a way into the ship and then the warp core. Broke down the containment field or caused the reaction to go critical." He turned to Nog and asked, "Can you run some scans and see if there's any way to know more about what happened? It might not be important now, but maybe later . . ."

"*Oh,*" Bharad said, strangling on her words. "*It's important now.*"

"Why?" O'Brien asked. "What do you mean?"

"*I mean,*" Bharad said, her voice dropping again, "*that our transport is falling apart around us.*" She looked down at the console before and must have manipulated some setting on the communication station, because it slowly pulled back to show the passenger cabin. A few of the researchers were sitting, but just as many were clustered near Bharad. Every thirty seconds or so, a dark shape moved through the top edge of the frame: Ginger and Honey moving from side to side. The scanner made it difficult to see exactly what was happening, but it appeared that the arachnoforms were spinning a frothy web that was slowly filling the cabin.

"What are they doing?" O'Brien asked. "What's happening?"

"*The* Wren's *internal sensors told us that she's losing hull integrity. I explained it to the girls and they, well, you can see. I think they're preventing the ship from falling apart. If nothing else, we have atmosphere to breathe. For now . . .*"

Nog whispered, "Good girls."

"*Can you get us out of here?*" Bharad asked, her voice cracking. "*We're afraid to activate the engines. Even impulse might—*"

"Stand by," O'Brien said, cutting the audio feed. "What do you think? Can we break through the interference?"

"I've been trying to get a lock on something . . . *any-*

thing," Nog said. "But the transporter beam won't stabilize. Frankly, I'm amazed you can even talk to them. There's so much radiation."

"Can you scan their hull? Is she really breaking up?"

Nog peered at the sensor readouts, but shook his head in frustration. "I can't be sure. *Something* is happening to the hull's structural integrity. It's eroding, but not like it's being bombarded. Something slower . . . more like *digested*."

"Should we risk the tractor beam?"

"You heard what Captain Maxwell said. We might tear the ship in half."

"Can we just go over and bump it back toward the station?" O'Brien asked. It was a ridiculous suggestion, and the chief clearly knew it.

Nog shook his head. "Even if there isn't a cloud of Mother cells around the *Wren* now, risking physical contact would be bad. We just don't know enough about how this thing functions. Sometimes, it seems to be responding like a simple colonial organism. Sometimes, it seems to be acting with intention."

O'Brien and Nog stared at the image of Nita Bharad as she looked from side to side and then back over her shoulder, talking to her fellow refugees, clearly attempting to reassure them. She was also waiting for O'Brien and Nog to come back with a solution or a lifeline or just a good old-fashioned miracle.

Nog's mind raced, working through their tools and options, but no casually brilliant solution came. Finally, with all the authority he could muster, he said, "I think our duty is clear here, Chief."

"Which is?"

"To alert Starfleet to this very rapidly evolving—" He stumbled, realizing his phrasing may have been inopportune. "Okay, degrading . . ." He pinched the bridge of his nose with his forefinger and thumb. "Never mind. This is *bad*, Chief. And not just for these people. We need assistance to help them, and the only way we're going to get any relief is if we can get clear of this interference."

"But by the time we do and get back here," O'Brien said through gritted teeth, "the transport may come apart at the seams." He looked at the monitor. Bharad was talking to someone behind her, trying either to fend off or reassure an off-screen personage. "They'll panic soon, try something stupid."

"Which is another good reason for us to get out of range," Nog insisted. "I don't like this any better than you do, but we're out of options."

O'Brien appeared as if he very badly wanted to use harsh language. Then he sighed and his face went slack. "If Julian was here, he'd think of something clever."

Turning away, Nog said, "He probably would. This would be the point where the two of you would come up with some improbable solution, something crazy, something that *just might work*." He sighed. "I wish he were here, Chief. I really do. And I wish I were back on the station. We'd all be a lot happier. I think this is one of those times, though, when we all do"—he waved his hands helplessly—"what we have to do." He turned back to the chief, hoping he had set his face in a look that said the conversation had to end.

On the screen, Bharad was speaking sternly to someone off-screen, waving them away. One of the arachno-forms descended into the frame, stared into the pickup for a count of three, and then leaped away. Another person's hand flapped into the frame, but Bharad roughly shoved its owner back. Nog actually felt like he was watching the tumblers inside O'Brien's mind click into place. Flatly, he said, "That's actually a very good idea, Nog." He tapped the comm and said in his very best *everything is going to be fine* voice, "*Wren*, please stand by. We're coming to get you."

Bharad turned back to the monitor. *"How? Are you transporting us—"* she began, but O'Brien cut her off.

"Stand by," he said, "and tell everyone to calm down. *Amazon* out." Before Bharad could ask another question he wasn't prepared to answer, O'Brien closed the channel. Spinning on his heel, he strode purposefully to the runabout's storage lockers, which he began opening one by one until he found what he was seeking.

When Nog saw what O'Brien was lifting out of the locker, he squinted at it with mingled curiosity and something that might have been awe. "What are you planning, Chief?"

"Nothing clever," O'Brien said. "Probably something very stupid." Falling back into one of the passenger seats, he began to undo the fasteners on his uniform. "If I survive," he added, "please don't tell Keiko what I did. She'd kill me."

Chapter 11

Doctor Michael Clark sat in the waiting area, struggling with the urge to prop his feet up in the chair across from his. His left knee ached, the remnant of a recent hiking injury, the sort of thing that could have been set right with a judicious application of an anti-inflammatory. His wife had been pestering him to visit the infirmary and have the strain treated, but Clark was precisely the sort of doctor who hated to be poked and prodded by other physicians. Instead, he rubbed the knee and took another sip of the lukewarm tea the desk sergeant had been thoughtful enough to bring him a half hour earlier, along with the promise that the processing would take "only a few more minutes."

Only a few more minutes. Clark let the phrase roll around in his head as he studied the empty waiting area. *Otahuhu District,* he decided, *is not in the grip of a crime wave tonight.* He patted his raincoat folded over the back of the neighboring chair. The fabric was almost dry. Looking out the window, he could see the trunks of the palm trees bending in the wind, their tattered crowns rattling and shivering in the cold rain. He thought about his warm bed and his equally warm wife. He thought about Ben Maxwell and the mistake he, Michael Clark, made when he gave Maxwell his personal contact information and the instruction to "please call if you ever need a hand."

His trip to Otahuhu District was a result of the third call he'd received over the past four months. The first call—from Maxwell—had been a pleasant surprise (despite coming at a late hour), and they had spent a mostly enjoyable hour catching up on recent events. The second call had been annoying, though fortunately the police hadn't required him to come downtown, but only vouch for Maxwell. When the officer had called this time, she had politely insisted that Clark come retrieve Maxwell personally. "And perhaps consider getting him into some sort of treatment program."

"I'm not his doctor," Clark had explained. "Not anymore, at least."

"You might want to reconsider that," she had said firmly. That was five hours ago. Clark rubbed his sore knee.

A red light embedded in the wall beside the innocuous door that led from the waiting area into the mysterious inner workings of the police station blinked twice. The door slid open. Ben Maxwell emerged looking much as he had the last time Clark had seen him: fit and trim, though sporting a two-day growth of stubble on his chin. Some of the whiskers, Clark noted, were growing in gray. He was standing in profile to Clark and speaking to someone on the other side of the door, who then handed Maxwell something that looked like a sack of wet laundry. Clark couldn't see precisely what it was, but it was heavy enough that Maxwell made an *oof* noise and reset his legs to compensate.

"Thanks," Maxwell said. "Really, thanks a lot. Thanks

for taking care of him. Did anyone check? No?" He shook his head questioningly, but did not appear to be receiving an answer. "Okay. Well, thanks." Maxwell stepped aside so the door could slide shut. Through the low-level force field where the desk sergeant sat, Clark heard the sound of what might have been muffled laughter. Possibly a moan. Neither was a good sign.

Maxwell turned around and saw Clark. He smiled his damnably charming smile. "Hey, Doc," he said. Unable to extend a hand because of the load he was carrying, Maxwell gave a slight bow. "Thanks for coming. Sorry for the trouble. I didn't think they'd call you in the middle of the night when I gave them your name. They said they needed to speak to someone local, but I thought they meant tomorrow morning."

Clark was only half listening to what Maxwell was saying. He was too intent on what Maxwell was carrying to be able to give anything else his full attention. "That," he said, "is the ugliest dog I've ever seen."

Maxwell nodded. "Can't argue with you there."

The dog appeared to be some kind of dachshund, though its coat was longer and scrubbier than anything Clark had ever seen on the breed. The dog's body hung down over Maxwell's forearms in a manner that indicated it had no bones. The front and rear paws dangled limply. For a moment, Clark thought it might be unconscious or even dead, but then it opened its eyes, which were bloodshot. The dog looked at him and then looked away, staring into the middle distance as if it was watching its own death approaching, which, Clark judged, was entirely possible. It yawned, exposing yellow teeth. A rancorous stench emerged, penetrating every nook and cranny of the room. It closed its mouth and appeared to fall back asleep or, possibly, into a coma.

"Is it yours?" Clark asked, praying for a denial.

"As much as it belongs to anyone." Maxwell shrugged. "Sure."

"*Why?*"

"It's a long a story," Maxwell said.

"Does it have a name?" Clark was reasonably sure he didn't want to hear the story, so his brain was manufacturing evasion techniques. Interestingly, his knee didn't hurt anymore. The dog's overwhelming stench had driven away every other sensory input.

"The attendant in the holding area was calling him Horrible."

"Horrible."

"Yes."

"Okay," Clark said. "Let's get you and Horrible back to wherever you belong tonight."

"Well," Maxwell said. "About that . . ."

In the end, after much double-talk and fudging of forms, Maxwell and Horrible settled in one of the guest cottages. "While not exactly a patient," Clark explained to the matron, "neither is he a member of the staff."

The matron looked dubious, though she had the good manners not to point out how ludicrous this sounded. "So, then, an alumnus?"

"Let's go with that for now."

The next day, after sleep and the scrubbing of the stench of Horrible from his hands, Clark paid them a visit. Maxwell had shaved and showered, but was still wearing the same clothes, though they had obviously been cleaned or at least blotted. Horrible was curled up on a small rug near an open window. A layer of filth might have been removed—he looked less matted than before—and the cleansing made it possible for Clark to see large patches where the dog's fur had been rubbed away or, possibly, scratched off. Clark bent down over the dog, feeling it was incumbent on him to offer some kind of greeting.

"I wouldn't," Maxwell said. "I don't think he likes to be touched."

Clark withdrew his hand. "Oh," he said, "that must have made washing him an interesting experience."

"It was. I already told the matron that I'll clean up the bathroom," Maxwell explained. "Bit by bit. When my strength returns."

"Lovely." Clark sat down in the single guest chair. Maxwell was already seated on the small couch, sipping at a mug of tea. The doctor noted that his left hand was very pink, as if a knitter recently repaired the flesh. He hadn't recalled seeing an injury the night before, though Maxwell had been carrying the dog in his arms. "I think it might be time for your story. I've cleared my schedule for the afternoon just in case . . ."

"No worries," Maxwell said. "I've been rehearsing the condensed version."

"Good," Clark said, crossing his legs. "Pray commence."

Maxwell inhaled deeply and then let the breath out slowly. He steepled his fingertips, then parted them, presenting his palms as if he was holding an offering. "I've been in Auckland for a couple weeks. I came here because

I wanted a beer. I'd been staying in a common house, but I lost my billet because I came home late one time too many. I like walking the streets at night, so that's not so bad, but finding a place to sleep during the day has been difficult." He folded his hands on his lap.

"Last night," Maxwell continued, "it rained, as you probably noticed. I was hunkered down in a doorway, weathering a squall, when I heard a sound. It was distant, but piercing. Eventually, I decided it was a howl."

"Horrible," Clark said.

"No," Maxwell said. "Not Horrible. Another dog, a bigger dog. I could see him from where I was camped out, sitting near a streetlamp. This was back near the waterfront, close to the docks, the small warehouses out by—"

"I know where you mean," Clark said. "The police told me."

"Okay, fine. The bigger dog was sitting under a streetlight, his head back, howling. I went over to check it out, to make sure no one was hurt. When I got close enough for him to notice me, the howling stopped. This dog, he was a healthy specimen, probably forty kilos or more. Big. Head like a cement block. Couldn't tell what breed, but powerful looking." Maxwell paused, interrupting his narrative. "Did you grow up with dogs?"

"Yes," Clark said. "My father loved dogs. We always had at least one. Did you?"

"No," Maxwell said. "There was a succession of cats that hung around our house whenever my mother was on shore for more than a few days, but that was mostly because we always had fresh fish. They were like our garbage collectors. But dogs?" He shook his head. "So, honestly, I'm a little cautious with dogs. And this fellow looked like the kind of dog that was accustomed to having his way. He watched me as I came closer, the rain running off his head and dripping down his back. He waited until I was within a few meters, and then he looked down at the street, at the curb. He stood up and pointed his nose at the grate where the rainwater was rushing down. Then, he looked at me like, I swear to you, like he was saying, 'Okay, this is yours now. I'm going home.' And then he turned away and trotted off down the street."

"And you looked down into the grate?"

"Yes."

"And there was Horrible."

"Yes."

"How did you get him out?"

"It wasn't easy. I had to remove the drain cover, which must have set off some kind of sensor, which is probably why the police came to investigate. Apparently, there've been some burglaries in the area. One of the break-ins must have been through the sewer system."

"I'll take your word for that. How did you get the grate off? That must have been a challenge."

"I had a probe," Maxwell explained. "And the clamps holding the grate in place were worn."

"A probe?" Clark asked. "You mean you had exactly the kind of tool a burglar might carry?"

Maxwell shrugged. "That, more or less, is what the police officer said."

"My question would be, why didn't he also *arrest* you?"

"I think it's because my story held up."

"Your story?"

"Yes, my story: that I was rescuing a dog from a sewer."

"Why would he believe that?"

"Mostly because I had a dog dangling from my hand." He held up his left hand, the one with the recently repaired skin. "When I reached down to get him, the damned dog must have decided that the best way to get out of the sewer was to grab hold and not let go. When the police arrived, I was sitting on the curb trying to pry his mouth open."

Clark pondered the image. "Ow."

"Yes," Maxwell agreed. "Fortunately, his teeth weren't sharp enough to break the skin. Or maybe he was just being careful."

"Soft mouth."

"Huh? In any case, they got Horrible to let go at the station when they offered him food. They bandaged up my hand, and then I visited the infirmary this morning." He flexed his fingers. "Good as new." Maxwell waved his hands like a performer concluding his act. "End of story."

"All right," Clark said. "That explains last night. Now get to the part about why you're back here in Auckland living what might generously be called 'a vagabond existence.'"

"I told you," Maxwell said. "I wanted a beer."

"They have beer in other cities," Clark said. "Indeed, in *most* cities. On most *planets*, I've been told."

"Not Klingon planets. It makes them gassy, which is not something you want to be around."

"Ben," Clark said, "the last we spoke, you decided it was time to go back to work, back to space. My memory may be dim due to extreme exhaustion, but my recollection is that you greeted the idea enthusiastically."

Maxwell crossed his arms over his chest and looked away. "It didn't work out."

"I know. I did some checking. Though I may argue with your definition of 'didn't work out.' You saved the lives of all of the people on that ship."

"Yes," Maxwell said, "but not the pirates."

"Not the pirates?"

"Right."

"Why did you think you should have saved the pirates?"

"Not *save* them. I don't think I should have saved them. Just found a way to avoid killing them."

Clark let the statement linger in the air for a long moment. Then he asked, "Do you think that was even possible?"

Maxwell shrugged. "Everything's possible."

"Probable, then?"

"I don't know. That's the point. I couldn't figure out a way."

"And if you couldn't, Ben Maxwell, former starship captain and ace pilot, if you couldn't, then who could?"

Maxwell turned to look down at Horrible. "That's not the point," he muttered. "The point is that I decided I didn't like being in a situation where there was the possibility I might have to make that kind of decision. I did what I had to do, but I don't want to have to make that choice again."

"You told me once," Clark said, "that what you wanted more than anything was to serve again. I remember that phrase very distinctly: 'to serve.' What is service if not being in a position to save lives if you have the ability to do so?"

Maxwell did not reply. He was staring down at the dog, who was now lightly snoring.

"You still haven't said why you came back to Auckland. And please don't say it was to have a beer. I saw the tox screens from the police report. You haven't had a drink in days. Probably more like weeks."

"No," Maxwell said. "I mean, not for a while. I had one and then I called you, like I had planned."

"Yes, I recall. We had a pleasant chat. I take it you hadn't originally called to have a pleasant chat."

"No," Maxwell admitted. He rubbed the new, pink flesh on his left hand with the fingers of his right. "I called planning to tell you that you're a terrible therapist."

Despite himself, Clark laughed. He had been prepared for a lot of different responses, but this had not been one of them. "Okay," he said, noting that Maxwell was not at all amused, "please explain, why am I a terrible therapist?"

"Because you let me leave here. You let me leave after I built those stupid robotic legs, which were specifically engineered so that you'd think, *Oh, he's all better now.* You released me back out into the world even though I'm still . . ." Maxwell couldn't look Clark in the eye when he finished the sentence. Instead, he locked eyes on the dog. ". . . still *broken*," he finished, practically spitting out the word. Having had his say, he laid his hands on his legs and turned his gaze on Clark. His posture said, "Prove me wrong."

Clark sat still. He badly wanted to cross his legs or

clear his throat or tap together the tips of his fingers, but he knew Maxwell might misinterpret any of those gestures as signs of weakness or surrender. Instead, he pointed out the window, which faced the ocean. "Broken," he said. "Interesting choice of words. And speaking of those robot legs, they're still out there. Still walking around. They tend to stay away from the beach, probably because you programmed them to be careful about stepping on people. Yes?"

Maxwell nodded.

"So, they tend to wander around a little way offshore. Tourists like to try to sail near enough to touch them."

"They shouldn't be able to do that," Maxwell said, mildly alarmed. "I made sure—"

"No one does. Or no one has yet. As soon as a boat gets close, the legs either stride off or go too close to shore for the boat to follow. You should see it. I swear the legs look like they're playing a game, like a dog with a ball it doesn't want anyone to have. You know that about dogs, don't you? How some of them don't like to give the ball back after they get it?"

Maxwell nodded, one eyebrow arched.

"I never saw the giant robot legs," Clark resumed, "as a sign that you were 'cured.' The effort required to project that illusion—that was significant and I thought it was a good sign. If nothing else, the legs were a sign that you were ready to *go*. Somewhere. Anywhere but here. You'd been here too long." He allowed himself the relief of crossing his legs. "And I'm sorry, Ben, truly sorry if I let you leave thinking you had somehow been fixed—as in, *no longer broken*. Psychiatry, therapy, psychoanalytics—whatever you want to call it—doesn't work that way. You'll *always* be broken. Or *have been* broken. Some terrible things happened to you. And, perhaps as a result, you did a terrible thing."

"Perhaps?" Maxwell asked.

"The mind," Clark said, "or, more precisely, the psyche is not a series of pulleys and switches. It isn't as simple as tug on this thread and here's the apple cart getting upended. And snipping that thread doesn't mean the apple cart will never be upended again. The best we can hope for is to make sure the individual has a modicum of self-awareness, enough so that they might think twice before putting themselves in a situation where there's an exposed thread or an apple cart that can be tipped and if they do, give them the tools to deal with it."

Maxwell said, "I had hoped for more."

"You got more," Clark said flatly. "You saved an entire ship full of people, and when you felt that something was wrong, you had the good sense to come back here—"

"To tell you that you're a terrible therapist."

"And give me the pleasure of proving you wrong." Clark folded his hands in his lap.

Maxwell sat for a time and stared at Clark. Then he shifted his gaze and studied Horrible, who had opened his eyes and was blankly staring back. Horrible lost interest and performed some personal grooming. He fell back to sleep. Maxwell rose, walked to the window, and looked out toward the ocean for a time, probably waiting to see if the robot legs would wander into view, but, obstinately, they did not.

Maxwell turned back, saying, "I need to find something else to do."

"Yes," Clark said. "I've been thinking about that. Perhaps it's your use of the word *broken*, but you've got me thinking about an old colleague of mine. Well, I should be honest: a better word to describe him would be *patient*. Or a little of both. He has some problems with grandiosity."

"Lovely. Sounds like I'd hate him."

"You would. Everyone does eventually. But that doesn't mean he doesn't need your help. Anatoly breaks things a lot, and I can't help but think he could use help from someone like you."

"Like me?"

"Someone who likes to fix broken things."

Maxwell considered for just a moment and then asked, "Where is he?"

"Far away. Very far away. Even by your standards."

"Sounds nice," Maxwell said. "Do you think they'll let me bring my dog?"

"*This* dog?" Clark asked. "On an extended space voyage? I think that would be an extraordinarily bad idea."

"Me too," Maxwell admitted. He let the idea sink in for a minute and then said, "I think that means he'll have to stay here."

Clark saw where he had made his mistake, but couldn't figure out a means to back out of it. He surrendered. "Yes, because you'll want to come back and visit."

"Naturally," Maxwell said. "Do what you can to keep him alive."

Chapter 12

Finch was annoyed. Nothing was going to plan.

There *had* been a plan. Once. Not too long ago. Everything had been moving along very smoothly. "Like it's on rails," Finch's mother used to say. He had been five years old before he understood she meant, "Like it's a maglev," as in "smoothly and without interruption." Before the insight, his only other understanding of the word *rail* was associated with *railgun*, so he thought she had meant, "Shot out abruptly at incredible velocity."

He had been an unusual child.

Now, being dragged down a corridor of his research station by his janitor, all Finch could do, besides try to stay on his feet, was ponder how he had come to this deplorable state. Blame *should* have settled on Sabih, but hadn't or, at least, not entirely.

They stopped outside laboratory two. The janitor mouthed some words at Finch, but it was impossible to understand the grunting, as Finch was distracted by the memories of his mother—his strange, lovely mother. *Mother,* he wondered, *where are you?* Finch stared at the janitor, a vain attempt at feigned courtesy. The janitor stared back, the corners of his mouth pulled down in an ugly snarl.

The janitor struck him. *In the face!*

Finch watched as beads of spittle arched through the air, beginning in a perfect parabola, but then, to his great surprise, swerved up, as if gravity had temporarily taken leave of its senses.

A moment later, Finch's feet left the deck and his stomach lurched against its moorings. The food and drink he had consumed over the past several hours left his body and hung in the air like a cloud.

Briefly—all too briefly—despite the nausea, despite the fear and worry, Finch felt a sense of peace settle over him. *Here it comes*, he thought. *End of the line.* And then he was amused to recognize that this expression, too, was associated with maglevs. *Everything,* he decided, *is about maglevs today.*

Gravity returned, and the deck rose up to greet him.

As hard as the janitor—*Maxwell,* Finch recalled—had hit him, it was as nothing to the titanic fury of gravity reasserting its dominance. The cartilage in the bridge of his nose went crunch. Fluids leaked from his body. *Will the indignities of this day never cease?*

Sound returned. The world was screaming at him: voices, alarms, rending metal. Maxwell. Maxwell was shouting at him.

Finch realized that until that moment, the world had been silent. Or veiled. He felt his gut quiver and the tiny bones in his ear—the malleus, the incus, and the stapes—resonate and chime. In his head, Finch recalled the calculations that determined the arc of his present circumstances, the movement here and there, up and down, back and forth, with gravity and without it. *Force and motion*, he recalled, thinking about his remedial physics lessons from his boyhood. His mother's hand, his mother's smile. *Force and motion.*

"—and then we're going to *explode*!" Maxwell was shouting. "Unless you help me."

"Yes," Finch replied.

Maxwell, losing the thread of his diatribe, subsided. He was on his knees. Both of them were on their knees. Finch's nose was bleeding, but already beginning to clot. He had always been a good clotter. The terrible sounds of rending metal subsided briefly. In that pause, Finch heard Maxwell say, "What did you say?"

Finch replied, "I said, 'Yes.' "

" 'Yes' to what?"

"To whatever you want."

"Whatever I want?" Maxwell looked incredulous, and then merely confused. "Whatever I *want*? What I want is to find a damned environmental suit! What have I been screaming about for the last two decks?!"

"I'm afraid I have no idea," Finch explained. "I believe I was in a state of shock, a fugue state of some sort. Possibly from seeing poor Sabih die?" The deck rumbled under their feet as something—no doubt something large and expensive—exploded or broke free from its moorings and crashed to the deck. "Possibly the undoing of all my worldly affairs?" He waved his hand casually, beckoning to Maxwell to take in the carnage around them. "I'm sure you understand."

"But you're all right now?" Maxwell asked dubiously.

"I seem to be myself again," Finch replied. "I suppose I should thank you for striking me." He rubbed his jaw. "I expect this will be swelling soon."

"Do you remember what we were doing?" Maxwell asked, ignoring Finch's potential injury. "What we were looking for?"

"You're seeking some kind of environmental suit, the sort of thing that would protect you from the vacuum in what's left of my lab."

"Right. Unless you've thought of some way to reseal the vents and get some atmo in there."

"If the lab has not already sealed itself and pressurized, we'll have to assume it cannot."

"So I figured." Maxwell turned away to examine the environmental indicators beside the door to lab two. "This doesn't look promising. Was there any radioactive material in here?"

Finch scrolled though his mental inventory. He knew Maxwell considered him a lackluster landlord, but Finch had a good memory for the work his tenants were conducting in his laboratories. *Zerkowski*, he remembered. *Chemist. Saponification.* "No radioactive material. Unless he was incorporating it into his soap."

"Soap?"

"Indeed," Finch said. "Everyone has their dream, Mister Maxwell."

"So the Mother probably hasn't tried to make her break through the hull here."

"What do the indicators say?"

Maxwell pointed at the display. "They say *no*. They say it's stable in there. I'm just not feeling too trusting right this moment. Do you know if there's an environmental suit in there?"

Again, Finch scanned his mental inventory. He

hmmmed. "Possibly. Doctor Zerkowski liked to be prepared for all contingencies." The gravity burped again,
and their feet left the deck. Maxwell grabbed the cover
of a power coupling in one hand and Finch in the other
so that neither of them would drift away. Finch grasped
Maxwell's arm with both hands, trepidation rising in his
gut (along with whatever remained of his lunch). Gravity
returned abruptly, but this time Finch was able to land on
his feet rather than his face.

"I think we need to take a look," Maxwell groaned,
crouching by the door. He wore a pained expression, as
if he had landed poorly. "But if this doesn't work out, I'm
heading straight to the storage area outside the generator
room. I have a suit stashed there."

Finch nodded in reply. He didn't sense that he would
be invited along for the excursion, which would leave him
free to do . . . what precisely? Return to ops? Attempt to
send out a distress call? Curl up in a ball and wait for the
station's hull to crack open? *No,* he resolved. *I will not surrender. There may still be a way to survive this.* He stole a
glance at his chronometer. *Not long until he arrives.*

"Go stand over there," Maxwell said, indicating the
doorway on the opposite side of the corridor. "Grab something stable. If there's no pressure behind this door, it
probably won't open anyway, but be ready in case it does."

Finch did as he was instructed. Maxwell raised his
thumb over the lock, but Finch held up his free hand, an
indication to pause.

"What?" Maxwell asked.

"Before you do that," Finch said, pitching his voice
low so the words would carry across the hall. "I just want

you to know, Ben, how very much I appreciate what you've done . . . and, hopefully, *will* do . . . for myself and my tenants. You've truly gone above and beyond the call of duty for an employee to his employer."

Maxwell stared at him, eyes narrowed. Then his face relaxed and the janitor said, "Since we're speaking our innermost thoughts, I'd like you to know that I sincerely believe you've been criminally negligent today and committed acts that may have resulted in the deaths of a dozen people." He paused, considering, then added, "And arachnoforms." He nodded, satisfied. "As long as we're clear on that, Mister Finch."

"Absolutely clear, Mister Maxwell." Finch added, "One more thing?"

Maxwell sighed and sagged. "Sure," he said. "Since there's no real time pressure here."

Finch grinned falsely. "A question: Am I correct in my guess that, once upon a time, there was a *Captain* Maxwell?"

The janitor cocked his head to the side and said, "There may have been, but he's gone now. Why do you ask?"

"Simply a thought that came to me after listening to how Chief O'Brien spoke to you." Finch shrugged. "It was a whim and a fancy. I thought I'd satisfy it since, in all likelihood, I may die in the next few minutes." He paused and waited for Maxwell to take his stance again. "I'm sure," he added, "that there's a fascinating story behind the loss of rank."

"I can assure you," Maxwell said, turning his back to Finch and squaring his shoulders, "there isn't." He waved his hand so the door sensor would be aware of their presence.

The door opened soundlessly, and Maxwell peered through it.

Inside lab two, lights flickered on.

The pungent aroma of industrial chemicals wafted out into the corridor, dogged by the florid stench of artificial lavender. Both Maxwell and Finch held their noses.

Finch crossed the corridor and peered into Zerkowski's lab. The inconstant gravity had tossed about containers and experimental arrays, but, overall, the damage was nothing compared to what they had seen in the rest of the station. "Doctor Zerkowski is a very organized fellow," Finch observed.

Maxwell crossed the room, careful not to step in any of the puddles that dotted the deck, and stopped before a wide, high cabinet. He slid open the door and extracted a neatly wrapped cube, a half meter on each side. "Helmet," Maxwell said, tossing it to Finch, who caught it with two hands. Maxwell extracted a second, smaller package. "Suit." And a third of similar dimensions. "Exchanger." Leaning into the cabinet, he saw another set of cubes stacked farther back: a second suit. He turned back to Finch and smiled. "Doctor Zerkowski *is* a very organized and very cautious fellow."

Runabout *Amazon*

"What do you figure the mass of the *Wren* is?" the chief asked as he removed the foam padding from the thruster pack. Nog was certain O'Brien already knew the answer and was simply making idle chatter.

"With passengers? Forty thousand kilos," Nog said. "Forty-five, tops."

"What's this thing rated?" O'Brien shifted his shoulders inside the suit. It was a one-size-fits-all model, and the intelligent material was expanding and contracting around the chief's limbs and torso, seeking an optimum configuration.

"It's a type four," Nog recited. "Meant to be used to shift cargo in low-*g* environments. I've seen them used to tow small barges." He concluded, "It should work. Maybe. Assuming you can find a spot on the *Wren* to attach a tow cable."

"I don't want to get too close." He hefted the harpoon gun. "What's the range on this?"

Nog wanted to grind his teeth. Again, he had no doubt the chief knew the answer, but the question-and-answer session must be helping somehow. "One hundred meters maximum. You'll only get one shot that way, but you won't need more than one. The *Wren* is a big target. Also, I would recommend you use the epoxy tip. The magnetic grapple might tear a hole in the hull if it's been compromised."

"Good thinking," O'Brien said, and adjusted the settings on the launcher accordingly.

Every Academy cadet, especially those aiming toward an engineering degree, spent hours wearing thruster packs, though usually in the relatively safe environs of a spacedock. Heading out into open space was another matter. "When was the last time you used one of these?" Nog asked.

The chief answered, "When we were building the station. Didn't I?" He tugged on the gauntlets, then cycled through the diagnostic programs. "You?"

"Inspection tours," Nog said.

"Right. Help me with this," he said, indicating the helmet and yoke assembly. Nog lifted it while O'Brien squatted as low as he could in the snug spacesuit. The helmet slid into the power pack and Nog felt locking mechanisms click into place.

O'Brien straightened and shifted the weight on his back. He spoke, but all Nog heard was a faint murmur. O'Brien touched his thumb to the tip of his forefinger, activating the suit's pickup. *"Why do these things always smell like someone was storing their old socks in them?"*

Nog shrugged. He *liked* the way spacesuits smelled.

"Give me a once-over," O'Brien said as he slowly turned. Nog checked seams and connections while the suit's diagnostics ran one more check.

"Looks good," Nog said, and then repeated a question he had asked a couple times. "Are you sure you don't want to bring a phaser?"

"We've been through this," the chief said. *"Anything with that kind of energy signature might draw the Mother. I'd rather not take any chances. Besides, what would I shoot at?"*

"Still," Nog said, but wasn't able to finish the thought. "It's your decision. You should be okay for up to four hours. If I'm lucky and find help quickly, I might even be back before you've finished towing the *Wren* back to the station."

"Right," O'Brien said, and gave a thumbs-up.

"If something goes wrong, if the *Wren* breaks up, hit the thrusters and get as far away as you can. I've got the suit's beacon frequency locked in. That's an order, Mister O'Brien."

"Aye, aye, sir," O'Brien said, no doubt attempting to sound jaunty and certain. *"Let's get moving. We don't know how long they have."*

"Coordinates locked in," Nog said, and stepped away.

"Energizing," Nog said, lifting his hand in salute as the beam encased the chief.

A moment later, Nog was alone in the *Amazon*. He checked the sensors to make sure the chief had materialized where they had wanted him to go—close to the *Wren*, but not too close. Everything looked good. Nog hailed O'Brien. "Chief," he said. "Status?"

"Fine," O'Brien replied. *"I wish I had never touched that beer."*

"Should I beam you back?"

"No," O'Brien said. *"I'll be fine. Be on your way, Commander. I'll be here when you get back. Well, hopefully not right* here, *but you get the idea."*

"Whatever you say, Chief. I'm . . ." He realized he was about to say *sorry,* but Nog bit his tongue. He *wasn't* sorry. He was doing what he was supposed to do. He was doing his *duty.* "Acknowledged. *Amazon* out."

Open Space
En Route to Robert Hooke

O'Brien counted to ten in his head and let his stomach settle. The suit's medical program must have sensed his discomfort and pumped something into him. Nausea dissipated and his mind cleared. Activating the suit's sensors, O'Brien quickly swiped through several views: the Hooke; the *Wren*; the status of local space (no meteorites or other debris); and, finally, the *Amazon,* a distant white dot. Nog must have pushed her a little way off.

Manipulating the sensor feeds with a combination of the wrist interface and eye blinks, O'Brien zoomed in on the runabout. Just as he reached maximum magnification, a blue disk appeared, the runabout seemed to elongate, and then she was gone. Nog had gone into warp. *Good*, O'Brien thought. *No troubles, then.* He turned his attention to the next problem.

Mindful of working in zero g, O'Brien tugged on the cord that tethered him to the thruster pack, gently imparting a bit of spin. Both he and the pack twirled, though slowly and in opposite directions. O'Brien extended his arm and waited patiently for the pack to align with his suit's yoke. When they were close enough, the locking mechanisms found each other and activated. O'Brien bent his other arm and waited for the yoke to snug into place.

A green light indicated that the magnetic connection was complete and the yoke and thruster were talking to each other. The right control arm extended until it aligned with his hand. The throttle control unfolded. "All right," O'Brien said aloud. "Let's see if I remember how to do this."

"Repeat," the suit's computer droned.

"Belay," O'Brien said. "Also, ignore my voice commands unless I address you directly. I'll say, *computer.* Understood?"

"Understood."

"I just like to talk through things sometimes. Out loud."

The computer, as instructed, did not reply.

Grasping the harpoon gun, O'Brien said, "Computer, turn me so I'm facing the *Wren*." Tiny chemical rockets puffed and spun O'Brien around ninety degrees until other chemical jets halted his movement. The *Wren* hove into view.

"Distance?" he asked, but then remembered the directive he had made only a moment earlier. "Computer, distance?"

"Ninety meters."

He hefted the harpoon gun and checked the sights. "Computer, fix target. Epoxy tip. And keep me in place when the harpoon is fired."

"Understood."

"Computer, fire harpoon."

O'Brien couldn't hear the chemical charge fire, but felt the recoil through his gauntlets. Chemical jets mounted on his back kept him in place as a thin, silver cable unspooled in a long, lazy arc behind the rocket-powered harpoon. To the naked eye it appeared fragile, but O'Brien knew it was woven from monofilaments and sheathed in flexible plasteel. Nothing shy of a plasma torch could cut it.

As the harpoon neared the transport's hull, a mechanism in the head cracked open the tiny heated chambers that held the various resins so they would be stirred together on impact. If the timing and thrust were accurately calculated, the harpoon's head would crack open just as it was kissing the transport's hull.

All O'Brien had to do was wait and find something to keep his mind busy. He decided to count stars.

At the count of nineteen, the cable ceased unspooling. The computer announced, *"Contact made."* A small display on the harpoon gun lit up and told O'Brien that the resins had mixed as anticipated, the line was secure, and the transport's hull unpierced. He doubted anyone inside the ship even knew the tow cable was in place.

O'Brien had hesitated contacting the *Wren* again before he felt there was a reasonable chance his plan could succeed. All things considered, the odds were looking better. It was time, he thought, to share some good news (though he appreciated that the idea of being towed back to a disintegrating space station could only be considered "good news" under the most charitable circumstances).

Checking the background radiation, O'Brien confirmed his suit could transmit a signal the *Wren* could receive. He smiled. *I don't know how much more good news I can take.*

"O'Brien to *Wren*," he said. "*Wren*, Nita, are you receiving?"

"Yes! Yes, hello! This is the Wren*!"* The signal dissolved for a moment, and O'Brien thought he detected someone whispering, *"Leave that alone, Javi!"* The signal cleared again and Bharad's voice came through clearly. *"Is that you, Miles? Have you figured out a way to beam us back to the station? Things are getting rather, uh, dicey here. Ginger and Honey are exhausted."* Whispers again, but of a more tender sort. *"Yes, my darlings, you're exhausted, aren't you. Just rest. Please rest. You've done beautifully."*

"I can't beam you back," O'Brien said. "But I think I can give you a tow."

"No!" Bharad said. *"The hull can't take a tractor beam!"*

"Not a tractor beam," O'Brien said, using his calm, reasonable *I'm-just-a-simple-engineer* voice. "More like a tractor."

"What?"

"I said," he began, but then stopped. If she hadn't gotten the joke the first time, repeating it wouldn't help. "Just hang on. I'm going to get you back to the station as fast as I can. Commander Nog went for help, so there should be a Starfleet ship heading our way soon. If we're really lucky, we'll just be settling in for our next round when the cavalry comes up over the hill."

"Cavalry?"

O'Brien was stymied. *How could you not know about cavalry?* But then he considered his wife's admonishment whenever he made this sort of observation in front of her: *Not everyone has fought in the Alamo as many times as you have!*

"Stand by."

"All right, Miles. But, tow gently, please."

"Will do. Gently. I'll be monitoring your hull integrity. But once we get moving, Isaac Newton will be doing most of the driving, so don't worry."

Bharad didn't reply for a long moment, but then asked, *"Didn't Robert Hooke and Isaac Newton hate each other?"*

"I'm sure that's a myth," O'Brien replied.

Chapter 13

"Weren't you supposed to tell me the story of your life last night?" Nita Bharad asked as she pulled on the tap and let stout flow into a pint glass. When she was finished with the pour, she handed the glass to Maxwell, who admired the artful swirl she had drawn in the head.

"Where did you learn to do that?" he asked.

"I told you last week," she replied, drawing a smaller amount into what had probably started its life as a juice glass. Bharad didn't believe in letting anyone drink alone, even if she only intended to have a small amount. They tapped glasses and both said, "Cheers."

"Remind me," Maxwell said, setting his padd on the bar. He had a vague recollection of a rambling conversation— the only kind with Bharad—about the circumstances that had brought her to the Hooke.

"I did post-grad work at Trinity. You learn a lot about pouring beer in Dublin."

"Ah, right."

"You may also recall that after our conversation, you said you'd share some of the details of your no-doubt extremely interesting life story. Do you?"

"Do I what?"

"Recall?"

"Alas, no." He sipped his beverage. "I can't imagine why. Was this the same evening where I proclaimed my undying affection for you?"

Bharad chuckled and turned away while tucking a strand of jet-black hair behind her ear. "No," she said. "And has that line ever succeeded in distracting a woman from what she was saying?"

"Only the one time," Maxwell said, thinking of Maria, despite the fact that such comments had as little effect on her as they seemed to have on Bharad. Maria had tucked her hair behind her ear too, when she was mildly embarrassed. The memory of her doing so made him smile.

She leaned forward, elbows on the bar, and peered at Maxwell. "I'm not sure if I've ever seen that before."

"Seen what?"

"A smile. A genuine smile and not that fake grin you pull when you want people to think you're listening to them. You should try it more often. It works for you."

Maxwell smiled again. He couldn't help it. Bharad's no-nonsense manner was irresistible. He asked, "Where's your entourage?"

"I don't know. That's half the reason I came here. I thought you'd be here and figured Ginger would be hovering."

"Where do you think they go when they're off on their own?"

"I have ideas," Bharad said, taking the tiniest sip from her glass. "I think they watch people: not just you, but everyone. I think they may be a lot smarter than they let on sometimes."

"How smart do you think they are?"

She considered comparisons. "Smarter than a dog," she said. "And smarter than many university administrators I've met." Maxwell laughed. "But, seriously, I'm not sure. Sometimes I find them poking at things on my workbench like they want to pick them up."

"Tool-using intelligence. Like apes and ravens?"

"Maybe."

"And you made them."

"I did." She smiled. "Makes you want to treat me with more respect, doesn't it?"

"I respect you," Maxwell said.

"Mmmm." Bharad crossed her arms, but did not comment. She nodded at his padd. "What are you reading? Anything good?"

He shook his head and groaned. "No," he said. "Nothing good."

"Bad book?"

"Bad news."

"Oh," Bharad said, and her eyes went soft. "Something wrong? Everything all right at home?"

"No. I mean, yes, everything's fine at home. It's here. Someone's coming to visit."

Bharad's eyes went back to flinty. "Really?" she asked, her voice flat. "You're complaining because someone is willing to come out here to the ass end of space to pay you a visit?"

"He's checking up on me."

"You *need* checking up on. I'd do it more often myself except you live in the bowels of the station where no one can find you."

"Except Ginger."

"Except Ginger."

They clinked glasses.

"Why is he checking up on you?" Bharad asked.

Maxwell winced. "I think he feels responsible for me."

Bharad's eyes changed again. They narrowed, wary and distrustful. "You mean," she asked, "this is someone who actually *knows* you? And *likes* you?" Her mouth twisted into a skeptical moue. "I don't believe you. It doesn't make sense. Are you sure you don't owe him?"

"Possibly, but that's not the point." Maxwell's neck and shoulders ached. He recognized, from several years of psychological counseling, that the ache was likely more due to psychic factors than physical ones. "We served together."

"This is part of that life story you aren't going to tell me, isn't it?"

"Yes," Maxwell said. "No. Possibly. I don't know."

"Is it the part where I find out how a man who is obviously capable of doing pretty much anything he wants is instead burying himself in the bowels of a research station filled with second-rate nut jobs?"

"Present company excluded, naturally."

"Naturally," she said. "I note that you aren't disagreeing. You haven't answered any of my questions."

Maxwell shrugged and surveyed the nearly empty room. He rubbed his hands together, then said in low tones, "I'm fairly certain he saved my life—my correspondent."

"And he feels responsible for you," Bharad said, rolling her eyes. "In that way that men do."

"Yes," Maxwell agreed. "I guess we do."

"Will he try to pry you out of here?"

"What?" Maxwell asked. "I don't think so. Why would you even ask something like that?"

"Because those of us with eyes can see that you've pretty much buried yourself here. I thought maybe your friend was coming to do an excavation."

"I thought I was keeping the place held together," Maxwell said, pinching the bridge of his nose.

"You are, Ben," Bharad said. "And as much as I appreciate it, I can't help but think there are more worthwhile places to keep together."

Maxwell tapped his glass against hers. "I'll drink to that."

January 9, 2386
Open Space
En Route to Robert Hooke

Miles O'Brien thought about his mother. He did not think about her often or, at least, no more often than he thought proper. He had been sad when she died, mourned her, and then moved on. O'Brien had always considered his love for her to be, as she had been, voluminous and well balanced. Thinking back on it, the only thing about her death that bothered him had been the obituary: *Megan O'Brien died quietly in her sleep after a short illness.* Inside his helmet, O'Brien shook his head. His mother had never done anything *quietly* in her entire life. If there was a state of mind that could be defined as *quietly*, Megan O'Brien had always existed on the opposite pole from that theoretical condition.

He wasn't sure why he was thinking about his mother, other than the plainly obvious reason that there had been a great deal of discussion about the Mother over the past few hours. Since firing the thruster and getting under way, O'Brien had been thinking about his entire family—wife, children, parents, brothers, and sisters—but, more than any of them, his thoughts kept circling back to Megan. Maybe it had something to do with the fact that she was the only one of his immediate family who had died. Or maybe it was because he was once again facing the possibility of his own death.

No one who had been in battle let the prospect of death slow them down when confronted with enemies to fight, comrades to protect, or machines to repair. Unfortunately, none of these circumstances described his current situation.

The thrust against his back was barely perceptible. The same, alas, was true of the glimmer of light that he knew to be the Hooke hull.

O'Brien checked his velocity and distance to his destination. He checked the remaining fuel in the thruster pack and the remaining oxygen in his suit. He did the math in his head, then mentally erased it, and then did it once more. *This may have been a mistake*, he thought.

The communicator chimed. O'Brien said, "Hello, Nita."

"How much longer?" Bharad asked.

This was the fourth time in twenty-five minutes she had asked. The math was still the same, so the answer had not changed. "Another twenty-three minutes," O'Brien replied.

"Can't we go faster?"

"Like I explained earlier, yes, we can. But then I can't guarantee that we'll be able to brake so that your transport doesn't just tear out the bottom of the station. It's going to be dicey as it is."

"Something just peeled away from the hull," Bharad said. *"Something large."*

"I'm sure it wasn't anything important."

"Why do you say that?" she asked.

In his head, O'Brien thought, *Because if it was important, you wouldn't be calling me.* To Bharad, he said, "Ships like the *Wren* have lots of extraneous parts on the hull: sensors, communication arrays . . ." He stumbled. "Flanges," he resumed. "Don't worry."

"I thought the tow cable might have torn loose."

"No worries, Nita. Everything's secure." O'Brien wanted to say something better, something more reassuring, but now he was thinking about his wife, wondering what Keiko would say if she knew what he was doing at that moment. Out in space with a thruster on his back, tugging a disintegrating spacecraft back to an infected space station. Most likely, she'd say, in a mildly disappointed tone, "Miles O'Brien, you're a damned fool."

A sour knot twisted in his gut. When was the last time he had consumed anything that wasn't liquid and alcoholic? *Might not be any other options anytime in the near future.* He wondered if Nog had made it past the interference and was on his way back. He wondered whether the Hooke was holding together. He wondered if Captain Maxwell was still alive.

Feeling a lump of self-pity and woe forming in the pit

of his gut, O'Brien did what his mother had advised him to do. He began to sing:

"The minstrel boy to the war is gone,
In the ranks of death you'll find him;
His father's sword he has girded on,
And his wild harp slung behind him."

A voice crackled over the comm channel. *"That's an awfully sad song, Chief."*

O'Brien turned to look to his left and then to his right. Nog was coming up beside him, skillfully piloting his own thruster pack. A second cable was stretched out behind him. He must have fixed his harpoon as he had flown past the *Wren*. When his cable went taut, O'Brien applied a little more thrust, confident that the two of them would be able to slow down the transport when the time came. He checked his velocity and did the mental calculation. He smiled, though only when his head was turned away from Nog. "Aye," he replied. "It is a bit. It's a song we used to sing back in the day on the *Rutledge*. Captain Maxwell liked it."

"Is there more?"

"There is, but it doesn't get any more cheerful."

"Another time," Nog said.

They flew along in companionable silence for a few minutes, Nog nervously checking their velocity and course. O'Brien watched the stars until Nog settled, and then asked, "What happened with the *Amazon*? I saw her go into warp."

"You did," Nog said. *"After you left the ship, it occurred to me that I could program the runabout to get clear of this distortion zone and send a message to the station. There was*

another thruster pack—I'm going to find out who stowed two of these on a runabout when we get back—so I figured I'd come and lend a hand."

"Ah," O'Brien said. "Well, thanks. Appreciate it."

"Should have thought of this sooner." He checked their course again, then added, *"I'm sure Doctor Bashir would have thought of it sooner. I'm just not as smart as he is."*

O'Brien let the sentiment echo around inside his helmet for a few moments. "Well," he offered, "who is, Commander? Who is?"

"True," Nog agreed.

Neither spoke for what was probably a long spell, but O'Brien found that he didn't mind the quiet. At the appointed time, the pair of engineers began to shift their configuration in an attempt to bring the *Wren* to a safe stop. Before heading off on the necessary vector, Nog added, *"If we survive this, I swear I'm never going anywhere with you ever again."*

Ops Center
Robert Hooke

"There are a lot of uncertainties here," Maxwell said as he tugged the legs of the environmental suit up over his trousers. "A lot of things we don't know."

"This is true," Finch allowed. He was seated in the chair in front of the primary environmental control panel, which showed a slowly spinning schematic of the Hooke, replete with blinking colored swaths to indicate problem areas. There were, Maxwell noted, lots of blinking red and orange blocks, and not very many yellow or green bits. The situation was rapidly going to hell.

The ops center had fared better than most of the rooms they had visited on the other decks, though this was likely because there were fewer pieces of fragile lab equipment here. "Just for fun," Maxwell said, standing and slipping his arms into the sleeves, "let's list some of them. Seeing as we're not doing anything else."

While no longer semicomatose, Finch had lapsed into recalcitrance. "Fine," he murmured. "Let's."

Maxwell pushed his hand through the suit's rigid cuff and extended his index finger, counting off. "We don't know how much of the Mother is still upstairs in your lab."

"True," Finch agreed. "Though we believe she was jettisoned."

"Belief is not evidence. And we don't have any working sensors in there, do we?"

"Sabih made sure of that."

Maxwell frowned, but did not reply. On the trek back to ops, he had been thinking about Sabih and his disastrous attempt at theft. While he hadn't known the young man well, he had never struck Maxwell as either particularly enterprising (beyond the venture capitalist model) or larcenous. Current circumstances, alas, did not lend themselves to additional investigations. One thing Maxwell knew for sure was that he wasn't going to allow Finch into the lab without being carefully supervised. As insurance, he had locked the second environmental suit into a cabinet for which the station owner no longer had the access code. "And if any remnant of the Mother is up there, do we know if she would be attracted to this suit's energy signature?"

Finch unfolded his hands and tapped together the tips of opposing fingers. He stared into space. "We do not," he drawled. "Although evidence indicates she is attracted to radioactive energy sources. Your suit runs on a battery with a modest energy signature. I doubt she would find it appetizing, especially with so many other tasty morsels to consider."

As if on cue another section of the Hooke's hull changed from orange to red on the display. Maxwell felt a shudder through the soles of his boots, though, thankfully, the gravity remained stable. "So," he said, "good news for our side. Any other bits you'd like to offer?"

"It will be very cold," Finch said. "Do not tarry. Your suit was not meant for prolonged exposure to vacuum."

"Noted."

"Otherwise, my only question is simply this: What do you hope to accomplish besides determining whether the Mother is still in residence?"

"And retrieving Sabih's body," Maxwell said.

"Naturally. And that."

"I want to see why the radiation blast didn't fire," Maxwell said. "I want to see if someone tampered with it. I want to see if it can still be used."

"Really?" Finch asked, his brows knitting together. "To what end?"

"I should think that would be obvious, Doctor," Maxwell said, standing up and lifting the recycler onto his back. "If I can, I'm going to reset it so we can fire the damned thing."

"And kill the Mother?" Finch had come back to life again. Maxwell doubted if Finch realized it, but he was gripping the arms of his chair with both hands.

"If the opportunity arises," Maxwell said, snugging up the straps on the harness. He mentally added, *And with a small amount of pleasure.*

"You couldn't," Finch said through gritted teeth. "You *mustn't!*"

"I could," Maxwell said, retrieving the helmet and brushing off the last of the packing material. "And while I'm not sure if I must, I'm pretty sure it would make me feel a lot better." He inspected the helmet's visor to see if a layer of thin film protected it. He found one, which meant the helmet had never been used. Peeling it away, Maxwell wondered how long the gear had been sitting in Zerkowski's storage closet, unused, unchecked.

He glanced at Finch, who was silently seething, and wondered if the big man's rage would get him out of the chair. Maxwell half wished it would. Though Finch probably had twenty or thirty kilos on him, Maxwell felt confident he could take him if it came down to an altercation.

Finch disappointed him by clenching the chair arms and turning back toward the monitor. Another square of the station's hull turned from yellow to orange. "We're not going to last long at this rate," Finch said.

"Then I'd best get on with it," Maxwell said, fitting the helmet into the suit collar. The servos meshed and he felt a rush of cool atmosphere flow into the helmet. It smelled like lavender soap. He found the communicator control on the left gauntlet and tapped it. "Is this working?"

Finch looked at him and nodded.

"Are we reasonably sure the hatch into the lab is sealed?"

"We are," Finch said. His voice sounded tinny through the helmet's small speaker.

"When I open that door there." He pointed to the closed hatch that led to the foot of the short stairway. "We won't lose all the air in here? It'll serve as an airlock if I close it behind me?"

"It should," Finch said. *"But why would you care? I'm the one who doesn't have a suit."*

Maxwell considered his point. "That's true," he said. "But then I wouldn't have anyone to chat with."

"How dreadful for you," Finch drawled.

Maxwell walked to the hatch, all the while trying to find his balance. The suit's joints were stiff, and he felt like he might tip over at any moment. He tapped the door's control stud, half expecting it to beep at him ominously, but, no, it swooshed open with only a small pop. He glanced back at Finch to make sure he hadn't collapsed. The station owner was still upright and alert, watching Maxwell attentively.

Suddenly, Maxwell felt very exposed, very at risk. If Finch could somehow seal the door behind him, then he would have to . . . do what? Maxwell had the environmental suit. If he must, he could figure a way out of the lab and back into the station through one of the many, *many* gaps in the hull. He might have to contend with the Mother in some fashion, but there was no proof yet that she . . . it was dangerous as long as you weren't housing a radioactive power source. *So, things are going my way,*

Maxwell concluded as he mounted the stairs. *Nothing to do but recover a body and fire a small thermonuclear device. Janitor's work, really.*

Reaching the top step, Maxwell stopped and considered his options. Firing a thermonuclear device might be a bad idea. Considering the creature seemed to like radiation.

He stopped in front of the door and pondered, but then decided he wasn't required to make a decision at that moment.

Light. He would need light. Feeling foolish for not checking it earlier, Maxwell found the control stud for the torch embedded in the suit's right gauntlet. It lit up, seeming unreasonably bright in the narrow space. He touched his helmet about the faceplate and felt another lamp, but couldn't find the control switch to turn it on. *Probably won't need it*, he decided, though he didn't like the idea of having to hold up one arm all the time to see where he was going.

He laid his left palm on the door and felt the chill of vacuum radiating through it.

When Maxwell tapped the control stud, once again his expectations were defied, and the door silently swooshed open.

Emergency lights cast long, distorted shadows. Maxwell moved his arm back and forth, looking for familiar shapes. He hadn't visited Finch's lab often, so he wasn't sure which console contours were correct and which had been disrupted or distended by the Mother's escape.

The tank. He knew the tank was in the middle of the room. Sabih had been there when he died. He would use the tank to get oriented. Maxwell half turned and extended his arm to frame the tank in the beam from his torch. He expected to find nothing more than a frame with cracked sides and the frozen remains of the Mother smeared against the inner walls, but such was not the case.

"Finch," Maxwell whispered. "It's still here."

"You'll have to be more specific, old man. What is still there?"

"The Mother," Maxwell said, speaking louder. Why shouldn't he speak in a normal tone of voice? It wasn't like there was atmosphere to carry his voice. Or like it would be able to hear him even if there was. "It's still here. Floating. How is that possible? Shouldn't the liquid have been sucked out? Shouldn't it be frozen?" Other questions rose up out of the murk of his mind, many of them quite logical and sensible. His calm state of mind was surprising, considering how completely and totally disturbed he was feeling at that moment. *Starfleet training is still holding strong,* a distant part of his mind said.

Finch did not reply immediately, though Maxwell heard him breathing deeply, just shy of panting. *"It's possible,"* he said finally, *"that Sabih reprogrammed the environmental controls."*

"Why would he do that?"

"I don't know," Finch said. *"One cannot predict the actions of a criminal. Or the young. Can you describe her condition?"*

Maxwell rolled his eyes and thought, *Yes, it's a blob. Next question?* But he knew Finch was asking for actionable information, so he tried to comply. "I don't really know what it looked like before, but it's floating in the middle of the tank. Tendrils are moving slightly. Some of them are pressed up against the walls of the tank. Wait . . ." He stepped closer and shone the torch onto the face of the transparent surface. "What's the tank made out of?"

"A form of transparent aluminium." Finch pronounced the word like a British person would. *"Reinforced with ceramic fibers. Very durable. Why?"*

"It's cracked," Maxwell said. "But the cracks are very fine. It seems to be exerting pressure against the cracks. I think I see . . ." He had to move at a forty-five-degree angle away from the surface of the tank wall and shine the light from above to make sense out of what he was seeing. "There's something coming out of the tank: a thread or fiber of some kind." As much as Maxwell hated the idea of moving closer, curiosity had gotten the better of him. He shifted his stance and lifted his right arm at an awkward angle.

The knuckles of Maxwell's gloved fist brushed against Sabih's face.

He was standing up, his head canted at an awkward angle. Sabih's eyelids were open, the muscles around them twitching, but the eyes looked like frosted glass, discolored by broken and distended vessels. His mouth moved slowly, soundlessly.

Maxwell stared. He imagined he could feel the young man's breath through his gauntleted hand, though, of course, that was ridiculous. There was no atmosphere, no medium for breath to move through, and no heat to be transferred.

He watched Sabih's lips as they moved over and over

again in the same pattern, even though no other part of him moved. He looked, Maxwell decided, like a marionette, one controlled by an amateur puppeteer. Maxwell took a cautious step away, the better to see the nightmare.

Poor, dead Sabih's lips and tongue kept making the same movements over and over, slowly, but precisely. Connections clicked into place inside his head. Words were shaped.

Let.

Me.

Out.

Chapter 14

"To old acquaintances," Nog said, lifting his glass.

"Not forgotten," Jake replied, and tapped his glass against Nog's.

Despite the fact that (or possibly because) he had spent much of his youth working in a bar, Nog had never developed a taste for alcoholic beverages, though he had never lost his love for root beer. On the occasions when Nog visited Jake Sisko on Earth, his old friend always made sure to lay in a couple of cases of the soft drink. If the two of them ever wanted something a bit stronger, they would mix in a bit of *sanar*, which, his uncle (who was a bit of a snob on such matters) used to say, was nothing more than Terran vodka, but with none of the complexity. Neither Jake nor Nog cared. It was the inebriant that the two of them had first shared as boys, and the ceremony of its consumption meant a lot to them. They clinked their glasses together and the ice cubes jingled merrily.

Both smacked their lips, admired their frosty tumblers, and settled back into their chairs. They grinned at each other, but neither spoke for a time, not wanting to spoil the moment. Finally, Nog couldn't resist and exclaimed, "Happy New Year!"

Jake smiled like he had won a bet and said, "And to

you." For more than a decade, assuming they were in the same sector of space, Nog and Jake made it their practice to seek each other out on the turning of the Earth year and toast each other.

"To twenty-three eighty-five," Jake declared, taking another sip of his drink.

"Good riddance," Nog added.

"Really? That bad?" Jake set aside his beverage and eyed the spread of snacks he'd prepared, a cross section of goodies that both men had either tolerated or enjoyed for the other's sake since they were boys.

"That bad," Nog said, scooping up a handful of pistachios and cracking the shells. He wasn't crazy about pistachios, but enjoyed the cracking.

"The station opened."

"And the president was assassinated there."

"Garak became castellan."

"And Doctor Bashir was court-martialed."

"He saved the Andorians."

"Only by doing something so illegal that we don't even know what it is."

"But . . . wait. Never mind," Jake said. "No matter what I say next, you'll think of something terrible to counter it."

"Probably," Nog allowed, brushing the wisps of pistachio shells off his uniform. "It doesn't take much to think of bad things."

Jake studied his friend out of the corner of his eye. "Or one bad thing," he added. "The one you're not telling me about."

Nog didn't reply, focusing all of his attention on the

snack selection. Korena had raised a rueful eyebrow at the glaringly mismatched items before slipping out of the house to visit some friends.

"Or," Jake continued, "*can't* tell me about."

Nog shrugged, picked up his drink, and sipped it.

"Ah," Jake said. "Okay. Must be pretty bad."

"Pretty," Nog replied.

"Did something you regret?" Jake asked. "Or . . . ?"

"*Almost*," Nog said, feeling like he was skirting the edge of the permissible. "But close enough that I felt . . . what's the right word?"

"I'd say *rattled* covers it."

"Right. *Rattled*." He nodded. "I'm rattled." He shook his empty glass, making the ice tinkle. "I'm also empty."

"The mixings are over there," Jake said, pointing at a low table where bottles and a bucket of ice were artfully arranged. "Korena set that up for us."

Nog went to the table, splashed liquids into his glass, studied the color, and adjusted. "She's too good for you, you know."

Jake lifted his half-empty glass in acknowledgment. "Punching out of my weight class." He took a sip. "I recommend it, by the way." Nog was certain his reaction was being carefully recorded.

"I'm sure."

"Having any leanings in that direction?"

Nog settled back down in his chair and stretched out his legs.

"Nog?"

"Hmm?"

"Leanings?"

Nog didn't know how to reply. This wasn't like his classified work for Active Four, the Federation black ops team. He *knew* what he wanted to say about that incident, but Nog also knew he shouldn't and wouldn't. He knew his friend's casual question about potential relationships was meant to sound boyish, even silly, but Nog felt his tongue swelling up in his mouth and his shoulders tense. Finally, he said, "It would be nice, but it doesn't seem to be in the cards these days."

"No prospects?"

"Oh, well, sure," Nog said. "Prospects. Always prospects. The station is busier than ever and you know . . . the uniform."

"It's very flattering."

"It is," Nog agreed. "Remind me to tell you later about this little Arcadian I ran into last month."

"Little?" Jake asked.

"By Arcadian standards, yes."

"Okay. Though I gather that's not your point."

Nog looked at his friend—his oldest, closest friend—and then looked down into his again-empty glass. His ears felt warm. He set the glass aside, suddenly mindful of the too-many beings he had watched drown their sorrows (and their cerebral cortexes) at his uncle's bar. He looked back up at Jake, who was leaning forward, a slight frown on his face. He hadn't bothered to shave that day (or maybe the one before), which, Nog thought, must be one of the perks of being a writer. Or maybe Korena liked her husband with a little stubble. *Before I leave,* he thought, *I'm going to have a long talk with her. Every time we see each other, I say that and yet it never seems to happen.* "No," he said. "Nothing to do with leanings. Just frustration. Just . . ." Nog thought, *No one to talk to,* but then, in a fit of generosity, decided this comment might make his friend feel guilty. And he didn't want Jake to feel guilty, and most certainly not about following his dream, finding a life, or falling in love. *Why should anyone ever feel bad about that?* And so he said, "Not enough time. Too much work! And no one to complain to!" He laughed and thought it sounded like a pretty convincing laugh.

Jake laughed too. Rising, he walked over to the table and poured himself another drink. "Sounds like you just need someone to hang out with," he observed and then, as if struck by inspiration, added, "Hey, what about the chief?"

January 9, 2386
Hangar Deck
Robert Hooke

Fortunately, the evacuees had left the Hooke hangar doors open. If they hadn't, O'Brien wasn't sure what they would have done. Maybe he or Nog could have raced ahead of the slowing transport and found a manual override, though, naturally, there was no guarantee that there *was* an override or, if there was, that it would still function.

As it turned out, using the thruster packs to brake the *Wren* hadn't been as difficult as O'Brien had imagined. He might have even been able to guide her in using only one pack, given that they got lucky and approached the station on the side with the hangar door and not the other. Luck might have gotten them through. *But probably not*, O'Brien admitted. Without Nog, the *Wren* would have been doomed, and O'Brien would have been faced with the painful choice of abandoning her or dying along with the researchers. *Does he know that?* O'Brien wondered, and then conceded, *He probably does. He can do the math as well as I can.*

The transport's port nacelle scraped against the edge of the hatch. O'Brien watched flakes of paint and hull plating flutter out into space. Peering past the ship's stern, he saw a couple of flares from Nog's thruster as he brought the *Wren* to a gentle stop, her bow barely bouncing off the rail at the back of the hangar.

Nog glided into the hangar and grabbed one of the security railings. *"Go ahead, Chief."*

O'Brien, positioned beside the hangar controls, slapped a big red button. He was momentarily surprised by the wave of nostalgia that washed over him for times in his life when important bits of machinery were controlled by big red buttons.

To the chief's surprise, the hangar doors silently slid shut. Overhead lights brightened. As soon as the hatches met and a seal was established, atmosphere hissed into the hangar. Artificial gravity activated and O'Brien's feet touched the deck. Sitting down clumsily, he slapped the harness buckles and gasped gratefully as the thruster's weight dropped away. A second thud made the deck shudder: Nog had likewise freed himself.

Thumbing the catch on his helmet, O'Brien listened

to the suit shutting off the flow of air into his helmet. He lifted it away and inhaled deeply, gratefully, smelling lubricant, the sharp tang of liquid fuel, and oxygen that had been recycled one too many times through an inferior scrubber. *Heaven*, he thought.

Struggling into an upright position, O'Brien walked ponderously over to where Nog still lay and extended his hand, proffering assistance. "Could have been worse."

Nog puffed out his cheeks and rubbed his brow with his gauntleted hand. "Speak for yourself, Chief. I was almost out of air."

"Huh," O'Brien said, "it must have been low to start. I still have a quarter left."

"No," Nog said. "It was full. I checked it. I, uh, just breathe heavily."

"Right." He decided not to pursue the point. "Let's check on these folk."

As they crossed the deck to the *Wren*'s primary hatch, both men tapped connection points on their sleeves and left bits and pieces of their suits, the parts they needed to interface with the thrusters, in their wake. Without discussion, both had decided to stay in their suits, helmets clipped awkwardly on their backs.

"Were you able to stay in contact with the pilot?" Nog asked.

"Nita wasn't the pilot," O'Brien said. "But no. The signal kept dropping out. Last I heard from her was ten minutes ago."

"No damage to the hull," Nog said.

"Not on this side either," O'Brien agreed. "But the hole wouldn't have to be very big to . . ."

"I know."

They both knew. Death by decompression or suffocation was a death in fear and darkness—not an end that O'Brien would wish on anyone.

They checked the hangar deck's interfaces. "Power's on," Nog said, studying the compact display. "And it seems to be interfacing with the *Wren*."

"Open her up," O'Brien said, adding a silent benediction for the passengers and crew.

Nog tapped a control (not a big red button, alas). The *Wren* did not respond immediately. O'Brien sensed a shudder in her frame, as if the ship was considering whether to wake or crumble into dust. Instead, the hatch popped, releasing a burp of stale air, but not opening completely. "Give me a hand with this," O'Brien said. Nog knelt low for maximum leverage. "Okay, heave."

While the door didn't slide open easily, neither did it fight them. "No lights," Nog said, and flicked on the small, bright torch on his suit's left wrist. "Interior hatch."

A second hatch had opened just enough for them to grip its lip, but it resisted more than the first. O'Brien worried that decompression may have warped the frame, but then remembered the puff of air. *Could have been caught between the hatches*, he thought, but then decided he needed to take control of his imagination.

The interior hatch slid aside, but reluctantly. "It's not warped," Nog said, huffing. "It's more like something is holding it on the other side."

"Wait," O'Brien gasped. "I think I know what this is. Hang on." He pressed his mouth to the narrow gap and said, trying to project his voice without shouting, "Can anyone hear me?"

He tilted his head, ear close to the gap. Muffled shouts and expletives. "There's someone alive in there."

"Why can't we open the door?"

"Someone gummed up the works."

"What?"

"Well, webbed it up."

"What?" Nog repeated.

"Help me move this just a bit more," O'Brien said, ignoring the question. Answers would be forthcoming soon enough anyway. He hoped.

Both engineers shoved at the door, Nog cursing under his breath as he tried to avoid being stepped on. O'Brien knew he was being clumsy, a combination of exhaustion and the bulky suit causing him to flail when he knew he should be trying to think strategically. *What time is it?* he wondered. *How long have we been here?*

It moved a few centimeters, enough so that the light from Nog's torch illuminated the space just beyond the hatch, a space filled with white threads. O'Brien cautiously pushed a finger into the cottony mass. "Ginger and Honey have been busy," he murmured.

"What?" Nog asked. He was, O'Brien thought, sounding progressively less patient.

"The spiders, uh, the arachnowatis . . . Nita's creatures," O'Brien explained. "I think they may have filled up the passenger cabin with . . . what should I call it? Uh? Webbing?"

"Really?" Nog said, though he had lost the impatient

tone. "Interesting . . . but *why*? They're not planning to, uh, you know . . . *eat* them?"

"No!" O'Brien exclaimed, yanking his hand away from the hatch, his long-dormant arachnophobia flaring to life. "I mean, of course not. I don't think they even eat . . . living things."

"They don't," said a muffled voice.

O'Brien turned to the gap and asked, "Nita?"

"Yes," the voice said.

"Are you all right?"

"I suppose." A pregnant pause. "I can't move."

"Okay," O'Brien said, trying to sound calm. "Why?" He knew why, but thought Nita might need to talk it out.

"The girls got a little enthusiastic."

"Right," O'Brien said, trying to be agreeable. "We can't open the hatch."

"I'm not surprised," Nita replied. "The webbing is everywhere. And it's very sticky." O'Brien felt certain he heard the sounds of struggle. "And very strong." The last statement had a note of pride in it.

"Any ideas what we can do to get you out?"

"Find something very sharp?"

Another voice from within shouted, "Use a plasma torch!" Other voices added suggestions. "Electricity!" "Phasers!" "A pointed stick!"

"Shut up, Winslow!" Nita shouted. "Always with the pointed stick!"

"I'll just go see what I can find," O'Brien said, and withdrew from the hatch. As he stepped back, with Nog at his heels, the chief thought he saw a set of green and gold orbs glowing through the gap in the hatch. "Ideas?"

"A plasma torch would work," Nog suggested.

"Unless the filaments are flammable."

"Hmm. Good point. We should cut off a sample and see."

"A knife might be best to start. Something sharp."

"But not pointy."

"No, not pointy."

Nog drew the short work knife from the sheath in the suit's leg. "I'll see what I can do with this."

"Okay," O'Brien agreed. "I think I saw a workshop at the other end of the hangar. Captain Maxwell will have something useful there."

O'Brien headed for the shop, but only got a few steps away before Nog asked, "How much time do you think we have?"

"Until what?"

"Until this all falls apart?"

O'Brien shook his head. "No idea. We don't know enough about what's happening. We have to get those people free first. Then we find out what's happened to the captain and to Finch." He bit down harder on the name than he had expected. Shrugging it off, he pointed back to the hatch and said, "Be careful back there. I think I saw one of them—Ginger or Honey—looking out. If you come at them with a knife, they might think you mean them harm."

Nog shook his head dismissively. "I'm not worried," he said, and smiled. "I think they know better. They're smart. You can see it in their eyes."

O'Brien shuddered. "Sure," he said. "In their eyes."

Finch's Lab
Robert Hooke

Sabih's body lurched forward, his mouth moving mechanically. Maxwell responded as he had been trained: he sidestepped to the right, grabbed his attacker's arm in both his hands, and used its momentum to propel Sabih into a bulkhead. The only sounds Maxwell could hear inside his helmet were his own accelerated breathing and the disconcerting crinkling sound the still-stiff suit made when he moved.

And then, joy of joys, Finch was there inside the helmet too, sounding (inexplicably) like he was genuinely concerned. *"Ben! What's wrong?!"*

The Sabih-thing careened off the bulkhead, then stopped, stunned possibly, and stared straight ahead, unresponsive. Maxwell had seen the posture before and expected his knees to buckle. In a moment, he would be facedown on the deck.

This did not occur.

Instead, the head twisted to the side like there was a crosshair on Maxwell's chest and the broken nose was the tip of a bowman's arrow. A thin stream of what Maxwell thought was blood seeped out, and then, to Maxwell's surprise, curled away from his lip to sway from side to side like a serpent preparing to strike.

The Sabih-thing bounced on his toes and snapped his body around to align with his head. His lips and tongue, black with burst subcutaneous vessels, continued to move in recognizable patterns, mouthing the same thing over and over: *Let. Me. Out.*

Maxwell took a step back and tried to clear his head, unsure what he was seeing. He wanted to keep his wrist-mounted lamp trained on the Sabih-thing but he couldn't suppress the fear that there was something else waiting in the shadows to either side of the beam, something worse, something unthinkable. *Let* who *out?* Maxwell wondered. *And where would he go?*

"Ben!" Finch shouted. "*What's happening?!*"

"Lights, Finch! If you can find them! Lights!"

"*What? Why?*"

The Sabih-thing pitched forward, arms extended, black fingernails clawing at Maxwell's helmet.

Maxwell sidestepped to the right. Instead of grabbing the arm, he squatted and extended his left leg. The Sabih-thing's legs became entangled in Maxwell's and it tumbled forward. With a sweep of his leg, Maxwell brought the creature down. Gasping for breath, laboring against the environmental suit's substandard exchange, Maxwell spun on the ball of his foot and snapped forward, intent on bringing the heel of his hand down on the base of the skull. If he aimed well, he would snap the Sabih-thing's spine. That was usually the solution in all the old horror stories, wasn't it? Break the connection to the undead brain.

Aiming with his torch, Maxwell cocked his arm and, encumbered by the suit, punched down as hard as he could. The heel of his hand stopped an inch from the base of the skull, his conscious mind finally recognizing what his unconscious had registered a second earlier: a black cord was coming out of the back of the head, exactly where Maxwell intended to strike him.

Maxwell froze.

The cord pulsed.

Maxwell shone his torch on it and followed its arc to the cracked face of the tank.

Finch picked that moment to find the light controls. A single light activated over the tank, casting the Mother in an ominous glow. The creature writhed, though whether because of the sudden light or some subtler stimulus, Maxwell could not say.

His knee collapsed, and he turned the movement into a clumsy roll.

"Ben!" Finch shouted. *"I found a light control!"*

"I know," Maxwell said, keeping his voice low and even.

"And I've got a sensor feed."

"Good. Super." Maxwell glanced at what used to be Sabih. He had managed to place his palms on the deck and was trying to push himself up. Without thinking, Maxwell scuttled away until he felt the bulkhead behind his back.

"My god," Finch murmured. *"Do you see?"*

"Oh, yeah," Maxwell said. "I see." There was enough light to track the Mother's movements and to see the Mother's tendrils extending from cracks all around the tank, each one stretched out in a different direction. Maxwell stopped counting when he got to eight tendrils, though he was sure there were more. Some were very, very thin, no more than cilia, probably just sampling the immediate environment. Others were thicker, ropier, and poking into ventilation and electrical outlets. One was plugged into what Maxwell assumed was a hole in the bulkhead. Another was plugged into a hole in the back of Sabih's head.

"*It's astonishing!*" Finch said.

Maxwell permitted himself a brief sigh. *Of course,* he thought. *Of course. Why not?* "I'm going to get out of here," he said, attempting to sound calm and reasonable.

Sabih—or the thing that now lived inside of him—figured out the correct series of movements and managed to get up on his knees. He—it—did that thing where he twisted his head around and fixed its sightless eyes on Maxwell again. Sabih's mouth moved. The tendril of the Mother that had come out through his nose seemed to move in time with his mouth. A couple of his teeth, Maxwell noted, had broken when he face-planted onto the deck, and thinner tendrils oozed out of the splintered remains.

Staring at what remained of the young man—Finch's lackey, Finch's minion—all he could think to do was murmur, "I'm so sorry." It came out of his mouth in one breath: "I'msosorry." Meaningless.

The Sabih-thing's mouth moved in the same rhythm, over and over, the movement just as meaningless as Maxwell's words.

Maxwell pressed his back against the bulkhead and levered himself up into a standing position. For a moment, he was moving so fast that he wondered if the artificial gravity had failed again, but his old friend's logic and training laughed at him and his middle-aged bones. *That's just fear. Fear and adrenaline.*

He ran through the hatch and punched the control with the side of his hand, too hard, as it turned out. *That's going to leave a mark,* he thought, cupping the side of his right hand and breathing through his teeth.

The airlock cycled, and, faster than it felt like it should have, the second hatch opened. Maxwell lurched through it, expecting any moment to feel the grip of a tendril around his waist, but the second hatch slid shut.

Finch stood before Maxwell, offering his hand for support, gibbering. Sound was muffled. *I used to be good at this,* Maxwell thought. *I used to be good in a crisis. What happened to that guy?*

Maxwell took Finch's proffered hand and waited for the deck to stop swaying. As soon as he felt steady, he removed his helmet, clenched his fist, and brought his arm back. He wasn't sure when he had formed the idea, but Maxwell had known for the last couple minutes that as soon as he saw Finch, he was going to punch him in the face. Damn warnings or fair play.

Finch, obviously, had also been thinking ahead. The hook jaw of a very large wrench met Maxwell's temple.

Blackness swam up or Maxwell dove down to meet it. He wasn't able to say for sure. Just before the darkness swallowed him, the strangest image swam up to meet Maxwell: a gerbil. Its shiny black eyes glittered and its tail twitched. Maxwell thought—just for a moment—*I know you,* but, before he could remember how, the darkness folded in over him.

Chapter 15

Captain Amelia Rojek tossed the padd on her desktop and frowned, disappointed. "So, that's it?" she asked. "No defense? Not even a statement?"

The defendant's attorney, Commander Vincent Zugay, settled into the visitor's chair. Rojek had always made it a point to make sure the opposition had a comfortable chair. She believed it made them sloppy, but this tactic never seemed to work with Zugay. He laced his fingers, cupped the back of his head, and stretched the muscles in his neck. "You're complaining? Be happy. Take the win and call it a day."

"Win?" Rojek laughed once, a short, sharp bark of derision. "It's hard to think of this one as a win." She shook her head, then brushed back her bangs, which, she knew, were getting a touch too long. Rojek disliked feeling unkempt. "I thought he'd fight it."

Now it was Zugay's chance to laugh. He took off his glasses (Rojek believed they were an affectation, but had not bothered to confirm her suspicion) and wiped the corners of his eyes. Noting the dark circles under the commander's eyes, the captain wondered if he had been working as many hours as she did. She wondered if they should work out a deal, one where they could each work a little less on certain cases in exchange for naps. Rojek shook her head sharply. *You need to get some rest, Amy.*

"There's no fight left in him." Zugay asked, "Do you really think that he'd have stood a chance?"

Rojek picked up her padd again and attempted to focus. Captain Maxwell's confession was a freely made admission of sole guilt and a request for clemency for the *Phoenix*'s crew for their actions that led to the deaths of approximately six hundred Cardassians, as they were "totally unaware that I was acting on my own." She shrugged. "No. There's too much evidence. It's all there in the logs. And I would have called Captain Picard as a witness. Have you ever heard him *speak*?"

"Yes," Zugay said. "If Jean-Luc Picard told me I was responsible for blowing up Praxis, I'd believe him."

She chuckled. Zugay was a pretentious ass, but he could be funny when the mood struck him. And he had nice hands. Rojek had always liked his hands.

"It's just that, well, even during the interview, I found myself thinking, *I like this man. This is a good, decent man . . .*"

"Who has confessed to killing over six hundred people."

Rojek stopped, appalled. "Aren't you supposed to be *his* attorney?"

Zugay pointed at the padd. "Not anymore," he said. "He fired me. The captain will offer no defense and will accept whatever the court-martial decides." The commander rubbed his head in exasperation, which made a mess of his usually carefully styled hair. "My role at this juncture is to deliver documents to the court. Tomorrow, I'll report and get a new case, hopefully, this time, for someone who will actually want me to *defend* them."

"And hopefully not be guilty," Rojek added.

Zugay waved away the idea. "That's not the point."

"Of course not." Rojek settled back in her chair. Neither of them spoke for a moment. Zugay stared at his glasses, which he still was holding. Rojek looked at her padd. No one, she guessed, wanted to get back to work.

"But I know what you mean. Maxwell has *it*, that air of command. You want to believe what he says. If he'd really wanted to defend himself, if he had been willing to get up in a courtroom . . ."

The captain nodded. "Maybe." She understood what Zugay was saying. He might not have won, but Captain Maxwell might have changed a few minds. He might have, as her mother used to say, stirred the pot. The peoples of the Federation were wary of conflict; they welcomed the truce with the Cardassians. But if a man of Maxwell's character came forward and presented evidence, a justification for what he had done—there was no telling what the repercussions might be.

"What do you think will happen to him?" Zugay asked.

Pointing at the padd, Rojek said, "With this? He'll be stripped of all honors and rank. Sent to New Zealand for treatment. If the panel is feeling particularly merciful, they'll wipe this from the public records so it won't follow him around for the rest of his life. Given time, maybe he'll be forgotten, maybe even forgiven, if that's possible."

Zugay nodded in agreement. "Ever been to New Zealand?"

"The penal colony?" Rojek asked, amused and aghast. "*No.*"

Zugay put his glasses back on his face. "Not the penal colony. I meant the country. New Zealand."

"Never."

Rising, Zugay retrieved the slim attaché case he always carried. His uniform, Rojek noted, was well tailored, but the slacks were wrinkled, like he had slept in them. Maybe he had. "You should go sometime. It's beautiful."

Rojek indicated the pile of padds before her with a wave of her hand. "Yes," she said flatly. "I'll get right on that as soon as I've taken care of a few things."

"There will always be things that need tending," Zugay offered. "But we all need to take a break sometime."

"Let me know the next time you're going," Rojek said, sounding a little more defensive than she wanted. "And I'll tag along."

Zugay nodded as if a deal had actually been struck. "Deal. I'll let you know. Pack a swimsuit if you're not afraid of sharks."

"I'm afraid of sharks."

"Well, that's just sensible, but you'll still want to bring a swimsuit." The door slid open as Zugay approached. Rojek wasn't sure if they were still kidding around, or if she had just agreed to go to New Zealand with this man. This *irritating* man. Who has nice hands. And a nice smile, she admitted, if she was willing to be completely honest with herself. "You'll get all the sign-offs and forward that to the court?"

Rojek shook her head, momentarily confused. *Right. Back to work.* She was fairly sure she was blushing, and so did her best to keep her head down so her cheeks were in shadow. "No worries."

"Shame about him, though," Zugay said. "I hate seeing anyone just . . . give up that way."

"Really?" Rojek asked.

"Maybe Maxwell should have taken a few vacations."

"It's a thought."

"See you." Zugay left and the door slid shut.

"See you."

Three months later, Zugay called Rojek to tell her he was headed to New Zealand for a week and left the address where he would be staying. With some family, he said. A family thing. If she had some time and the means to make it, he said, she should come and visit. "We have lots of room," Zugay said. "My brother-in-law has a house down there. Very nice. Big." Rojek listened to the message fourteen times before she thought, *What the hell? Why not?*

January 9, 2386
Hangar Deck
Robert Hooke

The webbing, or the silk or whatever you wanted to call it, was an engineering marvel. Nog couldn't get over it: light, pliable, and very strong. And sticky. Very, very sticky. He learned about the stickiness right away. Attacking the stuff with a knife was folly. *How do they make this stuff?* Nog wondered, watching the arachnoforms chasing each other around the interior walls of the hangar and among the struts. They had squeezed out of the exceedingly small opening in the main hatch. Their carapaces appeared to be the only thing their threads didn't stick to. Now, one of them—Ginger, he thought—was chasing the other, like she was playing a game of tag, while the second, Honey, seemed to only want to put as much distance between herself and her sister as was possible. *Sisters,* Nog thought, *are the same everywhere.*

He turned his attention back to the webbing. Fortunately, the plasma torch was working where a knife had not. A test had proved the webbing wasn't combustible. It appeared to Nog that the strands with a lot of adhesive were actually flame retardant (what could be done with *that?*), while the ends of the strands, the last bit that the arachnoforms spurted out, were not. When the plasma torch hit one of those bits, only a tiny percentage of the total, it would disappear in a puff of blue flame and leave behind an aroma like burned sugar.

Every flare of blue flame produced a squeak or squeal from one of the *Wren*'s passengers.

Nog couldn't blame them. As he reached each scientist, he had to explain what had happened. Each had been cut off from everyone else, ensnared and muffled in a sticky cocoon. Every one of them had likely expected Ginger or Honey to inject them with venom or attempt to extract their bodily fluids. But that didn't appear to be what the arachnoforms were. They had simply done what Nita had instructed: keep the transport from breaking up and doing whatever they could to protect the passengers. The girls had performed spectacularly. Nog couldn't imagine how many meters—scratch that, *kilometers*—of thread the arachnoforms had extruded.

O'Brien bent down over Nog and asked, "How're we doing?" Since there was only one torch, the chief was reduced to assisting newly freed passengers out of the *Wren* and periodically asking Nog the same question. "Progress?"

"About halfway back now."

O'Brien hovered a step and a half behind Nog, close enough to converse in low tones, but not so close as to be in the way. Not *physically* in the way.

"I think we can turn this over to Nita. We should get a move on." Without warning, Nog felt his feet leave the deck. The crown of his head cracked against the transport's low overhead. Behind him, O'Brien shouted, "Whoa! *Whoa!*" and felt fingers rake his back. All around, Nog heard the scientists, muffled yelps of fear and surprise.

Just as suddenly, Nog was on his knees, panting, his Ferengi metabolism pumping life-saving flight endorphins into him. Nog had been in enough similar situations to know that running away at top speed wouldn't improve his chances of survival (despite Ferengi instincts to the contrary).

Why after all this time, Nog mused as he forced his breathing to slow, *do I still feel this way?* It was a fleeting thought and likely would have been forgotten if he hadn't felt a gentle, reassuring touch on his right arm.

Nog turned around, expecting to see the chief, but, no, it wasn't O'Brien. One of the arachnoforms—Ginger, he thought—crouched on the deck beside Nog, lightly touching him with one of her slender forelimbs. She turned her head from side to side, her jewel-like eyes glittering in the low light. Nog had the distinct impression from the way her mouth pieces were moving that Ginger was asking a question, perhaps inquiring about his well-being. He said, "I'm fine. Just a bump on the head." He patted the top of his skull. "Ferengi have thick ones. Nothing to worry about."

Satisfied, the arachnoform withdrew a half step. When Ginger pulled the tip of her forelimb away from his arm, tiny hooks or suction cups pulled lightly at the fabric of his environmental suit. Nog carefully reached out with his free hand and gently patted the creature on the head. Ginger appeared to enjoy the contact.

Behind him, O'Brien cleared his throat, and then said, "We need to get moving. That was the artificial gravity generator being, er . . . irresolute. We're lucky it only lasted a moment."

"Agreed," Nog said, standing. He heard the tips of Ginger's legs tapping along behind him. "What's our play?"

The chief stepped into the hatchway and raised his hand, signaling to Nog to stay in the transport so they could speak in relative privacy. Ginger climbed the bulkhead beside them and appeared to be listening carefully to their exchange. "We head for ops," O'Brien said, speaking in low tones, "and hope the captain is still there. Maybe he's managed to break through the interference or has spotted someone headed our way."

"If not?"

"I've been thinking about that."

"And?"

O'Brien shook his head. "If the station begins falling apart, we'll have to put everyone back on the *Wren* and push her out the hangar. Hope for the best. Before we go, make sure your suit's been recharged. We may need them."

Nog hated to admit it, but he couldn't think of a better plan. "We don't really know if the *Wren* has been compromised, do we? I mean, it seems to be holding together."

O'Brien snorted. "With all that gunk on the inside? I doubt if it could fall apart if we wanted it to."

Beside them, Ginger clicked and chittered. Nog wasn't sure if she felt like she was being insulted or complimented, but O'Brien took a half step back. Nog very respectfully reached out again and rubbed the knob of chitin over the cluster of Ginger's smaller eyes. He was pleased when she seemed to be pressing back.

"Interesting." Nita was peering into the hatch.

"What?"

"She's warmed up to you quickly. Ginger usually likes to watch people for a while before she lets them get that close."

Nog felt unexpectedly self-conscious, like he may have broken some unknown taboo. "She came up to me after I hit my head."

"You'll have to let me record your interactions later."

O'Brien raised both of his hands, fingers pointed up, a gesture designed to end all unnecessary conversation. "Nita," he said, "we have to go. You'll need to finish cutting out the rest of the passengers. Nog, can you show the doctor how to use the plasma torch?"

"I know how to use a plasma torch," Nita replied. She plucked the tool from Nog's hand and set about adjusting the flame, all the time grumbling to herself about ingratitude and "just wanting to do some damned science."

Stepping out of the *Wren*, Nog was greeted with the sight of a half-dozen weary, frightened, sticky scientists either lying on the hangar deck or perched precariously on packing crates. No one spoke, but their eyes followed Nog and O'Brien as they crossed to a wall-mounted unit where they could replenish their suits. Nog didn't enjoy the sensation.

The replenisher pumped asthmatically, and the gauges on Nog's suit took forever to turn green again. Speaking low and attempting not to betray any emotion, Nog asked, "Should we bring the thruster packs?"

O'Brien shook his head. "It would send a bad signal," he said. "Besides, they're pretty close to tapped out."

"And heavy."

"Very heavy."

"How long could we last in these suits in open space?"

O'Brien squinted, calculating. "Six hours. Maybe a little longer if we really squeeze down on the nitrogen mix."

The hangar deck shuddered and the supine scientists, as one, briefly levitated. Nog's feet left the deck for a second, and his stomach lurched. Behind him, Ginger chittered in agitation.

"We really have to go," O'Brien announced loudly enough for everyone to hear. "We'll be back soon."

"How soon?" asked a random researcher.

"As soon as we can," Nog replied.

One of the scientists shouted, "And what if you can't?"

The corner of Nog's mouth twitched in annoyance,

and he briefly, involuntarily, closed his eyes. "We will," he said when he looked back up. "One way or another." No one responded and Nog felt their collective disbelief.

Behind them, another scientist emerged from the hatch of the *Wren,* blinking, disheveled, and covered in threads. Nita Bharad guided the besieged soul to a resting spot, then addressed O'Brien and Nog. "We know you'll do everything you can." She held up the plasma torch. "I'll keep everything together here until you get back."

O'Brien disconnected his suit. "Thanks." He jogged toward the doorway to the main stairwell where Nog was waiting.

One of the researchers called, "And what do we do if the gravity goes off again?"

Nog was surprised by O'Brien's reply. "Ask Ginger to stick you to the deck."

"It doesn't look like Ginger is planning to stay with us," Nita replied, pointing at a spot behind Nog. The commander looked up. Ginger was dangling from a thread just above the doorway, her eyes fixed on him. "She appears to have taken quite a shine to you."

"Wonderful," O'Brien said.

"Oh, come on," Nog said. "I bet she could be really useful."

"Sure, if we run into some giant houseflies," O'Brien said, but then stopped short. "Which, considering this place, we shouldn't dismiss out of hand." He slapped the switch that unlatched the hatch into the station's core and peered into the gloom. He beckoned to Ginger and said, "Ladies first." The arachnoform obeyed without hesitation, dropping to the deck and skittering into the darkness.

"See?" Nog asked, following his new friend. "She just wants to help."

"I am thrilled and delighted," O'Brien said. "Look at my face. Can't you tell?"

Ops Center

The image of the gerbil flickered in Maxwell's mind's eye, shimmied, and melted into a close-up of Finch's round face and heavy brow. Maxwell's head throbbed and his throat was dry. He tried to move his hands, but the fingers were numb and swollen. His shoulders ached. Licking his lips, Maxwell tried to think of something witty and disarming to say, but the only sound that came out of his mouth was an indistinct whine of misery.

"You're awake."

It had been, Maxwell reflected woodenly, a very long time since someone had knocked him unconscious. There had been a time when this would happen often enough that Maxwell had become familiar with the sensation of struggling back to consciousness while the world shivered and pulsed around him. Back during his Starfleet days, especially during the Cardassian conflict, the experience was commonplace enough that, when it occurred, Maxwell was able to get through the stomach-lurching wretchedness by thinking, *Oh, right—this again. I can do this.* And he could, too, usually with his dignity intact.

Starfleet officers needed to be able to take a blow without vomiting on their shoes.

But you're not Starfleet anymore, are you, Ben?

Maxwell turned his head to the side, opened his mouth, and emptied his gut.

To his great surprise, Finch held a bottle of water to Maxwell's mouth. Maxwell sipped, swished, and then spit. He drank some more, grateful. His stomach settled and his head cleared. When the room stopped surging, he saw that his arms were bound to the chair's arms with repair tape, probably from a roll that had come from Maxwell's own tool box.

Finch stepped away, holding the now empty bottle aloft. "More?" he asked.

"No," Maxwell said, shaking his head. "Thank you."

"You're welcome. Feeling better?"

"I have a bit of a headache. Also, I'm tied to a chair."

"Just a precaution," Finch said. "I felt the need to keep you in one place until I've had a chance to explain."

"You don't have to explain anything to me," Maxwell said.

"I don't?" Finch seemed both confused and surprised. Also, Maxwell noted, he had taken off his jacket—one of the rare occasions Maxwell could recall seeing Finch without one—and had sweated through his shirt. There were two large stains under Finch's armpits and perspiration dripped off his forehead. Maxwell realized that he, too, was perspiring heavily, though his environmental suit was attempting to compensate. Without the helmet, there was only so much the suit could do.

"No," Maxwell said, attempting to sound calm. "You

don't. I understand what's happened. You've made some bad choices. Events have gotten out of control and you're trying to compensate."

Finch's mouth screwed up and his brow furrowed. "You're talking to me like I'm crazy," he said. "You're trying to keep me calm. Like I might lose control any moment." Finch took a step closer and laid his hands on the tops of Maxwell's arms, near enough that when the beads of sweat dripped off his nose they landed in Maxwell's lap. "I'm not going to lose control," he said, his voice quavering. "And I don't have to compensate for anything."

"Okay," Maxwell said, trying to hold Finch's gaze. His legs weren't taped to anything. The chair was fixed in place by a central pillar that he could use to spin around, though for many reasons—including his unsettled stomach—Maxwell decided he wouldn't. There wasn't much point in kicking Finch in the groin at just that moment, though it could arrive soon. *Time enough for violence.* "I believe you." Maxwell swallowed hard and turned away. The reek of fear rolling off Finch was too much to bear. "Am I correct that the environmental controls are offline?"

Finch pulled away and looked around the room. "I don't know," he said. "I hadn't noticed."

"It's a little warm in here."

"Is it? I thought that was just me. I've been busy."

Yes, Maxwell thought. *Dragging me into this chair and taping me to it. That must have been exhausting.* On the best of days, Finch was not an impressive physical specimen. On the kind of day he was having today, the station owner was probably close to passing out. "If the environmental systems are down, we only have whatever air was pumped into this room," Maxwell explained. "It may start to get stuffy in here soon." He looked around at the debris on the deck. The room looked like someone had scattered every loose object off every flat surface. Maxwell recognized the pattern. "And the artificial gravity has turned off and on. At least once."

"Yes," Finch admitted. That probably accounted for some of Maxwell's queasiness. Also, a mild concussion was probably a factor. "I've rerouted the power to our deck to compensate."

"And the rest of the station be damned."

Finch swallowed hard, his Adam's apple bouncing like a rubber ball. His eyes flicked from side to side. "I'll be leaving soon. After I leave, you can readjust the grid however you like."

"You've arranged for a ride?"

"No," Finch said, wiping his shirtsleeve across his brow. "Not exactly. But I can't imagine he'll mind giving me a lift. Especially after he sees what I've done. And I'll be able to pay him. Oh, yes." Finch drifted over to the sensor station, which appeared to still be functioning. "Not picking up anything yet," Finch mumbled. "Not that I would, I suppose."

"Subspace interference still pretty bad?"

"What?" Finch asked, distracted. "No. I mean, yes, but clearing out. Things should settle soon. That's not what I meant. Never mind. Shut up. I'm not talking to you."

Maxwell groaned. *If he's not talking to me, then who?* "Who's coming, Finch?" *Keep him focused.* Maxwell dissected Finch's comments. "Especially after *who* sees what you've done?"

Finch spun around. For a moment, Maxwell worried that he had pushed the wrong button. Maybe Finch would decide he didn't need company. He grimaced, light from the console flashing disturbingly on his teeth. No, not grimacing. *Grinning*. Finch was very pleased about something. "My customer!" he crowed. "My *first* customer. Maybe a bit of a loss leader when you factor in the loss of . . . well . . ." He waved his arms dramatically to take in the entirety of the Hooke. ". . . all this. But acceptable. Acceptable."

"Customer?" Maxwell repeated. He'd spent enough time in mental health facilities and knew enough therapists. He even counted some of them as friends. He knew their techniques. Repeat the last significant word, and let the patient do the rest.

"*First* customer," Finch repeated. "And when others find out what I've done, the first of *many*!"

"First customer for what? The Mother?" He couldn't help himself. Maxwell knew he should just let Finch talk, but there was the urge, the damnable desire, to set things *right*. "She's eating your station, Finch. She did something terrible to Sabih."

"Or is she trying to *fix* Sabih?" Finch rebutted. "I think . . . I think that's what she's doing. Maybe . . ." He rubbed his hands together in what Maxwell imagined was supposed to be self-assured glee, but there was no conviction behind it. Finch knew the truth as well as he did.

"More likely the Mother is trying to talk through him. Could you read his lips from in here? I could." Maxwell strained against the tape, trying to get the blood flowing. Finch had wrapped him too tight. He knew that Finch was getting too agitated, but he couldn't help it. *Bad air,* a part of his brain told him. *You're getting stupid.* "I *could* read his lips. You know what he was saying, Finch? You want to know what Sabih was saying?"

Finch stood stock-still, his arms at odd angles, his hands limp, like he might reach forward and grasp Maxwell by the throat. "What was he saying?"

"He was saying, 'Let me out.' Over and over again. His dead lips. In the airless room. And that . . . that *thing* with its tendril jammed into the back of his head. Like a puppet."

"Or a communicator," Finch said softly, his eyes suddenly bright with wonder. "Or a translator."

Maxwell knew he had gone too far. He tried to reel Finch back in. "No," he said. "No. Not like that. She . . . *it* . . . is not trying to talk to us. It's not alive. It's not intelligent. It was just repeating the last thing that went through Sabih's mind, *his* last thought. Even if it *is* talking through him, it's the only thing a creature in a cage would say! '*Let me out!*'"

But Finch was no longer paying attention to him. Something on the console flashed. Maxwell studied Finch's face, watching as the grin bloomed again. "Then the Mother is getting what she wants," Finch said, eyes gleaming in victory. "Her ride is here."

Chapter 16

"**S**o," Julian Bashir asked as he carefully settled onto his barstool, "what is the best day you've ever had?" The doctor attempted to perch his foot on the bar rail, but he was either too bruised or too deep in his cups to get good purchase. Instead, he contented himself with planting his elbow on the edge of the bar and his head on his fist. He grinned happily at his friend Miles O'Brien.

The chief, obviously equally sore and equally inebriated, placed his half-empty pint on one of the six coasters Nog had deposited in front of him. He squinted thoughtfully and rubbed his palm over the front of his leather coat. Looking from side to side, O'Brien continued to look contemplative until he spied his broad-brimmed hat, which he carefully retrieved and placed on his head. "Well," he said, and then repeated, "Well . . ." He looked at the fingernails of his left hand, which were all purple, as if his fingers had been nearly crushed. He grinned at some memory. "Well, I know I'm supposed to say something like, the day I met Keiko. Or, my wedding day. Or, the day my daughter was born." He held up his hands. "And, to be sure, all good days. *Very* good days."

"I'm sure," Bashir said, grinning. "Was I there for any of those?"

"No," O'Brien said. "Son being born, *yes*. As I recall, you were instrumenta . . . instrumentative . . ." He collected himself. "You were vital."

"It was a good thing I was there."

"Yes!"

They both retrieved their glasses, clinked them together, and drank deeply. "Happy I could help," the doctor said.

Bashir looked around as if suddenly remembering where they were. "Ah," he said, pleased. "Nog!"

Nog, who had been leaning back against the shelf where the liquor bottles were stowed, waved. They were the only ones still in the bar, the rest of the patrons having been shooed out an hour earlier, at closing time. It had not been a very busy night—not many patrons to shoo. Bashir and O'Brien would have made up for the evening's slow trade *if* Nog made them compensate Quark for their drinks, which he didn't. Maybe he would make up the difference out of his own pocket. He hadn't decided. He was having too much fun.

"Nog!" O'Brien cried. "We're out of drinks! Be a good lad and find us something adequate to our needs! One more round!"

"Just one. Something special. While you answer my question."

"Nog, something special," O'Brien agreed.

Nog reached around behind him and retrieved a bottle. "On the rocks, gentlemen, or straight?"

"Straight!" O'Brien cried.

"Rocks!" Bashir exclaimed.

"One of each, then." Nog poured. He knew what they wanted before either of them knew. He didn't get to play bartender often, but he knew he was good at it. He knew he could tend bar as well as the station's power plant or the *Defiant*'s engines. He poured them each a shot of the very old, very real precious whiskey, one over the rocks and one not. He set down the drinks on new coasters. After a moment's consideration, he poured himself a half a dram, though he didn't usually much care for Terran spirits. *Special occasion.*

"So, pray continue, sir," Bashir said. "Love, marriage, children, and et cetera. Best day ever . . ."

"Yes, as I was saying. I know what I *should* say. I know what I probably will say any other time anyone ever asks me this question for the rest of my life, but I also know that, in some small way, I'll be lying a little bit if I don't admit that the best day I ever had"— O'Brien raised his glass—"was the day we saved the Alamo."

Bashir lifted his glass and sloshed about half of the very precious liquid on the sleeve of his torn, stained wool shirt. "The Alamo!" he saluted.

Nog lifted his glass an inch or two, though he knew better than to intrude on the moment. He sipped the amber liquid. Wincing, he felt it burn down the back of his throat and up into his sinuses. "The Alamo," he said softly while the two men laughed and pounded each other's backs.

January 9, 2386
Central Core
Robert Hooke

"So," Nog asked as he and O'Brien jogged up the stairs to deck four, "is this day reminding you of anything?"

"What?" O'Brien asked, his panting echoing loudly off the hard walls and stairs. "Reminding? What?"

Nog, younger, carrying less mass, and, honestly, fitter, breathed through his nose and pumped his legs. "The Alamo," he said.

"The Alamo?"

"Sure," Nog said, reaching the next landing and pausing, pretending to be winded to give O'Brien a moment to lean on the railing and pant. "Remember the Alamo?"

"Well," O'Brien said, obviously confused, "of course. I mean, that's the whole point."

"I'm not following you."

" 'Remember the Alamo.' That's the quote. That's what everyone says." The chief shook his head. "You're supposed to remember it. The day they all died defending it. Davy Crockett, Jim Bowie, William Travis. All of them . . ."

"Except that one time," Nog said. "Back on the station . . . toward the end of the war. You and Doctor Bashir closed down the bar. You were . . . well, very happy. I remember you had been in the holosuite, and you were very pleased because I thought you'd finally won."

"Won?"

"The one you'd been playing for so many weeks," Nog said, suddenly aware that he may have made a misstep. "The one based on the Alamo"

O'Brien squinted as if looking off at a foggy and distant horizon. He wiped his perspiring forehead with his gloved hand and then smiled wanly. "No," he said, looking away. "I mean, yes, I remember. That was a strange day." Standing straighter, collecting his thoughts, the chief continued, "But everything was strange in those days. The Dominion closing in. Victory seemed like a dream. And there we were right at the center of it all, right on the anvil." O'Brien paused, momentarily lost in memory, and then continued. "I don't remember whose idea it was to change the Alamo simulation. Probably Julian's." He shook his head. "He didn't always play fair, you know. Anyway . . ." O'Brien looked directly at Nog and, for a moment, just a moment, Nog felt as if *he* was actually being seen. "I guess you didn't know. Did you?"

"Know what?"

"Didn't you wonder why we changed it?"

"Because you were tired of losing."

"Right," O'Brien said. "Exactly right. Sometimes you just want a win. Especially when times are dark. You want the bright sunrise over the mountains, the birds singing, and the sap rising. I think Julian was feeling it more than anyone back then." He laughed. "So, he changed the parameters. Davy Crockett lived. Bowie lived. Everyone . . . well, mostly everyone lived." O'Brien unclipped a water bottle from his leg and took a sip. "The good guys won."

"Oh," Nog said, embarrassed, though not entirely certain why. "I always wondered. I was glad to be there that night."

"Julian felt terrible afterward. And not just because of the vodka or rum or . . . bourbon?"

"Whiskey."

O'Brien reclipped the bottle to his thigh. "Though it's really very . . . well, it's kind of you to remember it. Haven't thought about that night for a long time." He grinned. "Thanks."

"You're welcome, Chief," Nog said. O'Brien looked like he was ready to tackle another couple flights of stairs, and Nog turned to recommence their ascent, but was suddenly struck by a thought. "Where's Ginger?"

O'Brien shook his head. "Don't know. Lost track of her. Probably run off, doing whatever it is she does. Hunting something. Trapping it. Wrapping it up in webbing."

"I don't think they do that," Nog said. "Besides, what's here that she could hunt?"

O'Brien leaned out over the stairway railing and studied the gloom. "I don't know. Lost lab animals?" They had only climbed a couple decks, yet the lighting was so poor that the deck was barely visible. O'Brien straightened and flexed his back. "She'll find us if she wants to. Don't worry." O'Brien mounted the first step. "All ready now? Got your second wind?"

"Sure," Nog said.

"Good," O'Brien said. "Let's be off. Find Captain Maxwell." Nog did not detect any sign of condescension or irony.

Ops Center

The large viewscreen Finch had used to show O'Brien and Nog his presentation flickered and flipped from display to communication mode. Finch fiddled with the control panel and tried to sharpen the signal. Maxwell squinted at the screen, still feeling woozy. A face appeared, though the features were poorly defined, either intentionally scrambled or badly tuned.

"*Finch,*" said a deep and resonant voice.

Klingon? Maxwell wondered, trying to place the accent.

"*What transpires? What happened to your station? Is the product safe?*" Definitely not Klingon, Maxwell decided. *Too polite.*

"There was an accident," Finch said, attempting to sound blasé. "But the product is fine. Better than fine, actually. Performing admirably."

"In what version of reality," Maxwell said, attempting to project his voice, "could anything that's happening here today be described as 'performing admirably.'" Or, at least, that's what he intended to say. He got as far as "In what version—" before Finch struck him across the face with the back of his hand.

Maxwell was unprepared for the savagery of the blow. Something in his neck popped, and he felt a bright spark of pain inside his mouth. He might have blacked out for a second, because there was a sense of a gap in the flow of time. When he awoke, Maxwell felt his head hanging down and watched a thin stream of pinkish saliva drip from his mouth down onto his lap. "Ow." That single word cost him. Maxwell tentatively probed the inside of his mouth with the tip of his tongue and found a large gash on the inside of his left cheek, probably where he had bitten himself.

Finch had returned to speaking to the face on the screen. ". . . disgruntled employee," he was saying. "Really no way I could have seen it coming, though, looking back, he was an unstable sort. Fidgety."

"Fidgety," the face intoned. Maxwell blinked away the pain and the fog. The image must have been intentionally garbled.

"But, as I have so often said," Finch continued, sounding more and more like his old self with every word, "any setback should be viewed as an opportunity. In this instance, this is doubly true. I've collected a great deal of data on the Mother's responses to adverse conditions and she, as I said, is performing admirably. The Shedai metagenome data you provided has been *invaluable* in finding solutions to problems that otherwise would have taken—"

"Finch," the voice intoned.

"Yes?"

"Excuse me, but I do not care."

"As you say," Finch said, head back. He rubbed the back of one of his hands against the front of his shirt.

Probably hurt it when he hit me, Maxwell thought. *Good.*

"I do tend to overshare when I'm excited."

"Yes," the face agreed. It appeared to turn as if it was reading something, possibly a sensor output. *"Readings indicate the product—"*

"The Mother," Finch added.

"Yes," the face agreed. *"The product is* not *in a containment device. How am I to transport it to my ship?"*

"Ah," Finch said. "Valid question. I need to—how

shall we say?—wrangle it? I may require some assistance on that score."

"Then I suggest you ask one of your associates," the voice said. *"My scans say you've several to choose from. I am prepared to wait for—"* He paused, either to check a chronometer or to convert the right unit of time. *"—one half hour. Before I entered this area of localized interference, my long-range scanners detected vessels headed to this sector. Were you expecting visitors?"*

Maxwell listened carefully to the speaker's intonation. He'd met so many individuals from so many worlds that he felt that he had a pretty good ear for accents, but the speaker's world of origin eluded him. There were some strange sibilants at the ends of words, but he couldn't place the long consonants.

"None that I wish to receive," Finch explained. "I may require a lift."

"A lift?"

"A ride. I'd like you to bring me along with you."

"You do not wish to go where I am bound."

"Probably not, but you can drop me somewhere along the way. I can compensate you."

The pilot of the spacecraft paused as if considering his options. Finally, he said, *"Prepare my delivery. I'll consider your request."*

"A half hour," Finch said. "I'll be ready."

The screen went blank.

"And he's been so polite up until now," Maxwell said.

"Be silent, Ben."

"He clearly wants your product, whatever he thinks it is."

"Be silent. I'm thinking." Finch looked as if he was, indeed, thinking hard. Hand on his chin, staring in the general direction of the stairway to the lab, he appeared to be pondering options.

"What's a Shedai metagenome?" Maxwell asked.

"You wouldn't understand even if I explained it to you."

"Try me," Maxwell said. His head was clearing, and he was attempting to subtly put pressure on the tape. If he kept at it, he thought he could stretch it enough that he might be able to yank his arms free. "I'm a very clever fellow."

"Perhaps," Finch said, turning toward Maxwell. "But are you clever enough to know when you may be looking at your last chance? We may die here if we're not careful." As if to prove Finch's point, the artificial gravity briefly blinked, just long enough that Finch's feet left the deck and Maxwell felt the strain on his arms.

"I thought you said you rerouted power to this room's grid."

"I did," Finch said, rising from a crouch. He had landed badly when the gravity returned, and Maxwell saw him wince. "Imagine what that must have been like in the rest of the station."

"I am."

"Your friends, whoever made it back to the station, they may not like it if we have too many more of those."

"You're probably right."

"So what," Finch asked, limping closer to Maxwell, "if I can convince my friend in the ship to bring them along with me?"

Maxwell suddenly saw where the conversation was headed. Still, he had to ask, "You think he would do that?"

"I think," Finch said, rubbing his chin with the tip of his thumb, "that the only way I'll be able to ask is if I contain and deliver the Mother. I can't do it alone."

"You're a bastard, Finch," Maxwell said.

"I am," Finch replied. "So very true. And you, Ben Maxwell, are a very good man." He stood in front of Maxwell's chair and leaned down over him, gripping the arms in his hands. "And if you swear to help me in exchange for my offer to try to get us all off the station, I have faith you'll do as you say. You were a good Starfleet officer, I would warrant. A man of honor. A man who kept his word."

Maxwell couldn't help himself. He brought one of his knees up as fast and hard as could. Finch crumpled to the ground, groaning and gasping imprecations. Speaking loud enough that Finch could hear him through what he was sure was a high-pitched internal screech, Maxwell said, "Cut me loose. I'll help. You've got my number." He paused to better enjoy Finch's muffled whimpers. "Well, *mostly . . .*"

Hangar Deck

"You're the last one," Bharad said, leaning in with the plasma torch. She handed the trussed-up researcher a set of welding goggles someone had found in cabinet. The torch had a little shield that Bharad could use to keep herself from being blinded by the glare, but the ensnared scientists seemed to feel better if they could watch what she was doing and not be forced to shut their eyes against the light.

Bharad had become fairly proficient in the use of the torch over the past hour and hadn't done anything worse than lightly sear one or two wriggling scholars. The researcher—Bharad couldn't recall her name—watched her work and even seemed to relax a bit when the filaments began to singe and snap.

"Just another minute," Bharad said, happy to be almost finished with her task. The doctor was vexed that she would no longer have a distraction from the problem they were facing. They were stranded on the Hooke with whatever menace Finch had unleashed. When her gut began to surge, Bharad stepped away from the almost-free researcher and waited for the gravity fluctuation to subside. It was a long one this time, and she was glad to be in a confined space. Out in the hangar, everyone had taken to standing near a fixed object that they could grab hold of at a moment's notice. One or two of her colleagues, ironically, had tried to cut strips of the webbing, roll them into thicker cables, and lash themselves to railings, but the silk had begun to dry out and become brittle, a condition Bharad mentally noted to investigate if she had the opportunity.

"I really hate that," the researcher said when Bharad started in with the torch again.

"Of course you do. But I'm being careful."

"Not the torch." She lifted the goggles to cover her eyes. "The gravity."

"Don't fidget. Almost through."

"Do we know if anyone's coming to help us?" The researcher (*What was her name?*) didn't sound frightened, just mildly concerned.

"Our Starfleet friends have gone off in search of Finch and Ben Maxwell. They sent for help, but weren't sure how long it would take to get here."

"Or if this old rust bucket will stay together until then." The researcher dragged her left arm out of the tangle of burned webbing. "What in seven hells did Finch release?"

Bharad shook her head and helped the woman to her feet. Fortunately, she had close-cropped hair, so it wouldn't be necessary to cut any off to get loose of the filaments. Poor Mary Ratinoff had had to chop away most of her very nice, long, red hair with a pair of work shears. "I'm not sure," Bharad said. "Commander Nog explained it was some sort of tailored bug—you know the kind of thing Finch liked—that's supposed to eat contaminants. It got out. Seems to like radioactive material best. Chews through whatever might be in the way to get to them, including hull plating and reactor shielding."

"Then why isn't it eating this old thing's warp core?" She indicated the *Wren* with a wave of her hand.

"Not sure. Probably because we tamped down the core. Maybe it's just preoccupied with the main course and is saving us for a snack. Who knows?"

"Why does the gravity keep cutting out?"

"The hull is breached on several levels," Bharad explained. "I don't think the Hooke environmental systems are meant to stand up to this much abuse. If I know Ben, he's probably trying to keep the catastrophes balanced out, which means systems are burping from time to time." She had no idea what she was talking about, but Bharad figured there was no reason why anyone else had to experience the fear and indecision she was. Besides, for all she knew, she was right and Ben *was* behind the disruptions. As far as she could tell—whether anyone else knew it or not—his was the hand that kept the Hooke from flying apart at any given moment.

"So, we're probably best off staying down here for now?"

"I think so," Bharad said. "The hull appears to be intact. We have atmosphere and power."

"And if things start falling apart, we have your spiders to help keep things together."

"They're not spiders," Bharad said peevishly. "They're *arachnoforms.*"

The researcher—Bella (her name suddenly popped loose from the depths of Bharad's memory)—made a rude noise and shuffled stiffly out of the transport to join her colleagues.

Bharad switched off the plasma torch, saying, "I have no idea where the girls are." *Off with their boyfriends,* she thought ruefully. *Typical.*

Chapter 17

"I had a weird dream last night," Maxwell said.

"Oh?" said Doctor Clark, reaching for his padd. Over the years of psychoanalysis, Maxwell had gone from being a person who almost never remembered his dreams to someone who not only dreamed vividly, but also could recall the dreams in excruciating detail. Clark liked to take notes, possibly because it helped him to keep the particulars straight in his own mind.

"There wasn't much to it."

"What do you recall?" Clark asked.

"A gerbil."

"A gerbil?" Scratching on the padd. "That's what you recall, or that's all there was?"

"That's all there was: a gerbil."

"Not much."

"No."

"Was it doing anything?"

"No. Standing on his hind legs. Sniffing. The usual gerbil stuff."

"Not much of a dream, is it?"

"I guess," Maxwell said, and stared out the window. He was sitting in a chair today, so he could watch the clouds out over the ocean. "Oh," he added. "And he was wearing a red shirt."

"A red shirt? Like a T-shirt? Or a pullover?"

"No, I mean a uniform . . . a Starfleet uniform. The kind they wore when Kirk was commanding the *Enterprise*, before they redid the uniforms."

"Oh. Please excuse my ignorance, but what does a red-shirted Starfleet uniform indicate?"

"Back in Kirk's day, it meant engineering, service divisions, and security."

"Security?"

"Security officers." Maxwell grinned. "There was even a joke about that. A very old joke about redshirts." To his surprise, Maxwell felt the grin leave his face. He was feeling very, very sad and wasn't sure why.

"What is it, Ben?" Doctor Clark asked. "What are you thinking about?"

"Redshirts," Maxwell said. "I was thinking about the joke about redshirts."

Doctor Clark said, "Why don't you tell it to me?"

"No," Maxwell said. "No. I don't want to."

January 9, 2386
Deck Two
Robert Hooke

"Have I mentioned," Nog asked, his voice crackling in the intercom in O'Brien's helmet, *"how very much I'm not enjoying this?"*

"Yes," O'Brien replied, punching the giant undead

rat in the face. "You've mentioned it *several* times." The giant undead rat spun away in the indifferent gravity and crashed into a bulkhead. "Have I mentioned how happy I would be if we had thought to bring phasers?"

"By my count, ten times."

Only ten? O'Brien thought, mildly surprised. *Would have expected it was much more than that.*

Nog was doing well against his giant undead rat, though he had the advantage of receiving training in low- or zero-g battle while (presumably) the giant undead rat had not. *I must stop thinking "giant undead rat,"* O'Brien thought. *Probably not technically accurate. Also . . .* He wound up and booted the third giant undead rat down the corridor, its hairless gray tail twitching, glassy eyes whirling in their sockets. It careened off the ceiling and spun away. *Probably an insult to giant undead rats everywhere.*

Nog dislodged the giant undead rat's teeth from his gauntlet, braced his back against a doorframe, and then shoved the creature away. O'Brien had noted the thin purple tendrils poking out of the skulls of the two creatures he had fought, and this last one was no exception. The sudden acceleration imparted by Nog tore the tendril loose. The rat ceased flailing, though whether the reason was because of the kick or the tendril being torn loose, O'Brien could not say.

The tendril continued to move, waving back and forth in a probing motion. Its movement reminded O'Brien of one of those seemingly harmless sea creatures that clung to barrier reefs, eyeless, without discernable musculature, stirred only by the churning tide right up until the moment they struck.

Nog pushed himself off the wall and confidently soared past the creature to the door. He peered in, his head only a meter away from the tendril. O'Brien was impressed by how quickly Nog had adapted to the unstable gravity. *"Dark. Power's out. Hang on."* He jammed his arm through the crack. *"Hull breach. Not a big one, but big enough. And I think the rats—or whatever they are—came from here. There are cages on the ground, but they're tiny. Much too small for these monsters."*

"Do you think the Mother made them grow?"

"The Mother broke into the small reactor in here. I can see the damaged casing." The Mother's tendril must have sensed Nog's proximity. The tip turned in his direction. *"Or something else that was here in the lab,"* Nog continued, oblivious. Maybe a biological agent? Or a combination of all of the above?

O'Brien tried to cry out in warning, but decided direct action was required: he pushed off from the wall and angled his trajectory so his wide heavy boots landed squarely on the tendril's "neck."

Nog looked back over his shoulder, surprised that O'Brien was suddenly so close. He looked down and saw the tip of the tendril squirming slightly. O'Brien half expected it to contract, to try to withdraw, but, apparently, the Mother didn't work that way. *"Thanks."*

"No worries," O'Brien replied. "We should get moving."

"I was just wondering if there might be something in there we could use as a weapon, but I don't think we could get these doors open." He looked down. *"What do you think it will do when you take your foot off it?"*

"Want to stick around and find out?"

"Not really, no." Nog withdrew from the door and landed gently on the deck. Suddenly, O'Brien felt the gravity come back. The tendril squished under his boot and broke off.

Stepping away hastily, O'Brien asked, "What has Finch made?"

"A monster," Nog said. *"If it's responsible for what happened to these creatures, possibly a very dangerous one."*

"And who knows what else is in this place it may have affected."

"We'll have to contain it."

"We may have to destroy it."

"Destroy it? But if it's a new life-form . . . ?"

"I don't like the idea either. But what if it gets free? Spreads? We don't know what it could do and we're not in a position to study."

"Still," Nog said. *"I'm tired of death, Chief."* The corner of his lip curled. *"It's been a bad year."*

"I know," O'Brien said. "Let's see if we can keep it from getting any worse."

Nog nodded and turned back toward the stairwell. O'Brien knew they should have stayed in the core, but the signs of movement had been too tempting to ignore. *"I think I'd like to punch Finch if we find him again,"* Nog said. *"Really hard. In the face."*

O'Brien laughed, surprised but delighted. "You're starting to sound like me. Not officer material at all."

"Yeah, I know," Nog said, fighting a grin. *"I just wanted to hear how it sounded when I said it out loud."*

Ops Center

Fortunately, the environmental suits were accommodating and Finch was able to squeeze into the second suit despite his unorthodox frame. Maxwell noted, though, that his employer had curiously small feet. Sealing the front of the suit, Finch asked, "What's that you're holding? Not a weapon! I won't see her harmed!" Finch's insistence on giving the purple blob a gender designation was getting on Maxwell's nerves.

"Not a weapon," he said, speaking loudly so Finch could hear him through the helmet. Looking at the device he held, Maxwell understood why Finch might think it was a weapon. He hefted it by its stock, pointed it at the deck, and carefully pulled the trigger. A thick blob of glue squirted out of the barrel. "Glue gun. Used to seal hull breaches and suchlike. Found it in the repair locker. Should come in handy."

"For what?" Finch said, shaking his head.

"Put on your helmet and you'll find out."

Finch did as he was bid, though he needed Maxwell's help to slot the helmet in the yoke. *"This way,"* Finch said unnecessarily, pointing toward the stairway to his lab. Maxwell followed without comment, the glue gun in a ready carry.

In the airlock, the two men awkwardly stood on either side of the small window, both of them trying to peer inside without bumping helmets. The lighting was worse than when Maxwell had been there. A few emergency lamps still burned, casting muted shadows. "Sabih" was nowhere in sight.

"Where is he?" Maxwell asked.

"I have no idea," Finch replied peevishly. *"In a broom closet, perhaps? Clinging to the ceiling?"*

Maxwell ignored the attitude and focused on practicalities. "Looks like there's power to the door. I'm going to push the button, step in, and take two large steps to the right. You hang back a minute and wait to see if anything jumps out and says, 'Boo.'"

"There's no atmosphere in there," Finch said. *"Nothing is going to say, 'Boo.'"*

"I didn't mean literally."

Finch gave Maxwell a sidelong glance, which was difficult with a helmet, but he managed it.

Maxwell didn't wait for permission to continue. He pushed the button and the door swooshed open. He did what he said he would, except instead of moving to the right, he shifted to the left. No sense in giving Finch the option to anticipate his movements.

He scanned the room. Nothing stirred, at least not within the limited sphere of illumination, which meant he needed to inspect only about ninety percent of the remaining available space. "Do you know how to activate the torch on your wrist?" Maxwell asked.

"Of course."

"Light it up. Point it toward the tank."

With only the slightest pause, Finch did as he was asked. The light did not waver or shake. Whatever fear or uncertainty had gripped the station owner earlier, clearly his anxiety had eased. *He thinks he has a plan,* Maxwell thought. *That's bad.*

As before, the Mother floated serenely in its tank. It

had more tendrils extended than the last time. A bad sign. Now it resembled a sea anemone rather than a blob of mucus.

"Swing it around," Maxwell ordered. "Light the whole room."

Finch followed his order, perhaps because he wanted to rather than he was obeying Maxwell. Moving from left to right, he paused every couple meters to inspect and marvel. *"Astonishing!"* he gasped. *"Breathtaking!"* The Mother had been busy. Tendrils clung to the side of the tank and oozed down onto the deck. They crisscrossed the room and poked into panels. Some had climbed the walls and probed ventilator openings. It looked like it was trying to find a way out of the lab. Maxwell was certain it had succeeded.

As Finch moved the light, Maxwell followed, the glue gun raised to his shoulder. In his head, he counted off the quadrants: *One, nothing. Two, nothing. Three, nothing.* A shadow shifted unexpectedly. *There.*

The thing that had been Sabih a few hours ago lurched out of the shadows, stiff-legged, arms extended, mouth open wide, and purplish ooze extruded from every orifice. Maxwell let it take three steps, judging its rate of acceleration and direction. "Sabih" was headed toward Finch. Maxwell briefly considered letting it catch its quarry, just so he could listen to whatever sound came out of Finch when cold, cold hands closed around his throat. Sadly, more was at stake than his very temporary satisfaction. Maxwell crossed the room in three strides, pivoted, and kicked the ghoul squarely in the chest.

Bone crunched. The Sabih-thing crashed into the

bulkhead. Its legs crumpled, probably because the synovial fluid in its joints had long ago turned into sludge. Purple tendrils flailed.

Stepping forward, Maxwell inserted the barrel of his glue gun between the wall and Sabih's back. He depressed the trigger. Despite the cold, the glue flowed freely. *Thank you, internal heating unit.* The epoxy set and "Sabih" was stuck.

"Ah," Finch said, impressed. *"Clever."*

Maxwell pivoted, the glue gun's barrel level and steady. "Don't think I didn't consider cementing you in place too."

"But then how would you have gotten your friends off this station before the inevitable happened?" Finch stepped into the center of the lab, claiming it like a conquering hero.

Maxwell was annoyed. He tried—but failed—to think of a way to get the researchers off the station without Finch's assistance. "Let's finish this, Finch."

"Doctor Finch," Finch said. *"Not Finch."*

Maxwell hefted the glue gun. "I'm considering changing my mind."

Finch tilted the torch up so Maxwell could see the expression on his face. He was smiling. Fearlessly. Maxwell decided to let Finch enjoy the moment.

The station owner turned his light to study the Sabih-thing, which continued to struggle, though stiffly and without much energy. Its eyes were dead and useless, dried out and desiccated in the vacuum. *And no brain behind the eyes to interpret whatever they were seeing even if it still had them,* Maxwell thought. He realized that he had completely given up on the idea that there might some small spark of a human being inside the husk of Sabih. *Which is probably for the best.* Maxwell had never fought the Borg hand to hand—he had been incarcerated when last they invaded. From reading accounts, he understood that one of the difficulties the combatants faced was the fear that some small part of the drone's original persona was still there.

Maxwell studied the Mother's pulsing tendrils. *Into the vents, into the bulkheads,* he thought. *Why?* Finch's monster must be mindless, despite whatever a metagenome might be. It was doing the things all organisms do: looking for a safe environment, eating, excreting, and making little baby monsters.

Maxwell looked at the tendrils again. He smacked his forehead—or tried to, but the helmet stopped him. "Crap!" he shouted.

"What?" Finch said. He was standing near—but not *too* near—the tank, admiring his work, watching the Mother expand and contract.

Finch would not share his dread. He would be delighted at the thought of Little Mothers, assuming he wasn't already thinking about them. Maxwell decided to sidestep the topic. "Just realized how much time has gone by. Your friend in the ship is going to get impatient." He pointed at the tank where the Mother serenely floated. "How do we box it up?"

"You're the handyman," Finch replied. *"Recommend something handy."*

Maxwell fumed. *I could just leave,* he thought, but

there was the remote possibility that Finch would actually figure out some way to crate up his monster. He pointed at a row of storage lockers. "What's in these cabinets?" Maxwell asked, but didn't wait for an answer. He yanked open doors and drawers.

"Most of that is lab supplies or materials needed to sustain the Mother."

"Back before it became self-sustaining."

"Obviously."

"I don't have time to go get anything. If we remove these cabinet doors, we could glue them in place around the tank frame. What do you think?"

"What about her tendrils?"

"We'll have to sever them. Hell, I'd prefer to sever them. Who knows what it can do with them? Or what they're currently attached to?"

"I would like to preserve as much of the Mother as possible," Finch said. *"And I find your use of the word* sever *distressing. Alas, I cannot think of a better idea at present. All right, then—hurry."*

Maxwell set to work on the first set of doors. Fortunately, they slid off their hinges easily enough when loosened with a probe. Within a matter of minutes, Maxwell piled up eight large slabs of lightweight, durable plasteel composite. Eyeballing the tank, he felt confident that he had almost enough material. One more set of cabinet doors would do the trick. He crossed to the last set of unused doors, but, when approached, they did not open. "This is locked," he said. "Any reason? Something in there I don't want to disturb?"

Finch looked back over his shoulder to see what concerned Maxwell. *"Ah,"* he said, and waved his hand. *"The device."*

"The one that was supposed to sterilize the lab if the Mother escaped?" Maxwell took a respectful step back, then carefully tapped the door with the probe. He tugged on the door handles and they parted easily. While the rest of Finch's lab equipment was disabled, this device's control panel still appeared active. Status lights blinked on and off, suggesting life and purpose. Maxwell studied the controls, looking for something that obviously said, "Push me."

"Stop worrying with that," Finch snapped. *"It's useless. Help me with the Mother. Our time is almost up."*

"Useless?" Maxwell asked. "Why?"

"It's been deactivated," Finch said absently, fussing with the cabinet doors. *"Long ago, in fact."*

"Long ago?"

"Of course. Why would I want to destroy the Mother?"

Why indeed? Finch was still staring at his creation, not paying Maxwell the least mind. *I could just walk right up behind him,* he thought. *He wouldn't even think about me being there, wouldn't give it a moment's thought.* He straightened up from the spot where he had been crouching and mentally measured the gap between him and Finch. *Just a shove,* he thought. *And he'd be in the tank with his monster. Who knows what it would do to him? Maybe nothing. Maybe everything.* The Mother's tendrils waved in the void, as if beckoning. Maxwell took a step forward. *Maybe it's time to end this,* he thought. *Time to take the leap.*

Central Core

A dozen purple tendrils protruded from an open hatch at the top of the stairway. They waved back and forth, though Nog couldn't tell if they were beckoning or warning him back. He took a step down without looking back and bumped into the chief. Risking a look back over his shoulder, he briefly spied the mob of giant undead rats massing on the landing at the bottom of the stairway. Their naked, pink tails twitched expectantly. O'Brien changed his grip on the club he had fashioned out of a small crowbar, a mallet, and some duct tape. Nog lifted his fire ax, feeling the ache in his biceps. "Chief," he said.

"Yes?"

"Remember what I said earlier about never leaving the station with you again?"

"Yes."

"I'm amending that."

"To?"

"Never going anywhere with you. *Ever*. Not even to lunch. Not even if Keiko asks me nicely."

Nog risked another peek over his shoulder. The band of rats had edged closer, tails and the purple tendrils flailing. Nog felt queasy.

"Actually, Commander," O'Brien said, *"I understand. You're just being sensible. If we never go out anywhere again, the probability of another situation like this arising will be much lower."*

"Exactly. No hard feelings?"

"None," O'Brien said, but then was silent for a minute

because he was busy waving his club at something that had approached. *"I would be happy to shake your hand in acknowledgment of our newfound agreement."*

"Maybe later."

"Right." O'Brien paused, trying to steady his breathing after having fought off his attacker. *"Any chance we can make it down past your lot and regroup on deck two?"*

Nog assessed. More tendrils had appeared, including a couple really big ones. "Doesn't look good. Any other ideas?"

"Just the one."

"Over the rail?"

O'Brien tugged the small grapple hook from the reel on his belt and freed a meter of cord. *"Over the rail."*

Nog glanced down into the abyss. Six decks below was a hatch back into the hangar, the very one they'd left less than an hour ago. "These were meant to be used in low or zero gravity," he said, tugging out his own grapple. "Any chance they'll hold?"

"Of course," O'Brien said brightly. *"There is definitely an infinitesimally small chance that they'll hold. Or that the gravity will shut off while we're falling. Better chance of the latter, actually."*

"Always the optimist," Nog said. "We'll have to climb the stairs again if we want to find Maxwell."

"One problem at a time, Commander," O'Brien replied, setting one foot on the rail.

"Understood," Nog said. "I agree with your recommendation, Chief." He placed one foot on the lower rung in the metal railing.

The tendrils and the undead rats both surged forward.

Nog and O'Brien quickly wrapped their grapples around the railing. Tipping back, O'Brien said, *"I've been looking around for a new activity. Something to get me out of the quarters. Don't know why I didn't think of BASE jumping."* He fell back into the abyss.

Nog took a deep breath and tried hard not to think as he released his grip on the rail. "Can't imagine how you overlooked it."

Chapter 18

"Tell me about the gerbil, Ben."

"I've told you about the gerbil, Michael. I don't want to have to tell you again."

"Humor me," Doctor Clark said.

Maxwell sighed and stared at the lampshade. He was fond of the lampshade. As often as not, when he was lying on the couch he closed his eyes, but, on the occasions when he kept his eyes open, well, there was his friend the lampshade. The ceiling above was painted an uninteresting beige, though it was broken up by an interesting topography of cracks and ripples. The tropical air was not kind to paint, even in the climate-controlled inner sanctum of the director's office. Outside the office's single window, Maxwell heard the regular *cheet-cheet* of a fantail. "It was a gerbil," he murmured. "One of two."

"What were their names?"

"I don't remember," Maxwell said. "They weren't mine. They were classroom pets—my sixth-grade class. It was a very small school—a small town—so the whole class was maybe twenty-five kids. Most of us—the kids, our families—lived in the same town our whole lives up until that point. We went to school together for years, so they were more like my family. You know?"

"No," Clark said. "Not really. My family moved a lot when I was young, and most of the schools were very large. It must have been pleasant."

"It was," Maxwell said. "Mostly. I didn't know anything else, so I don't really know how to compare it. Some good days, some bad."

"The bad day?"

Maxwell nodded. He had grown accustomed to not looking at the doctor when they had these kinds of conversations even though he could have with the slightest turn of his head. He liked listening to Clark's disembodied voice, sometimes even treating it like it was another voice inside his own head. "Yeah, I guess you could say that." He paused. "It was all my own doing, though."

"What was?"

"What happened to the gerbil. I was . . ." He hesitated, gathering his thoughts, then resumed. "I thought I knew a lot about gerbils. When the class got them, when our teacher brought them in, I got very excited about them, about gerbils. I thought they were neat. My mother didn't really like to have pets in our house. It was too small, and she was away for days at a time sometimes. Sometimes cats would hang around for a few months—lots of fish, right?—but they were there for her, not me."

"You never made friends with any of the cats?"

Maxwell considered. "Maybe? A couple? But they were usually mostly feral, so it wasn't like they were sleeping on the foot of my bed. Outdoor cats."

"Okay. The gerbils?"

"Right. I did what I always did when I got excited about something: I looked up all the information I could find and read everything. The day after the gerbils arrived, I had learned everything about them." Smiling despite himself, Maxwell said, "Ask me about gerbils. Ask me anything."

Clark chuckled. "All right. Binomial nomenclature?

"Ah," Maxwell began. "That's actually a more complicated question than you would expect. There are many, *many* species of gerbils. You probably mean the domesticated or Mongolian gerbil, which would be *Meriones unguiculatus*. Also sometimes called the Mongolian jird. Don't ask me what a jird is. My knowledge is deep, but not quite *that* deep."

"Understood."

"Domesticated in the mid-twentieth century. Originally used as lab animals, until someone decided they were cute. Became quite popular for a while, though a large percentage of the world population died out in the Eugenics Wars due to the decimation of their homeland and general lack of pet stores."

"Of course."

"Interesting side note: gerbils are *persona non grata* in New Zealand. Or maybe that would be *Rodentia non grata*. My Latin isn't that good."

"Competition with native species?"

"Indeed."

"Very impressive," Clark said. "So you were an expert."

"And enjoyed proclaiming it," Maxwell replied. "And I was humored because, well, because they humored me."

"You were popular," Clark offered. "And respected. The other children recognized your qualities."

Maxwell squirmed on the couch. "Sure," he said. "Nothing to do with how unbelievably, obnoxiously self-assured I could be."

"Of course not." He leaned a bit closer. Maxwell heard Clark's suit jacket rustle, and the doctor's voice become just a bit louder and more insistent. "And you're digressing, Ben. What happened?"

"Not digressing," Maxwell said. "Very simple: I was careless."

"How?"

Maxwell's eyes felt itchy. There was something in the air, something the filters weren't catching, so he rubbed his eyes in long, slow, satisfying arcs. When he was finished, the room was blurry and his eyes were warm. "We didn't have a cage," he explained. "But we had an aquarium. A big one. I'm not sure why. Maybe it belonged to my teacher? Anyway, it was big and gave the gerbils plenty of room. When they were awake, they'd bounce around inside it like . . . like gerbils. I loved watching them. But they were good jumpers and we worried—*I* worried— that they would jump out of the aquarium, so we decided we needed a lid."

"That seems reasonable," Clark said. "What kind of lid?" He asked the question in the tone he used when he knew Maxwell might require a little assistance, a little bit of lead-in.

"The only thing we had to hand was a piece of transparent aluminum. I'm not sure where it came from, but it was a little too small to comfortably cover the top of the tank. So we kind of angled it across the top."

"Curious choice," Clark said. "There must have been something better available."

"Probably. But our teacher, he was a 'you guys figure out how you want to do this' sort of guy. Believed in leaving us to our own devices."

"How did that work out?"

"Not well," Maxwell admitted. He soldiered on with the tale. "It was my turn to feed them, and I was feeling all very full of myself, very knowledgeable."

"You *were* knowledgeable."

Maxwell shrugged. "Maybe. But sometimes being knowledgeable isn't enough. I have a very clear picture in my mind of this moment: reaching over to pick up the cover and set it aside."

"Okay. And then what happened?"

"I didn't set it aside."

"No?"

"No. I bumped it. It fell into the aquarium and landed on one of the gerbil's backs. I recall that detail very distinctly. I could see it—the gerbil—through the aluminum and I could see his back. Flattened out."

"What did you do?"

"I ran out of the room," Maxwell said. "And hid in the boys' lavatory."

"Lavatory?"

"Rest room. The boys' rest room."

"And you stayed there?" Clark asked. "No one came to find you?"

"No, they did," Maxwell said. He folded his arms

across his chest, knowing he was probably telling the doctor all kinds of things with his body language. "Eventually. My friend Chuck. He found me."

"And?"

"And what?"

"What did he say?"

"He said the gerbil wasn't dead, that they lifted the aluminum off him, and he started moving around."

Clark must have uncrossed and then recrossed his legs, because Maxwell heard a lot of rustling. "Then I'm confused," he said. "The gerbil didn't die?"

"No," Maxwell said. "Not right away. But the crack to the head or the spine or whatever must have done something bad. By the time I got back to the classroom, expecting him to be alive and, I don't know—forgiving me?—he was jumping all around in the aquarium like he couldn't stop. My teacher took out the second one because he was so alarmed. The injured one just jumped around maniacally until he died. Or so I assume."

"Why assume?"

"It was late in the day. It was a Friday. The bell rang and we all went home."

"You couldn't stay?"

"I don't know," Maxwell said, trying to recall how he felt that day. "Maybe. I don't really recall much else about that day. I just know that when we came to school on Monday, there was only one gerbil. And a piece of wire mesh over the top of the aquarium."

Clark was quiet for a minute, letting the story settle in. Finally, he asked, "Did you tell your mother about what happened?"

"No," Maxwell said. "That time of year she would have been out to sea for two or three days at a time. I probably didn't see her again until Sunday night or Monday. I don't remember exactly. I know I never told her about it."

"Anyone else?"

"You mean besides you?"

"Yes."

Maxwell considered and then recalled, "Yes. My son. I told him a version of the story back when he was on the *Rutledge* with me. Well, the whole family. He kept asking for a pet, some kind of pet. 'Something small,' he used to say, believing, I think, that if it was small, it would be less trouble. Our quarters were small, even the captain's quarters. Not like *Galaxy*-class quarters."

"So, your son asked you for a pet and you told him the story of how you killed a gerbil when you were his age?" There was only a slight note of incredulity in Clark's voice.

"No!" Maxwell said, exasperated. "I told him how there was a gerbil that I had known who was killed because his cage got jostled, and that aboard a starship, that kind of thing could happen all the time. It was too risky, I said."

"And what did Carlo say?" Maxwell was always impressed how Clark could remember the names of people from his stories. *Of course,* he thought, *that's probably something they trained him to do.*

"He said he understood," Maxwell explained. "He said it probably would be better to wait until we were living planetside."

"And did you?"

"Did I what?"

"Get him a pet." Maxwell paused for a long time before answering, so long that Clark asked, "Ben?"

"What?" Maxwell replied, speaking in a low tone. "Oh. Sorry. Yes. We did. I was just trying to remember its name. *His* name. The dog. We got a dog. A little mutt. He was shaggy. Smelled kind of bad when he got wet. Adored Carlo. Sofia was a little scared of him because the dog would protect Carlo from any perceived threat, including his sister when she got mad at her brother."

"That's . . . well, strangely sweet," Clark said softly.

"Yes," Maxwell said, the word coming out more like a wet breath than a word. "It was. Worried Maria a little, but the dog didn't have a mean bone in its body. I wish I could remember its name . . ."

"It'll come back," Clark began.

"We didn't find its body," Maxwell continued, unprompted. "I looked through the debris of the house, but never found it. I figure the bastard Cardassians probably vaporized it with their goddamned disruptors." He felt his fists clenching and couldn't stop himself. "Those . . ." He thought the word but didn't say it. Years of training as a captain made it practically impossible for Maxwell to say certain words. "Killing a little dog . . . that . . ." He unclenched his hands and held them up to look at his palms. There were tiny, crescent-shaped wounds there, four on each hand.

"That?" Clark asked.

"That was probably trying to defend my son," Maxwell continued. The next words surprised him, "Because I wasn't there . . ."

"No," Clark said. "You were doing your duty. You

were following orders and also, not inconsequentially, keeping your crew alive. You were a man, Ben, with many responsibilities. Maybe too many."

"Maybe," Maxwell said. "But still. They died." He continued to study the small crescent groves in his palms, his mouth tasting of ashes, and added, "Small things in my charge tend to do that."

January 9, 2386
Central Core
Robert Hooke

Falling isn't so bad, Nog thought, *as long as you don't obsess about the sudden stop.* A distant portion of his brain was attempting to do the math, to calculate the relationship between mass and acceleration, even factoring in variables like the drag on the cable and possible fluctuations in the artificial gravity, but it was all too much.

He fell without knowing where the bottom was because math is not your friend in the dark. Nog felt the vibration of the spool in his belt unreeling and knew in his gut that the mechanism wasn't engineered to take the kind of shock he was about to put it through. Still, they had to try and, after what seemed the appropriate number of seconds in free fall, he squeezed the brake. Legs and head snapped backward, and the pressure against his lower back made Nog want to curse, but the breath was squeezed out of his lungs, so the only sound that came out was a soft, high-pitched *feeeeee.*

It might work, he thought, and fixed his jaw so he

didn't accidentally bite off his tongue. But his engineer's mind returned to calculations, and the answer he arrived at was that he had already fallen too far. The deck was coming up fast; gravity would win out over the paltry amount of friction he applied to the line. *Probably just as well*, he decided. The amount of force he would need to stop his fall would probably snap his spine anyway.

Contact.

Nog expected to hear a *splat* or a *crack*, but instead the din filling his head was more of a *boooinnnggg!* This sound was quickly replaced by a sharp *thwack* and a piercing screech, which, surprisingly, didn't come from Nog.

His gut told him he was bouncing, even though his brain hadn't quite accepted the idea. When the big bounces turned into little ones, Nog awkwardly groped the surface behind his back. *Some kind of netting*, he realized. *A little sticky.*

The screech was still going on, though it had slowed down and was lower in tone, like a teakettle removed from the flame.

Something was touching him, probing, checking his suit (and his body?) for lumps, tears, and contusions. Finding nothing, the probe withdrew. Nog lifted his arm off the netting, the sticky fibers pulling the fabric of his environmental suit taut, and flicked on his light. To his right and above, he saw the stairway that ran up the sides of the central core. He turned and found the chief, bunched up into a ball, his back against the bulkhead. He had his own light on and pointed at the opposite side of the chamber. Nog turned and there, as expected, was Ginger, her eyes glittering and mouthparts moving. She chittered expectantly. "I'm fine," Nog said, sitting up. "Thank you." He turned to O'Brien. "You okay, Chief?"

"Swell, thanks," O'Brien said, keeping the light squarely on Ginger.

Nog decided he wouldn't bring up the screeching noise he had heard. Tilting back his head (which was difficult in the bulky suit), he shone his light up to inspect the stairways. He was sure he saw movement: squirming tendrils and undead rats lying in wait. "Any ideas?"

"Not just yet," the chief said. *"Still processing the existential horror of finding myself in a web with a giant spider staring at me."*

"Okay," Nog said. "Take a minute." He tried to stand, but the web was too springy and there was nothing to brace against. *Amazing stuff,* he thought. *Must be a million uses for it.* He looked up again, had a thought, and then looked over at Ginger, who had backed away to the edge of the net and climbed the wall. "Could you," he asked, "catch those rat things in a web and keep them out of our way?"

Ginger stared at him blankly. Probably she couldn't hear him, since there was clearly almost no atmosphere in the core. He was amazed that the lack of air pressure didn't seem to bother her, but who knew what Bharad had designed them to withstand? After a minute of constant eye contact, Nog got the impression that it wasn't so much that she didn't understand him as she just thought his idea was pretty bad. "How about this? When we get to a level where we can't get past them, you climb up the wall and drop a line?"

Ginger tilted her head to one side as if considering.

"*I'm vetoing that one,*" O'Brien said. "*But I think you've got the right idea. Go around, not through.*"

"Right."

"*There might be another way. Assuming your new best friend is willing to help.*"

Nog looked into Ginger's eyes and felt very sure she was more than willing.

Finch's Lab

Maxwell gripped the front of Finch's environmental suit with both hands and threw the man across the room, as far away from the Mother as he could. Despite his smaller stature, Maxwell had the advantages of martial-arts training, surprise, and Finch's precarious sense of balance. The big man arced across the room, arms windmilling, to collide with the command console and crumple into an untidy heap. Maxwell bounded after him and landed with his leg straddling Finch's chest. Leaning in, he struck his opponent's helmet with the heel of his hand. Finch's head bounced off the deck, the blow cushioned only by the insulation inside of his helmet. A moment later, he groaned, eyes half-shut.

"You told Sabih to do it, didn't you?" Maxwell asked, grabbing the collar of Finch's suit and shaking him. "The whole thing about him quitting was just a big ruse, some showmanship. You knew your customer was coming to take away your monster, and you weren't sure you could build another, so you told Sabih to come back in here and remove a chunk. You told him there was no radiation blast, which was true enough, and you thought you told Sabih everything he needed to do to bypass your failsafes. But he really wasn't very good at this sort of thing, was he?" Maxwell banged Finch's helmet against the deck one more time because he liked the sound. "He was just a kid, a guy who wanted to work in science, but couldn't actually *do* science. Admit it or I'll break open this helmet and throw you in that tank."

Finch struggled, but was too disoriented and, considering the day he'd had, probably too tired. He flailed, but Maxwell slapped his hands aside and then gave him a half-hearted shake. Finch subsided, breathing hard, much harder than he should have been. Maxwell wondered if the big man was having some kind of seizure or a breakdown, but then the sputtering turned into words.

"Get off of me, you filthy peasant, you worthless piece of trash!" He inhaled deeply and Maxwell thought Finch was getting himself back under control, but, instead, he used the breath to continue his tirade. *"You're worthless. I know . . . I know about you. Know enough! Things hidden, because of your Starfleet friends, but I can put the pieces together! I can guess the story."*

Suddenly very tired, Maxwell released his grip and let Finch flop to the deck. From the corner of his eye, he spied the Mother in its half-enclosed tank, its tendrils palpitating. Maxwell said, "I'll tell you the whole story whenever you like." Motivated by who-knew-what malice, Finch attempted to grasp Maxwell's leg and drag him down, but his grip was too weak and Maxwell only had to yank his leg away. For good measure, he gave Finch a little kick in the side with his heel. "But here's the punch line,

the part you should remember: I've killed a lot of people."
He paused to catch his breath. Their fight had taken more
out of him than he had realized. "Even more than you, I
bet." Maxwell reached down, clutched one of Finch's legs,
and slowly dragged him across the deck toward one of the
exits. "Fortunately for you, I've decided not to add to the
total." He looked over at the tank and the thrashing blob
within. Addressing it directly, Maxwell added, "You don't
count."

Finch grasped his meaning. *"No!"* he shouted, trying
to kick free. *"You can't! I won't! Your friends!"*

Maxwell tightened his grip and shut off Finch's channel. No sooner did blessed silence descend than a new
sound interrupted: a hailing frequency. Finch stopped
struggling, apparently hearing the hail too. Maxwell
groaned. *A half hour can go by so quickly when you're preoccupied.* He tapped his suit's comm switch and said, "This
is the Hooke."

Finch's customer replied, *"Time is up."*

Chapter 19

"**D**id they forward the manifest?" Nita Bharad asked. Wendy Newsham struggled to keep up with her friend's rapid pace. Whenever they walked together, Newsham always felt winded, despite the fact that she was half a meter taller and had longer legs. What it came down to was that Bharad just moved faster, she wanted to get wherever she was going sooner so she could start doing whatever it was that needed to be done. Or so Newsham thought.

"Not the whole thing," Newsham said. She defrayed some of the cost of her tiny lab space and quarters by working in the hangar as a freight handler. It was one of the "programs" Finch made available to his tenants to help them cover their costs. Working there had one other benefit: Newsham had a pretty good idea what was coming into and leaving the station. "Finch won't document his private stash."

"Private stash?" Bharad gave her a sidelong glance.

"You know what I mean. His stuff gets highest priority. If whatever you ordered didn't fit on the transport, then it's still sitting in the loading bay back in . . ." She lit up her padd and scanned for the most recent transfer point. "Vulcan? Can that be right?"

"Seems like an awfully roundabout route."

"Funny thing about Vulcan: they're very strict about following the letter of the law, but they tend to err on the side of the recipient on questionable items."

"That's a very circuitous way of saying something, but I'm not sure what," Bharad said. She stopped at the lift and pressed the button several times in quick succession: *click, click, click, click.* This bothered Newsham, who had once dated a turbolift technician. *"You only have to push the button once,"* Severan used to say. *"It gets the idea with just one push."*

"It means that if you know how to list things on an invoice—*le mot juste*—Vulcan will let it go through."

"I just wanted my damned vitelline membranes," Bharad said. "My research is at a standstill! The last batch I got was contaminated! I wasted six months and an entire generation of embryos!"

"Embryos?"

"Eggs, dammit!" Bharad pushed the button six more times.

"I know what embryos are. I just didn't know you were working with them. Never mind. It's better I don't know." Newsham knew Bharad was some sort of genius with genetic manipulation, but she'd never quite gotten her head around exactly how or why or even whether it was (strictly speaking) legal. Newsham's work in quantum beekeeping was, by comparison, dull, even when you factored in the fractal honeycombs.

The lift arrived. Several weary-looking scientists slumped out; Bharad impatiently pushed into the throng, not bothering to wait until the departees were clear.

"Hangar!" Bharad barked, and the elevator doors slowly slid shut.

"You need to calm down, Nita," Newsham said.

"Do I?" Bharad asked. "And if I don't? What's going to happen?"

"Maybe your head will explode?" Newsham grunted under her breath, but then Bharad's fuming silence got on her nerves. She suggested, "One of the biotechnology guys started brewing beer and is serving it at the lounge on deck four. Want to go check it out?"

"Beer?" Bharad asked. "Brewed *here*?" She shuddered. "Sounds unsanitary."

"Possibly," Newsham conceded. "Doesn't the alcohol make it sanitary?"

Bharad dismissed the comment with a wave. The lift descended slowly. Newsham sighed. She wasn't sure why she and Nita were friends. She wasn't even completely sure they *were* friends. The one fact she knew for certain was that they were the only two Terran women on the station. Both of them had tasted real vanilla ice cream and knew what a Scooby-Doo was. They had a bond.

"Do you know the mass of whatever Finch had shipped in?"

Newsham lit up her padd again. "Four hundred kilos."

"Four hundred!" Bharad shouted. "The transport only carries five hundred! How is anyone else supposed to get anything out here?"

"That does seem like a lot," Newsham admitted. She scrolled through the parts of the manifest that she had permission to view. "Oh, here's why." She pointed to a line item. "Meat space."

"Meat space?" Bharad asked. "He's having meat shipped out here? Through *Vulcan*?"

"No," Newsham said. "Sorry. Jargon. He's transporting personnel. A person. He hired someone."

"Someone?"

"A hundred and fifty kilos of someone."

"That's a big someone."

"He's probably bringing some personal effects," Newsham said. "You know: clothing. A pillow. *Things*."

"I didn't get to bring things. Or, I should say, I did, but I had to pay for them."

Newsham shrugged and felt her ponytail come undone. She handed her padd to Bharad, reached behind her head, and whipped her hair back into a loose knot. "Maybe he did too. We don't know, do we?"

"He? He, who? What's his name?"

"Maxwell," Newsham read from the manifest. "Benjamin Maxwell. He's going to be the maintenance engineer."

"Huh," Bharad snorted. "Janitor, you mean."

"Sure," Newsham allowed, "janitor."

"Sounds like a loser."

"He's been hired as a janitor—sorry, *maintenance engineer*—out on the ass-end of nowhere," Newsham said. "Of course he's a loser." She chuckled. "But we're all losers, Nita. Otherwise, why would we be here?"

The lift ground to a stop, and the doors slowly parted. The hangar deck was, as usual, chaotic and disorganized. Badly packed crates were piled just outside the *Wren*'s cargo hatch. Underpaid pilots and shipping clerks milled about uncomfortably, waiting for someone to sign off on manifests. Finch, naturally, was nowhere to be found.

Bharad waded into the fray and began tossing about shipping containers, looking for something with her name on it.

A man with newly (though unevenly) shorn hair stood off to the side of all the nonsense, a carry-on bag at his feet and a small shipping container hanging loosely from his hand. He was watching the hubbub on the deck passively, like he was trying to solve some kind of puzzle. When he noticed Newsham's gaze, he cautiously approached her, moving, she thought, like a horse that had been beaten. "Um," he said, "hi. I'm looking for Anatoly Finch?"

"Then you should just follow his stuff up on the lift," Newsham replied. "His will be the last stop at the top."

"Oh," Maxwell said, and retracted in on himself a bit. "Damn. Okay. Well, can you tell me where my bunk is?"

"I'm guessing you're the new maintenance engineer?"

"Janitor, yeah."

"I can help you find your way. As soon as my friend is finished tossing the place for her package. You have all your stuff?"

Maxwell jostled his bag with the tip of his boot. "All set."

"That's it? Nothing else? No . . . pillow?"

"There aren't any extra pillows here?"

Newsham thought for a moment. "I'm not sure. Maybe?" She nodded at the box Maxwell was cradling under his arm. "What's that?"

He shook the package gently. "Oh, right. I saw this on the flight deck. Read the label and realized it was perishable. Figured I wasn't bringing all the mass I was allotted, so I grabbed it." He shrugged. "Do you know who it belongs to?"

Newsham scanned the invoice label with her padd. *Bharad, Nita*, it read. *Vitelline membranes.* "Well, damn," she said. "You've just made a friend for life."

"O-kay," Maxwell said. For just a moment, his slack features twisted into a knot. It looked, Newsham thought, like he had forgotten how to smile, but was doing his best. "Well," he concluded, "that's good. Can't have too many of those, can you?"

January 9, 2386
Deck Five

"Do you think she can survive outside?" Nog asked.

"I don't know," O'Brien said. "But she seemed to be doing fine in the core."

"I think there was at least a little air pressure in there."

"Maybe," O'Brien said, leaning out through the crack in the hull, staring out at the stars. "But she seems to be doing well enough now. I think we thank our lucky stars and go with it." He looked back over his shoulder at Nog and his new best friend. Studying Ginger's face, O'Brien noted that there was some kind of thin film over the two largest eyes, while the half-dozen or so smaller orbs were shut tight against the vacuum. Her mouthparts were folded shut too, and some sort of carapace closed over them. The arachnoform might not be completely invulnerable to the extremes of open space, but O'Brien had a strong feeling Ginger could tolerate more hostile environments than any Terran spider could. O'Brien wondered if Nita Bharad really understood what she had brought into the universe, but he knew that the present moment was definitely *not* the time to ponder such questions.

"But we don't even know if she can cling to the side of the station," Nog said.

"You're looking for reasons not to do this, Nog," O'Brien said. He very badly wanted this part of the mission to be over.

"I am expressing a reasonable amount of caution about expending our scant resources, Chief," Nog retorted. O'Brien was impressed despite himself. The kid knew how to use officer language. *"In my estimation, we only have one shot at this, and I am hesitant to proceed until we fully understand the parameters of the mission."*

O'Brien chuckled. "That last bit was practically Sisko-esque," he admitted. "Well done." Nog scowled, but he couldn't maintain it and grinned. Performing a quick mental calculation, he asked, "Do you know we've known each other for over fifteen years?"

"Seventeen, Chief."

"Seventeen?"

"Seventeen."

O'Brien considered. There was, at minimum, a strong probability that they were about to die. The plan—*his* plan—was ridiculous, though he knew it was also their best shot at survival, based on the information they had at hand. "It's possible," he said, "that it might be time for you to start calling me Miles."

Nog seemed startled. He appeared to consider the

statement very carefully. Despite the clock that was ticking in his head, O'Brien let him. *"It's possible,"* Nog allowed, *"but it's just as likely that I really like calling you Chief."*

O'Brien turned the sentiment around in his head for a minute or two and then laughed, using, he knew, precious oxygen. "Okay," he said. "Fine. You win. Let's get on with this. I can't feel my toes anymore."

Nog hesitated. *"Hang on a second, Chief. We're all the way down here at the bottom again. Maybe we should go back to the hangar and get something that might help us."*

"No phasers there," O'Brien said. "Remember that conversation?"

"I do," Nog sighed. "And no, there aren't any phasers. But maybe there's something that could be almost as useful."

Finch's Lab

"People are stranded here," Maxwell said. "Civilians." He wasn't sure if the word would have much impact on Finch's customer. Was he a military man? Maxwell still couldn't place the accent; he couldn't detect anything in the customer's cadence that screamed military. While he didn't subscribe to the idea that there was such a thing as a military personality, he believed that being part of a service organization enhanced certain modes of behavior. If nothing else, military personnel were polite when there was no cause *not* to be, and Finch's customer was being a rude ass.

"I do not care," the speaker replied. *"I've come for my product. I paid in advance. It's mine and I want it now."*

In his corner, Finch, who had been rolled up into a ball, uncurled just enough to correct, *"Only half."* Maxwell had reopened the channel to Finch's suit, but considered shutting it off again.

The customer must have heard Finch, too. *"If it isn't ready, it doesn't matter if I've paid for half, all, or nothing at all. Any way you look at it, I have no reason to stay. Except, perhaps, to have the satisfaction of watching this place explode. It will soon, too. My scans have revealed several structural flaws."*

"And you could just watch that happen?" Maxwell asked. "To innocent bystanders?"

"Would Finch be one of the 'innocent' bystanders?"

"I'm not going to dignify that with a reply."

"So, then the answer is: yes, absolutely."

Maxwell nudged him with the toe of a boot. "Finch," he said, attempting to keep his voice under control.

"Leave me alone."

"I need information. Some kind of leverage."

"Leave me alone. I'm ready to die."

Maxwell grabbed the loose cloth of Finch's environmental suit and attempted to roll him over. "I'm not," Maxwell said. "And there are a dozen people down in the hangar who might have an opinion."

Surprisingly, Finch relaxed and turned his head so that he could look Maxwell in the eye. One of Finch's eyebrows was cocked up. Something had amused him. Maxwell guessed what it was: his desperation. *"Not ready to die yet?"* Finch asked. *"I'm surprised to hear you say it.*

Ever since you've come here, it seemed to me that you've been watching for it just out of the corner of your eye. Didn't want to see it coming head-on, but you've been bracing for it, when the moment came. Why else come to a place like this?"

"I'm the only thing that's kept this place from falling apart."

"Hmmm," Finch said. *"But only just enough. Just enough so that it wouldn't fly apart all at once. Just enough so that no one would think to blame you. You made things nice enough that your 'friends' thought well of you, clapped you on the back, shared their home brew with you. Couldn't be too obvious, could you?"*

Maxwell was compelled to ask, "Too obvious about what?"

"About how much you want to die. Out here. In the inky black. You just needed to find the right place to do it. Somewhere no one would even notice." Finch pointed at the center of Maxwell's head with his stubby finger. *"You live here, out in the black. Even when you're not here, you're here."*

Ben Maxwell's face felt numb and his eyes burned. He tried to recall what time it was and how long it had been since he'd slept, but couldn't get the numbers to add up. He couldn't think of anything clever to say, so he did the simplest thing he could think to do under the circumstances and told the truth. "You might be right, Finch. The evidence is stacked up behind your theory. Some days." He shook his head. "But not today."

Finch smirked, showing his pearly, white teeth. *"Doubt there's much you can do about it,"* he said. *"At least without my assistance."*

Movement at the opposite side of the lab caught Maxwell's attention. He was afraid to take his eyes off Finch, not believing the big man had given up. Indeed, Finch's entire monologue seemed designed to distract Maxwell and, if that was true, the ruse had almost succeeded. Now, across the room: signs of life.

Finch was on the deck with equipment lockers and consoles blocking his view of the Mother. He couldn't see what Maxwell was seeing, a fact that made Maxwell just a tiny bit sad. The creature's tentacles waved in agitation. The cluster of limbs that were thrust out through the cracks in the lab's hull were pulsing and throbbing as if the Mother was attempting to retract them into its body. The Mother was not happy.

A bright light flared outside the hull. Maxwell shut his eyes against the flash and turned away. When he looked back again, the light had faded and Miles O'Brien was standing in a wide gap in the bulkhead. Under one arm, he awkwardly held what appeared to be the still glowing nozzle of an ion thruster pack. Miles must have been using the thruster as an assault weapon or bludgeon or maybe both.

"Ah," O'Brien said, "Captain. Could you use a bit of help?" He stepped through the gap, staying as far away from the still writhing Mother as he could.

Behind him came Commander Nog and after him scrambled the all-too-familiar eight-legged silhouette of an arachnoform. By her markings and general demeanor, Maxwell knew it was Ginger. The three of them were tied together with a cable composed of, Maxwell guessed, Ginger's silk. Maxwell pointed at Ginger. "They go EVA?"

"Apparently," Nog replied, *"yes."*

"Wish I'd known that. Probably could have been a big help."

"She didn't really like it," Nog said. *"I think it made her dizzy."*

Maxwell glanced at O'Brien for an explanation, but the chief just shook his head.

"And the Mother doesn't like fire," Maxwell added. "Not surprising, but good to know."

O'Brien tossed the thruster pack down onto the deck. *"Tapped out."*

"Not that there's really anywhere to go."

Now it was O'Brien and Nog's turn to exchange confused glances. They both turned to Maxwell. *"Nowhere to go?"* O'Brien asked.

Nog pointed out through the crack in the hull. *"How about that Romulan ship?"*

Chapter 20

"**W**hat's this, Lieutenant?" Maxwell asked. Worf, the *Enterprise*'s chief of security, had escorted him from the transporter room and through the ship's wide corridors to what Maxwell had assumed would be the brig. Instead, they were standing in the doorway to a cabin more luxurious than his quarters back on the *Phoenix*.

"These are your quarters, Captain Maxwell. Captain Picard has assigned them to you for the duration of our transit to Starbase 8."

Maxwell leaned in and studied the room. "Isn't this a bit *posh* for a prisoner?"

"You have not been charged, Captain," the lieutenant said, his voice deeply resonating even in the large space. "You are *detained*. Until a board of inquiry has met." The Klingon cleared his throat. "The situation is murky."

"Legally, you mean," Maxwell said.

"Yes, sir."

"But not morally."

"It is not my place to say, Captain." Worf lifted his arm, indicating Maxwell should enter first. The gesture did not imply Maxwell had any choice in the matter, so he complied.

Feeling it was inappropriate to sit, Maxwell looked around at the furnishings and said, "This looks very comfortable, Lieutenant. Please tell Captain Picard I thank him."

Worf nodded and replied, "I will, sir. If you require anything, inform the computer, and it will be brought to you."

With the replicator taken offline, Maxwell knew he was in a cage, no matter how plush. "Thank you, Lieutenant. How about a fifth of bourbon and a noose?" The words popped out before Maxwell had any awareness that he was going to say them.

The Klingon tilted his head and regarded Maxwell carefully. "I can bring you synthehol, if you like. Suicide is a dishonorable response to your situation. Chief O'Brien has spoken highly of you, Captain Maxwell. You do not strike me as being a dishonorable man."

Maxwell was humbled. "Thank you, Mister Worf. I'm not sure why I said that. Please pardon me."

Worf nodded in acknowledgment. "It has been a stressful day, sir. You should rest."

Maxwell looked around the room, thinking that all the furniture looked very, very comfortable and also about how much happier he would be sleeping on a hard cot in the brig. "I suppose," he said. "I'm inclined to think I'm going to get a lot of downtime in the near future. Lots of time to rest."

"Perhaps," Lieutenant Worf said. "May I speak freely, sir?"

Maxwell nodded.

"The universe is an unpredictable place and none of us knows what the future may hold."

Chuckling, Maxwell replied, "I've heard quite a lot about you over the past few years, Mister Worf, but I hadn't heard you were a philosopher." Worf grunted, but did not otherwise reply. He turned away as if to leave, but Maxwell realized he had one more request. "One more thing, Lieutenant."

"Yes, Captain?" Worf asked.

"Would you have done what I did?"

"Sir?"

"Attacked the Cardassian ships. Would you have done it, knowing what I knew?"

Worf turned back toward Maxwell, saying, "I do not think that this is an appropriate topic for discussion, Captain."

"Then let me put it another way: Would a Klingon captain have done what I did?"

The lieutenant considered the question. After a time, he said, "I am not sure what a *Klingon* captain would have done under the circumstances. Klingons are not all of a kind, any more than humans or Romulans or even Cardassians." Worf paused. "I can conceive of a situation where a Klingon captain might attack a civilian vessel, especially if he was convinced it was transporting war matériel. It might be an honorable course of action." The security chief looked up and locked eyes with Maxwell. "But I do not think he would sleep well."

Maxwell let the words sink in and then nodded in acknowledgment. "Thank you, Lieutenant Worf. I appreciate your frankness."

"You're welcome," Worf said. "Would you still like the bourbon?"

"No," Maxwell said, shaking his head. "I've never really liked bourbon. Or any kind of alcohol, really. I find drinking makes it difficult for me to sleep. And I have enough trouble with that as it is these days."

"Understood," Worf said, and left the room. Maxwell remained where he was standing and stared at the featureless surface of the door for what seemed like a very long time.

January 9, 2386
Finch's Lab
Robert Hooke

"Romulan ship?" Maxwell asked.

"Absolutely," Nog replied. *"Kestrel-class, I think. Or a shuttle. We've seen more than a few of those on DS9. Hard to say for sure since it cloaked right after we spotted it."*

"Cloaked?" Maxwell asked.

"It was and then it wasn't and then it was. Were you talking to it?"

"Yes."

"Well, that explains it. They had to decloak to talk to you. Poor power distribution. Or the pilot doesn't know what he's doing. You always have to consider that possibility."

"Of course," Maxwell said.

"What is it, sir?" O'Brien asked. *"What's troubling you?"*

"I talked to him," Maxwell said, staring into the middle distance, thinking. *"I talked to him and he didn't sound like any Romulan I've ever talked to."* He glanced up at the chief. *"And stop calling me sir."*

O'Brien grinned. *"Sorry, Captain."* The smile disappeared when the entire deck squirmed under their feet. All of them, except Finch (who was lying on his back) and Ginger (who was clinging to the wall), stumbled against consoles and waved their arms around, searching for stability, their inner ears punishing them. *"That's not good,"* O'Brien said, and began searching for the environmental controls console. *"We have to push whatever power we still have into the gravity generator or we could all . . . Oh, crap."*

Maxwell and Nog steadied each other. "I know," Maxwell said. "Already did that. Pushed it as far as it would go. If it's bucking now, we don't have much time left."

"Make that no time, Captain," O'Brien said. *"And if it's this bad up here, then what must it be like on the hangar deck?"*

Hangar Deck

"We're too old for this, Nita," Newsham groaned as the deck lurched and bucked beneath them.

Down on her knees, retching and clutching her gut, Bharad tried to sound jaunty. When the gravity had shut off, the rope that kept her from flying off the deck had torn the flesh around her forearms. When it came back on, both her knees cracked against the rail. "Oh, come on, Wendy," she said. "Didn't you tell me you used to ride bucking broncos back in the . . . in the . . . *Hang on!*" The deck receded again. This time, Bharad was ready, having wrapped the rope around both her hands. When she dropped again, she was able to cushion her fall with a roll. Judging by the groans and cries she heard around her, not everyone had figured out how to fall. "Back in the Montana?"

"Wyoming," Newsham said. She was lying on her back, head lolling to one side, a thin stream of blood trickling out her nose.

"Aren't they the same thing?"

Newsham rolled her eyes. "Haven't you ever looked at a map of North America?"

"Have *you* ever looked at a map of India?"

"Shut up!"

"You shut up!"

"Do you have any idea why this keeps happening?"

"What do you mean?" Bharad asked.

"The gravity bucking. If it's just getting shut off, shouldn't we simply float away?"

"Rather than being battered?" Bharad added. "Probably. Something cycling? Who knows? Ben could probably explain it." Bharad looked to her left and found a woman—the last one she had cut out of the webbing inside the *Wren*—lying on her side, staring at the two of them, eyes wide but unblinking, her head tilted at an uncomfortable angle. "Oh, no," Bharad said.

"What is it?" Newsham asked, but she must have seen Bharad undoing her ropes and scrambling toward the prone woman. "Nita," she cried. "Don't! That's a bad idea! If the gravity kicks again . . . !"

The gravity kicked again.

Finch's Lab

"Sir, what were you saying about the Romulan?" Nog asked. *"What did you mean that he didn't sound like any you've ever talked to? You mean like an accent?"*

"No," Maxwell said, shaking his head. The ill-fitting helmet rattled as he moved. "Not how he sounded, but the words, the phrasing." He snapped his fingers. "I've got it!"

"What?" Nog asked.

"Working man."

"Sir?" O'Brien was wrestling with the feeds from the dying reactor, so he couldn't look at Maxwell.

"He's not military," Maxwell said. "Not service, not a bureaucrat." He pointed a bulky finger at O'Brien. "He's a guy who does a job." He swung his arm around until he was pointing at Finch, who was lying on the deck, though something about his posture suggested he was awake and listening. Maxwell took three giant steps toward his former employer and effortlessly lifted Finch's sagging bulk into a sitting position. "Isn't he? Not a government representative, not a praetor, not a diplomat, not a spy."

Finch snorted and grinned horribly. Because of Maxwell—or the deck—his head must have struck the facemask, as his gums were bloody and, when he smiled, a spray of pink spittle blemished the interior of his helmet. *"A farmer,"* Finch said. *"Just a grubby little farmer. You forget that about the Romulans, don't you? And the Klingons too, I imagine. Only so much can come out of replicators. If you do it right, planting something in the ground and letting it grow is ever so much more efficient."* He chuckled, but his ribs must have hurt, because the laugh turned into a groan. Finch sagged down onto himself. Muttering, talking to himself as much as to Maxwell, Finch added, *"Mother's people were farmers. She hated farmers. Hated mud and weather and . . . and . . . pollen. Trees. Hated them. Hated them."*

Maxwell shook Finch, probably harder than he really needed to, or so Nog thought. *Captain Maxwell has some anger issues.*

"Get him back on the comm, Finch!" Maxwell snapped. "Get him back and tell him the truth! The least you can do is tell him that there's no miracle here! You can't save him or his family or his farm or his planet! You give back his money and you say—"

"No," Nog said, reaching out and clasping Maxwell on the shoulder. *"No,"* he repeated, more calmly. Like an officer. Or a businessman. *"That's a mistake."*

"What?" Maxwell asked.

"What?" Finch repeated, relieved or, possibly, surprised.

Nog did not reply to either of the men, but looked back over his shoulder at the chief, who, unexpectedly, said, *"First Rule of Acquisition?"* He grinned. *"What's the play?"*

Romulan Ship

Cretak fumed, uncertain how to proceed. This was supposed to have been a simple transaction: go to the station, get the organism, go home, save his planet. He'd been selected to make the run for the simple fact that he was the only one, besides Lareth, who could pilot the ship. Lareth was disabled, his mind fried by despair and longing and ale. "Don't be unkind. Poor Lareth has suffered so," Hexce, Cretak's wife, would say over and over again and then shake her head.

Cretak always wanted to reply, "*He's* suffered?! We've *all* suffered! *I've* suffered!" He knew better. Hexce wouldn't have it. She was a better person than he was. He knew this and it ate at him, but not too much and not all the time.

So now, here he was, hiding behind the infernal, energy-sucking cloaking device, watching the station and wondering what to do next. Finch, the *shart,* had failed them. Taken their money—all that his community had been able to scrape together—and then lied to them. No miracle was forthcoming. The soil would stay poisoned, and they would have to leave their planet. If they were lucky. Cretak had spent the best part of the last five years hating the Borg and the horror they had rained down on his world, but, at that moment, he decided he hated Finch more.

The comm chirped again. Cretak ignored it. Should he beam over to the station and attempt to wrest something from Finch? He skimmed the sensor readings and shook his head ruefully. Cretak knew he wasn't a scientist, engineer, or metallurgist, but he recognized the signs of impending disaster when he saw it. Many terrible things were happening in or near Finch's station. Cretak knew he wasn't qualified to understand them, but when chunks of plating peeled away from a hull and atmosphere vented into space—that was bad. He scanned the reactor output, but the readouts were confusing: peculiar spikes followed by power-downs. Gravitons and other more exotic particles geysered out of cracks and broken seams. His ship's computer explained it was time to leave.

A part of Cretak really wanted to stay and watch Finch's bloated corpse pinwheel through open space when the station blew, but the brief satisfaction would canker and turn into existential horror. *Damn you, Finch.* A distant part of his mind, a part that spoke with his father's weary voice, told him he was as much to blame as the human.

The comm chirped once more.

Cretak slapped the console and opened the channel. "Damn you, Finch!" he shouted, surprising himself.

"Too late," a voice responded. *"I think that's been taken care of."*

Cretak knew he wasn't an authority on humans or their whimsies, but he also recognized that the speaker didn't sound human. For that matter, he didn't sound like someone who was inside a crumbling space station. He sounded . . . amused? Disaffected? "Who is this?" Cretak asked.

"Turn on your viewer," the speaker said.

"Why should I?"

"Because I like to look a man in the eye when I'm making a deal."

Deal? Cretak wondered. *What in the names of the D'ravsai?* But he couldn't resist turning on the viewer.

The speaker must have been sitting very close to the pickup, because his features—particularly his flat, ridged nose and his thick brow—seemed to fill the screen. He smiled very briefly, showing a row of sharp teeth, though the smile did not reach his eyes. *"My name is Nog."* The image shimmered and, for a moment, Cretak thought something was wrong with the signal, but then he realized the effect was due to the fact that Nog was wearing some kind of environmental suit.

"What do you want, Nog?" Cretak asked.

Once again, Nog—a Ferengi, Cretak guessed—grinned, but only very briefly, as if he couldn't resist enjoying a private joke. *"It's not about what I want, friend. I'm contacting you to discuss what you might want. Or perhaps I should say* need."

"What do you know of my needs?" Cretak asked, taking control of the conversation. He knew about the Ferengi, about their much-vaunted ability to extract wealth from the unwary. Cretak almost chuckled to himself, though ruefully. *How can he take something from someone who has nothing?*

"All too much, I'm afraid," Nog said. *"I have some very bad news for you, sir."* He shook his head, his voice filled with what Cretak knew he was supposed to believe was regret. *"Very, very bad."*

"If you mean that Doctor Finch has reneged on our deal, that I'm to return home without the aid he promised—" Cretak snorted. "I have been informed."

The image on the monitor appeared to jump, like the signal had dropped and then quickly been reestablished. The Ferengi appeared briefly disconcerted, but quickly regained his composure. *"Ah, yes. Of course. Finch's bug. Does that translate?"* he asked. *"Do you know what a bug is?"*

Cretak was on the verge of being insulted, but he

was also curious about what the Ferengi was saying. "Of course I know what a bug is. I live out in the land, the sky over my head, soil in my hands every day. Back when there was soil . . ."

"*No, no,*" the Ferengi said. "*I mean the other kind of bug. It might not translate.*" He lifted his hand, huge in the pickup, and held his thumb and forefinger so that there was only the tiniest space between them. "*Microscopic. A pest . . . No, wait, not a pest. Nuisance? No.*" He waved his hand. "*Wait. I meant* plague. *Finch's plague.*"

Now Cretak was very confused and unable to conceal it. At first, he had thought the Ferengi was attempting to weave a tapestry of lies, but now he sounded as if he was having problems even finding the correct terms. Or maybe the translator was flawed? "Plague?" he asked. "*What* plague?"

"*The one that's enveloping your ship,*" the Ferengi said. "*They're like a swarm of locusts. Does that word translate? Do you have locusts on your world? Yes? How about a swarm that can survive in space? Can you imagine that? Or that it's on your hull now, burrowing into the seams? Our sensors are offline, but yours might still be functioning. For a little while longer. You should be able to find the swarm if you know where to look.*"

"What?" Cretak asked. His stomach shriveled in his abdomen. "What are you talking about? What swarm? What *bugs*?"

"*I'm really very sorry,*" Nog said. "*I assure you that I had nothing to do with this situation.*" He must have manipulated the viewer controls, because the camera pulled back and the Ferengi's whole face filled the screen. He was wearing a helmet, though it was one of the larger sorts, so it was possible to see his entire face. That was it. No uniform was visible, but he recognized the suit. *Starfleet. The Federation.* Nog continued, *"I was sent here to try to resolve the problem, but have run into some additional problems."* He smiled and, this time, Cretak sensed a genuine warmth and sincere desire to assist. *"Fortunately, I think we can help each other."*

Finch's Lab

Nog put the transmission briefly on hold and looked back over his shoulder at the chief and Maxwell. "I think I have his attention," he said.

O'Brien and Maxwell both nodded appreciatively. Maxwell said, *"I believe you do at that."*

Hangar Deck

Nita Bharad lay on her side, staring into space. She panted hard. The back of her jumpsuit was damp, probably from perspiration, but possibly from blood, too. It clung to her skin. The air in the hangar had grown cold, and she shuddered miserably.

The last round had been the worst. She was fairly certain one of her colleagues had lost her grip and been bucked up into the air and then dropped, but Bharad was too tired to look around. *Tired and thirsty,* she thought. *I would sell my mother for a glass of water.* She closed her eyes and felt her mind drift toward exhausted slumber, though she got hung up on an odd thought as she so often did before sleep: *Glass of water. Why a glass of water?* Had she ever really drunk water out of a glass? Growing up, they had drunk out of mugs and tumblers and metal bottles, but a *glass? Ever?* Such were the thoughts that kept her restless mind astir at night.

What was the fate of her girls? Bharad rolled onto her back and groaned. Something was sprained or torn. Opening her eyes, she stared up into the gloom (everything but the emergency lights was out) and tried to imagine Ginger and Honey sliding down on their threads to find her, bind her up, and carry her away to her bed, safe and protected. In her mind's eye, the girls floated like a pair of soap bubbles.

No soap bubbles floated before her. The only thing she saw were motes of debris—flecks of plasteel and insulation— whirling in eddies and currents of thinning, increasingly toxic atmosphere. They were strangely beautiful. She began to drift away with them.

And then Bharad's right wrist began to vibrate, and the movement jerked her back into the here and now. She lifted her arm and stared blankly at the comm device on her forearm. It vibrated again. Unable to lift her left hand to activate the comm, Bharad dropped her wrist onto her forehead and the vibration ceased. "Who's there?" she asked dourly.

"Hello, Nita," Maxwell said. "How're things?"

"Get me a beer, Ben," Bharad replied, grinning.

"For you, anything," Maxwell said. "But I can do you one better."

"Better than a beer?" Bharad asked, and, despite her dehydration, felt her eyes moisten. "What could be better than that?"

"How about a way off this station?"

Bharad smiled. "You shouldn't make promises you can't keep, Ben Maxwell." Somewhere nearby, someone worked up the energy to moan loudly, and Bharad silently wished whoever it was would kindly please shut the hell up.

"Listen to me, Nita," Maxwell said. *"I promise you, there's a way. We've got it figured out. I wanted you to know because people are going to start being transported away any second now."*

Off to her right, Bharad heard the telltale sound of a transporter beam grabbing someone. She had only transported a couple times herself and hadn't either particularly liked or disliked the experience. *It is,* she thought, *a wonder, but not a mystery, if there is a difference between the two.* "Thanks for the notification," she said, her voice cracking. "Any idea where they're being sent?"

"A ship," Maxwell said. *"A passerby. A Samaritan."*

"Oh, lovely," Bharad replied. "And why isn't this Samaritan's ship falling apart?" And added, "Like the others?"

"We're not entirely sure it won't," Maxwell said. *"Their engines are different. We believe it won't attract Finch's bugs."* He chuckled. *"At least, that's the theory. Not that we're telling him that . . ."*

"What?" Bharad asked, feeling, for a brief moment, outraged on behalf of their Samaritan. She suspected, knowing Maxwell, that the Samaritan wouldn't be quite so generous if he knew the Complete and Entire Truth. "And why aren't we telling him that?"

Maxwell didn't acknowledge the question. Instead, he continued, *"It's going to be pretty cramped. Just so you know."* Another transporter beam locked and whirred off to the left.

The dust motes spun before Bharad's eyes. "Any sign of my girls?" she asked softly. "I'm worried about them. Something may have happened . . ."

"One of them is right here with me," Maxwell said. *"Ginger. With her new best friend."*

"Not Honey?" she asked.

"No sign of her," Maxwell said. *"But I'm sure she's fine. She's smart, Nita. As smart as her mom."* Another transporter beam activated.

And then Bharad felt the deck below her buck. As she was flung up into the dank and dreary space, she briefly— very briefly—found herself thinking about playing with soap bubbles, the kind you made with a dish full of soap and glycerin. She tried to imagine she was one of those iridescent globes—shimmering like an oily rainbow, carried along by a breeze—and that she would either float away or pop.

Chapter 21

Eleven Years Earlier
Starfleet Penal Colony

"Let's talk about firsts," Doctor Gunther said. He was sitting in his overstuffed chair and Maxwell was sitting—not lying, but *sitting*—on the couch. They had met several times since he had been assigned to the colony. Most of their interactions had been cordial, however Gunther found Maxwell to be a frustrating patient. *Insufficiently invested in the therapeutic process,* he had written in the patient file.

"Firsts?"

"Firsts. The first time something happened. *Personal* firsts."

"Oh," Maxwell said. "Like, first time sailing a boat or first kiss or first day of school. That sort of thing."

"All good examples," Gunther agreed. "Pick one of those."

"Or first child born or first time in space or first time drunk."

"Also good examples. Excellent. You've got the idea."

"Or," Maxwell continued, "first sexual encounter or first fight or first funeral."

Gunther sighed. "Sure."

"Or first time in battle or first time someone died by your hand or—I don't know—first time I thought I was going to die."

Gunther set aside his padd, asking, "*First* time you thought you were going to die?"

"Sure," Maxwell said.

"How many times have you thought you were going to die?"

Maxwell looked confused. "How many?" He turned and looked out the window. It was a typical summer morning. Heavy gray storm clouds scudded along the horizon. Shafts of golden light streamed down between the banks so that the ocean's surface was alternately glittering and gloomy. "I spent most of my career out there. It's part of the job."

"How many?"

Maxwell turned his head to stare out at the ocean. Gunther noted that his cheeks were darkened by black and gray stubble. It was the first time he could recall seeing the former officer appearing in anything less than perfect wardroom condition. "Times I thought, *I might die today*?"

"Yes."

Maxwell shrugged and turned back to look at Gunther. "More than I can count."

"That must be exhausting."

"I suppose," Maxwell agreed. "You get used to it."

Gunther let the words hang in the air for a few moments and then retrieved his padd. He knew he had just made a tiny inroad and wanted to take notes. "Tell me about the first time."

January 9, 2386
Ops Center
Robert Hooke

"Nita?" Maxwell called. *"Nita?"* He flicked the communicator control stud on his environmental suit's gauntlet on and off several times. Since returning to ops, Maxwell had tried to contact Bharad, with no success. His frustration was becoming palpable to Nog, even through the environmental suit. He turned to Nog and asked, *"What's happening? What's the pilot doing?"*

Nog moved closer to Maxwell, careful to make sure his back was to the screen in case the Romulan was watching their interaction. "Exactly what we asked him to do," Nog explained. "He's beaming the scientists out of the hangar and onto his ship. He can't beam them all at once. A shuttle that size, the transporter probably has only one pad."

Maxwell said, *"We've convinced him that his ship may start falling apart any second, so he's probably more than a little nervous."*

Nog glanced at the screen from the corner of his eye, but all he saw was the pilot's forearm and shoulder. The Romulan was busy, presumably manipulating transporter controls. "Probably," he agreed.

"But we are reasonably sure the Mother won't be attracted to his engine?" Maxwell asked. *"Aren't we?"*

Both O'Brien and Nog remained mute.

"You think," Maxwell asked, *"Nita was just caught up in the transporter beam?"*

O'Brien pointed at the environmental controls console. *"Based on the scraps of data I can get out of this thing, yes. The hangar had some hull integrity up to a couple minutes ago. Now? Systems are failing all over the station."* Waving a hand, taking in the bulkheads and deck below their feed, he added, *"It looks like you were rerouting a lot of the power up here."*

Maxwell nodded toward the still-recumbent Finch. *"His doing, not mine."*

"We're probably alive now because he did," O'Brien said.

Maxwell grunted, clearly experiencing mixed emotions. *"Let's just make sure we've got everyone we can. Then, he can beam us over and we can jump to warp."*

Nog gritted his teeth in preparation for delivering bad news.

"That was a grimace," Maxwell said. *"Why is there a grimace?"*

"I wouldn't recommend going to warp. We don't know how fragile warp space is around the station. We have to assume it's fragile."

"Impulse?"

Nog made a slightly less pained expression.

Maxwell sagged. *"Thrusters?"*

Nog and O'Brien nodded in unison. *"We just need to get clear,"* O'Brien said. *"And wait for Deep Space 9 to send a ship to pick us up."*

Maxwell acquiesced. *"All right. I'm going to let you two explain this when he beams you over."*

"What about him, Captain?" O'Brien asked, jutting his chin toward Finch.

"*What do you mean, 'What about him?'*" Maxwell asked. "*He comes with us. He goes to prison. I know a good one. Nice ocean view. Good doctors.*" He jabbed a finger at O'Brien. "*And stop calling me* captain."

Nog turned away so neither hew-mon would see him rolling his eyes. The Romulan was attempting to get their attention, probably had been trying for a couple minutes. Nog unmuted the audio. "Yes, Cretak. Status?"

"*I've beamed aboard everyone I could. Some of your comrades are in poor health. I have provided first-aid supplies. Now, may we please leave here as quickly as possible?*"

"Of course," Nog said, resuming his role as negotiator. "We'll be ready to beam over in—stand by." He muted the audio and pointed at the blinking red square of light in the lower right-hand corner of the monitor. "What's that mean?"

Maxwell stared at the light for just a fraction of a second too long. "*That?*" he asked. "*Nothing. Proceed with the beaming.*"

"You've become a terrible liar, Captain," O'Brien said.

"*You mean I was a good liar once?*"

"You were an officer, so I assume you were." The chief pointed at the light. "But you're avoiding the point. Problem?"

"*Yes. Problem.*"

"How big?"

"*Pretty big,*" Maxwell said. "*Something just ate a hole through the reactor shields.*"

"How much time do we have?" O'Brien asked.

"*Not much,*" Maxwell said, just as lights went out and

the artificial gravity failed. *"All right,"* Maxwell said from the darkness. *"How about none?"*

O'Brien grabbed the console, careful not to move too suddenly and go careening into a bulkhead. When he was sure he was stable, he flicked on his light. A moment later Nog and Maxwell did the same, two friendly pools of light framing worried faces. "Okay," he said. "What's the plan?"

"I go shut down the reactor," Maxwell said. *"Before this bad day gets worse."*

"Right," O'Brien said. "I saw a bag of tools over there. Yours? Yes? Let me see what we'll need." He pointed Nog toward the spot where Finch had been. "Secure him before he floats away. Try to raise our friend on your suit's communicator. If you can't, push Finch out the hole so the Romulan can see you."

"No, Miles," Maxwell said.

O'Brien, who was already making his way toward the tools, had to halt awkwardly. "Why? What's wrong?"

"Nothing's wrong," Maxwell said. *"It's just that there's no reason why we both have to go. It's my reactor. I rebuilt it from scratch. If I can't shut it down in the next few minutes, then it's not going to be shut down at all."*

"You might need help," O'Brien began.

"No, Miles," Maxwell said, pushing himself off the console and easily gliding to the tool case. He swung it up and fished for a clip on the back of his suit. *"This isn't one of those kinds of problems."*

"Either we all live," O'Brien said, trying to parse Maxwell's logic, "or we all die. I'm coming with you."

"No."

"Why not?"

"Because I'm the captain," he replied, fastening the pack.

For several seconds, the only sound O'Brien heard was the inhalation and expulsion of breath inside his helmet. Then Nog said, *"I think he might have you there, Chief."* O'Brien jerked around to face his fellow engineer as if he meant to throw a punch, but the sudden movement sent him into an uncontrolled spin that he could arrest only by grabbing on to Nog's shoulder. *"Got you,"* Nog said, bracing against the console.

O'Brien looked at Nog, still gripping his shoulder. Then, with a nod, he patted him, released his hold, and turned to Maxwell. "You better get moving," he said. "We'll get as far away as we can. If nothing happens in ten minutes, we'll come back."

Maxwell said, *"Good plan."* He pointed at the thruster pack that they had used to burn back the Mother. *"What about that? You're sure it's tapped out?"*

"Positive," Nog said. *"Though there's another one in the hangar that has some fuel left. Assuming the hangar is still there."*

"One problem at a time," Maxwell said. Just before opening the hatch to the core, he looked back over his shoulder. O'Brien thought he was making sure they were leaving, but then he shone his lamp on a spot on the ceiling, revealing Ginger, who was anxiously twitching her forelimbs. *"And, Commander?"* Maxwell called.

"Sir?"

"Make sure Ginger goes with you."

"Yes, sir."

"*If anything happens to her, Nita will* kill *me.*"

They spotted the Romulan ship as soon as they were outside the station. O'Brien thought that the pilot was much too close to the Hooke. Maybe one of his passengers was making sure he stayed near. *Probably Nita,* he guessed. *Probably looking for her girls.* And, predictably, Ginger was the first one to disappear in a swirl of transporter effect. *Which must be thrilling for the people on the shuttle.* Nog disappeared a moment later, followed soon after by Finch. O'Brien tried to look back over his shoulder at the station before the beam immobilized him, but there was nothing to use for leverage. *He'll be all right,* O'Brien thought as the transporter took him. *He's come through worse than this in one piece.*

Central Core

A long life, Maxwell thought as he shut the hatch behind him, *filled with many bad decisions, and this may be my worst.* The feeble glow of his torch barely pierced the gloom when he leaned over the handrail and looked down to the bottom of the core. Bits of debris floated past the cone of illumination. Six decks down, he knew, was the hatch that led to the generator room. He could take the safe route and pull himself down the metal stairs along the handrail, but that would take much longer than Maxwell imagined he had. This was one of the many problems he faced (but didn't want to share with O'Brien and Nog). He didn't have a clear idea what he would confront when he reached the bottom of the core. The blinking red light was a very generic warning indicating only that there was a problem with the reactor.

When the sensors detected a problem with the core, lockdown programs should have isolated the tiny blob of antimatter the station reactor used for fuel and brought the backup generator or batteries online. Maxwell's guess was that the first step in the lockdown had occurred, but not the second. *Why?* The logical assumption was because something had interfered with the program. *What?* Maxwell felt sure he knew, and a part of him really didn't want to go find out. A vivid mental picture formed: a gigantic, shivering blob of purple goo sprouting writhing tentacles. For some reason, this new version of the Mother had a red-rimmed, bulbous eye in the center of its mass. *Maybe it would be better to just wait here in the dark*, he thought. *Either the reactor goes or Miles comes back to get me in ten minutes.*

Sighing, he said, "That's not what they pay you for, Ben. Time to clean up the mess." He vaulted the railing, his tools poking him on the back when he moved his arms. Maxwell awkwardly clung to the steel rail, his feet pressed flat against the stairway's frame. Bending his knees, he pushed off and dropped down into the darkness, watchful for large chunks of debris.

The railing for the stairway on the opposite side of the core, but one (or possibly two?) deck down, whirled into view, much faster than Maxwell had expected. He was barely able to get his arms up in time, but managed to grab the rail and check his progress by swinging his legs around to brake against the stair. "Not too bad," he said approvingly. It reminded him of the time he and Maria had gone zip-lining through a forest canopy.

He turned around, aimed, and pushed off again, exerting a little more force this time, mindful of the ticking clock.

Halfway across, he almost collided with something large, curved, and with what looked like a long, hairless tail. The shape barely registered before Maxwell had passed it. He didn't even have time to shout in surprise before another railing zoomed into view. Maxwell raised his arms and bounced off. Realizing he had missed his chance, Maxwell tried to judge if he was going down or up or simply back toward the center of the core. If he was, he was in big, big trouble. *Nothing to push against, nothing to grab.*

Instinctively, Maxwell windmilled his arms, feeling foolish even as he did it, knowing it wouldn't help, but unable to calm the primitive part of his brain that told him he should be able to twist around or rise above the imagined flood tide.

Maxwell's hand brushed up against something. He grasped it before he could bounce off. If it was large enough, he knew he could throw it and use Newtonian physics to get moving again. He tried to bring the object around and shine his wrist-mounted lamp on it, but was surprised when the movement instead swung his body around.

Whatever he was holding wasn't ready to move. Maxwell gripped it tighter, steadied himself, and brought the lamp up.

He stared at a line, taut as the cable in a suspension

bridge and thick as a climbing rope. One end must have been anchored up above, on the core's ceiling, while the other end was fixed below. He touched it with the tips of his free hand. *Sticky,* he thought, *but not too sticky.* The glue or gum was meant to aid movement, he realized, and not immobilize. He shone the torch from side to side, searching for other threads or for a familiar set of glittering eyes, but saw nothing.

Pointing his head down, Maxwell tugged hand over hand, headed toward the lower decks, careful never to let go.

Reaching the bottom of the core, Maxwell flipped around and reoriented his inner gyroscope, fixing the hatch to the reactor room in his sights. Pressing his feet to the taut cable, he released his grip, pushed off carefully, and sailed across the gap. Grasping the hatch handle, he twisted and pushed while wedging his foot against the bottom step of the stairs.

The hatch swung open without resistance. *Good housekeeping,* he thought.

The stairwell to the generator room was predictably dark, but a quick sweep with the torch revealed it was unobstructed. It was narrow enough that Maxwell could propel himself down it without worrying about losing an opposable surface. Reaching the end of the corridor, he faced the door to the reactor room, which had been Maxwell's home, his lair, his place of safety. To his right was a stairwell of only a half-dozen steps that led to the hangar—or, judging from what Nog had said, what was left of it. *Tempting,* Maxwell thought, pointing the torch down the gloomy stairs, *though delusional. The only thing*

I'll find down there is open space and certain death. He turned back to the generator room door. *As opposed to only* almost *certain death.*

"Really no choice at all," Maxwell said, and yanked open the hatch.

The lights were all on, and Honey was home. Or, to put it another way, she had made herself at home. Zero gravity was not a problem when you could make web lines to scurry up and down and round and round.

Honey hung in the center of her web about five meters off the deck. She quivered when Maxwell stepped into the room, and her web jittered in response. Behind her, a sickly orange light spilled out of a crack in the generator housing mounted on the bulkhead. *Oh,* Maxwell thought, with more surprise than he would have expected. *I'm dead.* And then realized, with more relief than he expected, *Or maybe not.* If Honey wasn't dead, no matter how sturdy her alien physiology might be, then the reactor wasn't spewing out radiation. *Not enough to be immediately lethal, anyway.*

"To work," he said aloud, and then suddenly realized how thin the air in his suit felt. He glanced at the gauge on his gauntlet and cursed. Fifteen minutes left, maybe twenty if he stayed calm. *Ha!*

He approached Honey's web. Naturally, the controls to shut down the reactor were on the other side. "I have to get past this, Honey. No offense." Maxwell knew the arachnoform couldn't hear him, but he also knew she needed to feel safe with him. This is how he usually acted around her: he talked and went about his business. It was their little dance. Maxwell would work, and Honey would hover nearby, watching him, usually from a safe distance.

Maxwell pulled himself along the bulkhead—fortunately festooned with many knobs and handholds—intending to work his way around the room to the point where the control console met the wall. From there, it was only a few meters to the reactor controls. "I'm just going to turn this off, girl. And then we can sit here in the dark together until Miles comes back to get us. Won't that be fun?" The arachnoform didn't stir. He added, "Did you know I used to be in Starfleet, where I did all kinds of dangerous things?"

When Maxwell reached the junction of the bulkhead and the console, it was as if he had crossed an invisible line. Honey shuddered and scrambled down from the center of the web to stop a centimeter above the deck, no more than a short hop from Maxwell. If he wanted to reach the console, he would have to pull himself past Honey. Maxwell found this idea unaccountably distressing.

Beside him, one of the console's data screens flickered to life. Images and text rapidly scrolled down the screen, stopping occasionally as if an unseen reader had found some bit of information that was especially interesting. Maxwell tried to read it, but he found it difficult to focus his attention on the screen for more than a half second at a time. Whenever his gaze flickered back to Honey, she was still hanging where she had been, uncharacteristically still. She was watching him, Maxwell realized, as he watched the images slide past. Sensing she wanted him to see what was on the screen, he tilted forward to get a better look.

Most of the data appeared to be old Starfleet reports: log entries and accounts of missions, the sort of thing cadets read at the Academy. Some of them dated back to the twenty-second century, though others were newer. It looked like they had been taken from Kathryn Janeway's *Voyager* logs. The headings for all of the reports shared two words: *First Contact*.

"What is this?" Maxwell asked. He looked from side to side, expecting someone to step out of the shadows and announce their presence. "Who's doing this?"

Honey hung from her thread, her legs folded loosely along her sides. She twitched when he spoke, almost as if she could hear him despite the vacuum. Leaning closer, Maxwell shone his torch directly on her, carefully inspecting her. Before, when she had dropped down to the deck, he had believed the arachnoform had been hanging by one of her threads, but now, near as she was, Maxwell saw that it wasn't a thread at all. A strand of glistening purple goo protruded from the back of her cephalothorax. Slowly, carefully, so as to not make a mistake, he traced the strand back up to a spot where it emerged from the crack in the reactor vessel. "Oh, Honey," Maxwell said, genuinely surprised by how the realization grieved him. "I'm so sorry."

In response, Honey climbed down and pressed the tip of her abdomen, the spot where her spinnerets were, to the deck. She moved back and forth, her back legs shifting in a controlled, staccato action. The sticky stuff she had on the tips of her long legs that allowed her to climb walls was keeping her from bouncing around in zero g.

Maxwell felt the seconds ticking past. He knew he was

running out of air and that the generator needed tending, but he felt sure he owed Honey whatever time she needed to complete her task. Besides, he was pretty sure if he tried to get past her, she would find a way to stop him.

Honey's limbs fell still and she rose up off the deck, though whether the purple strand tugged her up or she climbed, Maxwell could not say. Something glistened on the deck where she had crouched only a moment ago. Braced against the console, he leaned down and shone his torch on the spot.

In jagged, blocky letters, Honey had written SOME BUG.

All Maxwell could do was look up at Honey exasperated and ask, "What?"

Her large eyes glistened. She cocked her head. If the Mother had taken control of her like it had Sabih's body, then it was doing a perfect impersonation of Honey's expectant stare. After a minute, expectation dissolved into disappointment. Honey dropped back down to the deck and painted new words.

When she rose again, Maxwell leaned in and read the new patch of lines: NO KILL I.

So many things depended on Maxwell moving, but all he could do was stare at the words and rack his brain.

NO KILL I. SOME BUG.

Maxwell was suddenly overwhelmed by the memory of his daughter, Sofia. She was, at most, five years old, and sitting in his lap, the back of her head smelling like sweet grass. She was leaning forward and pressing her fingertip to a padd, tracing the lines of words in an illustration.

All in a rush, the answer came to him.

Maxwell knew the clock was ticking. He knew that

his air was almost gone. He knew his friends were wondering whether he was alive or dead and whether *they* had much longer to live. He knew all of this, and yet, he couldn't help himself. He couldn't stop.

Maxwell started to laugh. His eyes were streaming, which was frustrating, because he couldn't clear them, and he was quickly out of breath because of the great, giant, oxygen-consuming whoops of hilarity. He had to grip the edge of the console or risk floating away into the center of the room or getting stuck in Honey's web, which was difficult, weak as he was. When the onslaught subsided and his ears stopped buzzing, he tried to steady his breathing and clear his head.

"'No Kill I,'" he said. "The Horta. It's been a James Kirk kind of day, hasn't it? And 'Some Bug.' That took me a minute." He shook his head in wonder. "Sofia loved that book. Cried every time we read that chapter. 'Some Pig.'" He readjusted his grip on the lip of the console, feeling steadier. When he glanced at the monitor, the well-remembered cover of *Charlotte's Web* appeared. "Poor Charlotte," Maxwell said, feeling genuinely sad, not only for the spider, but for his own behavior, his own suppositions and prejudices. He looked up to the crack in the reactor housing from where the purple strand descended. "Sorry," he said. "Not Mother, but *Other*."

The orange glow from the reactor was fading and the room was growing darker. Without needing to look at the control panel, Maxwell knew that the danger of the reactor overloading had disappeared, consumed. Whatever this piece of the Mother had wanted with the energy source, it had finished its meal, the energy used to give birth to . . . something. But what? He glanced at Hon‹ "What are you now?" he asked.

The arachnoform appeared to understand the questio‹ She shrugged. Maxwell laughed. "Well, that's strange," ‹ said. "A shrugging spider." Maxwell rearranged his grip ‹ he could continue to observe Honey in the lengtheni‹ shadows. "You know," he said, "when I joined Starfleet, ‹ those years ago, that was the promise they made to yc ' . . . strange new worlds. New life. New civilizations.' ‹ turned out that when you find strange new worlds, som‹ times the new life you find wants to kill you. The univer‹ needs soldiers just as much as anything else."

Honey took a step closer. The light from Maxwel‹ torch made her eyes gleam. He had the distinct feeling s‹ was listening to him.

"But I never got to do a first contact." He reach‹ out and the arachnoform took another step closer. "Un‹ now. What are you in there now? Mostly Honey? Mos‹ the Other?"

Honey took the last step forward and pressed her he‹ into Maxwell's open palm. He couldn't feel the bum‹ and ridges of her carapace through his gauntlets, but ‹ felt the pressure, even a little warmth. Maxwell was su‹ denly conscious of the cold. Whatever heat the room h‹ held was quickly dissipating.

He tipped his gauntlet, even as he kept rubbing Ho‹ ey's head. The gauge on his gauntlet was blinking fu‹ ously. The needle was inching into the red. "So, here's t‹ thing, dear girl. Small things do not do well with m‹ Even if we can get out of here, I can't really guarantee th‹ we'll make it very far."

Honey pulled her head away and stretched her many legs. Limbering up. Maxwell pointed at the purple strand that terminated in Honey's thorax. "Or can you even go?"

The arachnoform shivered. The strand broke away and crumbled like a dried fern.

"Easy as that?" Honey stared at Maxwell. "And how do I know you're not just going to try to take over the galaxy once we get out of here?"

Honey pointed to the message on the deck: NO KILL I.

"Okay," he said. Maxwell carefully worked his way back to the hatch, Honey at his heels, like a dog cheerful at the prospect of a walk on a sunny morning. "I'm going to hold you to that."

Chapter 22

"Is it this one?" O'Brien asked. "Or this one? Dammit, which button do I push?" The Romulan shuttle's controls were largely unlabeled, and though he was able to distinguish which panel controlled the sensor grid, he was unsure which switches were used to fine-tune the array.

The Romulan smacked his hands away from the controls. "None of them," he said. "Hands off. Give me a moment and I'll do it." He had done as O'Brien had requested and pushed the ship out as far as it could go on thrusters for ten minutes and then stopped. When O'Brien had requested that they turn around and go back, the Romulan had stared at him like he was an idiot. After five minutes of futile argument, they came to a compromise: firing up the sensors and pointing them back toward the Hooke.

The Romulan locked down the pilot station (not without giving O'Brien a warning glance) and set about adjusting the sensors. "Are you looking for anything in particular?" he asked.

"No," O'Brien said, trying to look over the Romulan's shoulder. He had managed to remove his helmet and gloves, but was still wearing the bulky environmental suit, which was difficult to manage in the snug pilot's cabin. "Well, yes. Radiation. A lot of it if the reactor went critical."

"An explosion, then," the pilot said, fingers moving over the controls. His hands, O'Brien noted, were etched with deep lines and there were crescents of dirt under his nails that no amount of soap could extract. "Working man," Captain Maxwell had said. *Farmer,* O'Brien thought, and felt safe.

Back in the very cramped passenger compartment, Nog had taken charge of triaging the injured scientists. Two of the scientists were dead from trauma sustained during the gravity fluctuations and three others, including Nita Bharad, were severely injured, though Nog had stabilized them. Not surprisingly, Finch had taken up what he probably believed was a safe spot just outside the archway between the pilot's cabin and the main compartment. O'Brien guessed that Finch thought a Starfleet officer would defend him if the shell-shocked scientists gathered their wits and came for him. The chief wasn't entirely sure what he would do if someone suggested shoving Finch out the airlock.

"Nothing," the Romulan whispered, slowly twisting a pair of tiny controls with the tips of his fingers. "Nothing, nothing, and noth—" He jerked his head back.

On the sensor display, O'Brien saw a bright orange spike peak and then slowly fade. "What was that?"

"I . . . I'm not sure," he said, shaking his head. He looked up at O'Brien, sheepish or apologetic. O'Brien had never seen that particular expression on a Romulan's face. "I'm not an expert with this equipment, but . . ."

"But what?" O'Brien asked, trying to make sense of the data scrawling up the screen.

The Romulan pointed at the ship's main viewscreen, which was still fixed (he had claimed) on the Hooke position. As O'Brien watched, a tiny yellow light briefly flared and quickly died, casting no more light than a match blown out the moment it was struck.

O'Brien stared at the screen, his mouth agape, uncertain what to say or do. He felt a hand on his arm and was surprised to see it was the Romulan's. "I'm sorry," the pilot said. "I don't really know what's happening here, but I know he was your friend."

"He was," O'Brien began. "He was . . . my . . ." He wasn't sure what word he wanted to say next, so, instead, he said, "We have to go back."

The Romulan just shook his head once and said, "No. There would be no point."

"What's happened, Chief?" Nog stepped over Finch and stuck his head into the pilot's cabin. Somehow, he had managed to remove his environmental suit and was wiping his hands on a cloth soaked in some kind of antiseptic.

"We think the Hooke just exploded."

"*Think*?"

O'Brien pointed at the pilot. "He . . . what's your name?"

"Cretak," said the Romulan.

"Cretak saw a spike on the sensors, and there was a flash. We saw it from here." He pointed at the monitor and suddenly realized his hands and face felt numb. *I'm in shock,* O'Brien thought. *How can I be in shock?*

"You should sit down, Chief," Nog said, guiding him

toward a tiny jump seat, the sort of thing a copilot would use.

"Sorry," O'Brien said, not sure why he was apologizing. "I just . . . I guess I thought we would make it back in time. It never occurred to me that . . ."

"I'm sorry, Chief," Nog said.

"He was a brave man," Cretak said. "Did he know what could have happened?"

"He did," Nog said, nodding. "He knew. He saved us all."

O'Brien looked at the screen, at the swath of beautiful, remorseless stars. "He did, didn't he?" He would not say it aloud; maybe, later, when discussing the day with Keiko, the chief would tell her, "All things considered, not the worst way to go."

Nog pushed his way through the throng of researchers, telling each of them softly what had happened to the station and Ben Maxwell. He made sure to tell them that they had contacted Starfleet and a ship was in transit. All of them thanked him, patted him on the back, and then let him pass. As he worked his way aft, Nog heard weeping and whispering, the sounds of relief and sorrow.

Bharad was at the rear of the shuttle, lying down on the deck with Nog's balled-up environmental suit pillowing her head. She had more space than the others, not only in deference to her injuries, but because Ginger was dangling from a thread above Bharad, occasionally reaching down to touch her creator with one of her long forelimbs.

Nog knelt beside Bharad. She had a frightening split in her scalp, but that injury was more terrifying-looking than life-threatening. Nog was more concerned about possible internal injuries, but there was nothing he could do for her except monitor her vitals. Her eyes were barely open, but he saw the light of consciousness in them. "Doctor Bharad?" he asked, touching her shoulder.

"Nita," she said. "Any friend of Ginger's can call me Nita."

Nog smiled. "Okay, good. Nita, then."

"My head hurts."

"Yes, I know. I told you that you might have a concussion."

"Did you? Oh, right, you did."

"Nita, I have some news."

"Tell me your news."

"We've contacted Starfleet. A ship is on its way."

"They'll have to figure out some way to get us off this ship without spreading Finch's bug."

"True. If the bugs are even here at all. But we're good at this sort of thing."

The doctor reached up and patted Nog on the cheek. "You're a good man," she said. He liked the way her hand felt there. "I'm going to bring Ginger to visit you when I'm better."

"I'd like that," Nog said. He hesitated, unsure if he should continue.

"There's more, isn't there?" Bharad asked. "Those aren't happy noises I'm hearing."

"No," Nog said. "We're pretty sure the station was

lost. And . . . and Captain Maxwell, he stayed behind to keep the reactor from blowing before we were clear."

"Honey?" she asked. "What about Honey?"

Nog shook his head, unsure what words were appropriate under the circumstances.

Bharad closed her eyes and reached up to clutch Ginger's dangling limb and then turned her head away. Nog pawed through his medkit until he found a suit patch, which was the closest thing to a hankie he could locate. He handed it to Bharad, who mumbled something that might have been "thank you." She didn't dab her eyes, as Nog had expected, but held on to his hand. Around them, the other scientists spoke in low tones, but none of them turned to look at the strange trio—the Ferengi Starfleet officer, the geneticist, and her creation.

When Bharad was cried out, her breathing slowed, she dabbed at her eyes and regarded Nog suspiciously. "I *must* have a concussion," she said. "I thought I heard you say *Captain* Maxwell. Which is about the silliest thing I've ever heard. Ben was a janitor." She smiled gently. "A very *good* janitor."

Nog couldn't suppress a smile. "I have no doubt," he said. "None at all."

Deep Space 9

In the end, getting everyone back to Deep Space 9 and through quarantine turned out to be both much simpler and much, *much* more difficult than Nog had anticipated. A cargo vessel, the *Kirby*, had been rerouted when Nog's message was received. The *Kirby* tractored the Romulan shuttle back to the station without incident and the researchers were moved to a quarantine area in Sector General. Using information grudgingly provided by Finch, the quarantine team quickly confirmed that there were no traces of the organism on or in any of the survivors of the Hooke disaster. Even Ginger, after some initial hesitation, by both parties, was processed and allowed to remain with her creator.

Twenty-four hours into the surprisingly relaxing observation period, Nog realized that he was enjoying himself. Chief O'Brien was on the mopey side at first, but after a visit from Keiko and his kids (outside of the sterilization field), he bucked up. He took charge of organizing an Irish wake, not only for Maxwell, but for all the lost. Beverages were consumed. Tales were told, many of them flatly unbelievable, though none were challenged. There was laughing and crying and even some dancing. Nita Bharad, much improved after some treatment, demonstrated a dance step called *Visharu Adavu* to the wonder and delight of all, but most especially Ginger, who spun appreciatively on a strand.

The next day, during a debriefing, someone must have uttered "Shedai metagenome." Starfleet Intelligence descended like an avenging god. Everyone was moved and kept in separate areas, they were questioned gently, but relentlessly. Finch, who had been seen skulking through the corridors of the quarantine area late at night, usually spewing dire imprecations under his breath, disappeared and was never seen again.

During one of his interviews, Nog asked if a team

had been sent to investigate the fate of the Robert Hooke. After much rumination, the captain in charge revealed that a ship had been dispatched. Nog was told that the evidence largely corroborated his account of events: an almost-healed patch of subspace and background radiation readings that were likely the result of the rupture of a matter/antimatter generator. There was no sign of any survivors.

A week later, the researchers were released and each received a stern warning to never speak of the Robert Hooke. Nog and Bharad exchanged contact information, promising to stay in touch. Ginger appeared to be confused about why they were boarding a ship without Nog, but Bharad shooed her down the gangway like a mother hen herding a chick.

O'Brien and Nog were held for an extra week. No one ever told them why. The chief's family was waiting for him when he and Nog were finally released, all of them appearing happy and relieved to see him again. Quark was waiting for Nog, his concern well concealed under a mask of aggravation and impatience. As they headed for their quarters, O'Brien said, "Let's never, ever, *ever* leave the station together."

"Agreed," Nog said, nodding.

Neither of them seemed quite ready to go. O'Brien looked down at Nog and asked, "What time does your shift start tomorrow?"

Nog thought for a second, "Zero-nine-hundred."

"Yeah," the chief said. "Me, too."

"Good," Nog said. "See you then."

O'Brien nodded. "Sure. Or . . ."

"Or?"

"Or we could meet at Quark's around zero-eight-thirty. Get a coffee?"

"I don't like coffee."

"Raktajino?"

"I like raktajino."

"What is the difference between coffee and raktajino?"

"It's the spices," Nog said. "It's all about the spices. I'm surprised you don't know that, Chief."

"It's not something I've really paid a lot of attention to up till now," O'Brien said, falling into step. "But I'm willing to try."

Epilogue

Bharad woke up early, much earlier than she would have liked, and padded around the house in her bathrobe and wool socks. *It's May,* she thought. *It shouldn't be cold.* Back in February, given everything that had happened on the Robert Hooke, the idea of living near the ocean and watching the sun come up over the horizon every day had seemed very appealing, but Bharad was having second thoughts. The weather wasn't what she had expected: foggy and cold some days, windy and dry on others. She decided she would give June and July a chance—to see what a real summer season was like—and then consider new options. She could go anywhere she pleased—the research grants were portable; however, she knew she would have problems with Ginger, who appeared to love the marshes of Absecon and the nearby dunes.

Loading the French press with ground coffee, Bharad flicked on the kettle and leaned her back against the counter to consider her options for the day. Lots of gene sequencing results to review, though that was drudgery and best left to the lab's automated systems. Maybe a drive up north to the Pine Barrens would be a better use of her time. Ginger was beginning to lose some of her anxiety about trees. Bharad had just assumed that Ginger would *like* trees, but that was not the case. On first viewing them, she had been awed, even intimidated, and hid under their vehicle.

Ginger, who typically stayed up late and woke late, surprised Bharad by poking her head through the kitchen door and waving her front legs excitedly. "What are you doing up?" Bharad asked as she poured the hot water into the press. Ginger disappeared, only to return a moment later, once more waving her forelimbs. Bharad set the kettle down and tightened the sash on her robe. Something was wrong. "What is it, girl?" she called. The arachnoform didn't return. Cautiously approaching the door, she heard Ginger slipping on the tile floors as she scurried away.

Bharad followed. *A visitor? At this hour?* Ginger liked visitors if she recognized them, but was wary of strangers. *A curious local? A kid making good on a dare?* That seemed unlikely, as the security system would respond to anything that appeared moderately threatening. Turning the corner to the back door, Bharad was briefly dazzled by the first ray of sunshine glittering on the ocean. She had to turn away, cover her eyes, and blink the swimming motes. Though temporarily blinded, she heard the *tick-tick-tick* sound of Ginger tapping at the window glass beside the door. Just on the other side of the door was the long porch that ran along the back of the house, the one where they spent hours after their return to Earth, the place where they both nursed their wounds over their mutual loss.

When she finally felt she could open her eyes, Bharad

did so carefully, shielding them from the glare with her right hand cupped over her brow. Squinting, she peered out onto the porch. Then the breath left her body and her knees grew watery when she was sure she was seeing what she was seeing. It didn't seem possible, but there wasn't anyone else it could be. Ginger tapped, tapped, tapped on the glass, so sharply that Bharad worried she might break it, but Bharad understood her excitement.

Her sister was home: Honey, twirling serenely on a web strand, hung from one of the porch's joists.

She needed a moment to remember how the door's lock worked. As Bharad fumbled with the mechanism, she heard herself burbling incoherently. Ginger had ceased poking at the window and was now poking at Bharad's legs, the sharp tips of her tarsus no doubt making tiny holes in the pajama pants. Finally, the lock surrendered and she flung wide the door. Ginger leaped past her, collided with her sister, and carried them both over the porch railing. Neither fell far. Web lines snagged a post, and they were both back up on the porch in a moment, bounding around each other, inspecting one another with their pedipalps. Bharad launched herself into the fray, and both sisters embraced her. Twenty limbs of various shapes and sizes were wrapped around and through one another. One of them wept loudly. No doubt, the neighbors were alarmed.

When the greetings and the tears finally subsided, Bharad felt at a loss. As she ushered the sisters into her house, all she could think to say, over and over again, was, "This doesn't make any sense. How is this possible?" And, of course, it didn't and it wasn't. The Hooke had been destroyed. Starfleet had accounted for nearly every scrap of debris, and the bits they hadn't were too small to have carried Honey to safety.

Bharad fell into her routine. She fed the sisters, both of whom ate ravenously, and then poured herself a cup of insanely strong coffee (it had steeped for quite a while). Sitting in one of the two kitchen chairs, she stared at the arachnoforms as they groomed each other and tried to account for all the possibilities. Only one made anything even close to sense. "Ben."

Honey ceased grooming her sister and looked up at Bharad. Then, with an air of having been interrupted, she rose, stretched, and clattered over to a desk Bharad had designated as her workstation. Very deliberately, Honey pulled the single chair away from the desk and clambered up into it.

Sunlight spilled in through the bay window beside the desk, and Nita noticed a couple of things she hadn't in the blurred haste of reunion. First, Honey's carapace was much more chipped and dented than her sister's, as if she had been through some kind of battle or violent explosion. "Well," Bharad said aloud, "I suppose you were, weren't you?" Second, Honey was wearing a belt. She wasn't surprised she had missed it, as the belt was quite thin, almost the same color as her carapace and strapped around the flexible membrane between Honey's abdomen and cephalothorax. The belt was festooned with tiny pockets.

Honey reached down under her body with her pedipalps and fished something out of one of the pouches. When the pedipalps reemerged, the tips were covered in tiny plastic caps. Then she reached up and tapped on the face of one of Bharad's padds. The padd's face lit up and displayed the passcode request screen.

Honey tapped the padd again, meaningfully.

Not sure what was happening, Bharad leaned forward and entered the passcode. Honey swiped at the screen until she found the text program and then opened it. A keypad appeared and Honey tapped away at it quickly and precisely. Feeling her breath coming in short gasps, Bharad leaned forward again and looked at the screen. Honey had typed, "Hello, Mother."

Bharad sat down on the floor. She hadn't planned to do so, but her knees had suddenly given out. Still perched in the chair, Honey gazed down at Bharad, patiently waiting for her creator to collect herself. "You can talk," was all Bharad could think to say.

Honey tapped on the padd, and then carefully carried it down onto the floor so Bharad could see the screen. "No," it said. "But Honey can type."

"Since when?"

Honey paused to consider a reply and then typed, "Since merging with the Other."

"The Other?"

"Finch's Other."

A score of questions flitted through Bharad's mind. For no particular reason, she settled on, "Can Ginger talk?"

Bharad couldn't say why, but she had the distinct impression Honey liked this question. "No," she wrote. "Not yet. But Honey has ideas."

Feeling one of her eyebrows creep upward, Bharad

asked, "You'll be sure to run those ideas past me before you try anything, won't you?"

"Yes, Mother."

Feeling a bit calmer, Bharad leaned her back against a hassock and pondered her next question. Unaccountably, she worried she might only be able to ask a few and needed to make them count. She asked, "What does Ben have to do with all of this?"

Honey needed to type for a couple minutes to complete her reply. Bharad was surprised to see that the arachnoform hit the backspace key several times, as if she was editing her reply. "Ben saved Honey. And Honey saved Ben. The *Wren* stayed together, because of Honey and Ginger. Ben had a rocket."

"The thruster pack," Bharad said.

Honey typed, "Yes."

"But you've been gone for months. What happened?"

Honey seemed to think about her reply for a time. Or, at least, she didn't start to type immediately. When she did, she wrote, "Ben and Honey were found by men. At first, we liked them, but then we didn't. Fighting. Adventures."

Bharad ran her fingertips over the dings and dents in Honey's carapace. "I see," she said. "Where's Ben?"

"Ben brought Honey home. Said he had to go."

"Well, I look forward to hearing his version of this story when he returns."

Honey typed, "Ben won't return."

"Why not?"

"Ben said he likes being dead. Ben says he likes being new."

Bharad thought about Honey's statements for a long minute and then replied, "Not a janitor anymore. Nor a starship captain."

"No," Honey wrote. "No."

Rubbing the tiny dent in the back of Honey's head, a long scarred-over battle wound, no doubt, Bharad asked, "Is there anything else you want to tell me right now?"

Honey typed, "Honey wants to go back to cleaning Ginger. She is very dirty."

"Really?"

"Yes. Really."

"All right," Bharad said, "but we'll return to this topic when you're finished."

Honey shoved the padd over to Bharad and returned to grooming her sister.

Bharad stood up slowly, clutching the padd to her chest. She glanced at the time and saw it was just a few minutes before nine. Looking out the window at the sky and the billowing clouds, Bharad knew it was going to be a fine day. Maybe they would go to the beach instead of the Pine Barrens.

Five Months Later
Starfleet Penal Colony

Michael Clark opened his eyes and was instantly, completely awake. He glanced at the chrono on the nightstand, moving only his eyes, wary of making too much noise. Zero-six-thirty.

No one else should be in the house. His wife and son

were on Mars, with his wife's sister and rest of the clan. Clark was supposed to join them when the workweek was done. If there was an emergency at the hospital, someone would have called first and not come to the house unannounced. There were protocols, dammit. The doctor closed his eyes and attempted to focus past all the usual morning sounds of an early summer's day. A few birds chirped outside, working their way through whatever seeds remained in the feeder. Downstairs, various bits of semiautonomous machinery whirred or hummed, but nothing seemed wrong or out of place.

Maybe the damned robot legs are outside, he thought. *Waiting.*

Then Clark realized that the problem wasn't an alien sound, but the absence of a sound. The wheezing was missing.

"Freud's sticky ghost!" Clark cried, and sat up. It was a stupid expression, one his father (an unrepentant psychoanalyst) used to shout whenever he was particularly annoyed. "Horrible!"

No response, not a hack nor a rattle, not a gasp nor an expulsion of gas. Clark didn't smell anything bad, so he knew the dog hadn't crawled under the bed to die—not that the odor would be much different than the one he expelled in life.

Clark rolled out of bed, careful to look where he planted his feet before doing so. The dog occasionally fell asleep (or lapsed into a coma) in inconvenient places. But, no. *No Horrible.* He swiped his hair back out of his eyes as he stepped into his slippers. *Why do I continue to call it by that terrible name?* Shuffling quickly from room to room,

Clark ordered the computer to turn on the lights as he went. He looked under tables and chairs, inside cabinets and under rugs, though he knew the last was utterly irrational. *No dog. No Horrible.*

He reached the kitchen, the last uninspected room, but it, too, was empty, though there was a lingering hint of the dog's funk, as if he had passed through recently.

Clark scanned the room for clues. His gaze alit on a padd leaning against the wall near the back door. He activated it, and there was a note.

Thank you, it read, *for taking such good care of him.*

And, below that, as if in an afterthought: *And me, too.*

Clark scrolled down to make sure there was nothing more. The note was unsigned.

Staring at the padd, Michael Clark considered the possibilities until he finally landed on the most likely explanation, as improbable as it seemed. Mulling over the idea, he smiled and said, "You're welcome." He wiped the note from the memory and placed the padd on the countertop.

Clark went back to bed and soon fell back asleep. He may have dreamed, but, if he did, he did not remember the dreams when he woke again.

ACKNOWLEDGMENTS

The seed of this story was first planted during a conversation with Michael Clark during a recording for his *Captain's Table* podcast (www.visionarytrek.com/category/the-captains-table). For that reason if no other, I felt I owed him a character name. I'll also buy him a pint the next time I'm in London.

Margaret Clark suggested that it might be worth exploring the idea of adding Ben Maxwell to the story. Right as ever, Margaret. Thank you for that and all the other righteous editing. Thanks also to Ed Schlesinger at Simon & Schuster for his assistance and to Scott Pearson for copyediting above and beyond the call. Also, I'd like to extend my profound gratitude and appreciation to the curators of Memory Alpha and Memory Beta. I've been doing this long enough to remember when you guys weren't around, so thanks for being there.

Thank you to beta readers Helen Szigeti and Tristan Mayer for their thoughtful criticism of early drafts and also for putting up with my whining and kvetching. I'm indebted to Annarita Gentile for any insights gleamed from her about the psychotherapeutic process. If anything herein sounds authentic, it's to ARG's credit; inaccuracies belong solely to the author.

As ever, I'd like to thank the writers, cast, and crew of *Star Trek: The Next Generation* and *Star Trek: Deep Space Nine* for developing the rich universe in which it is my privilege to play. In particular, this time around I'm beholden to Colm Meaney and Aron Eisenberg. Lastly, Bob Gunton and the *TNG* writing staff created an extremely memorable character in Benjamin Maxwell, and they have my sincere regards and admiration. I'd be curious to hear what any of them thinks of the rest of Ben's tale.

ABOUT THE AUTHOR

Jeffrey Lang has authored or co-authored several *Star Trek* novels and short stories, including *The Light Fantastic*, *Immortal Coil*, *Section 31: Abyss*, *The Left Hand of Destiny*, "Foundlings" (in the anthology *Prophecy and Change*), and "Mirror Eyes" (with Heather Jarman) in the anthology *Tales of the Dominion War*. He lives in Bala Cynwyd, Pennsylvania, with his partner, Helen, as well as Kirby, Puffy, and Tumble (cats) and Joey and Lili (dogs). No arachnoforms yet, but we're open to the idea if the opportunity arises.